Our Huckleberry Friend

JOHNNY MERCER

The Life, Times and Song Lyrics of

OUR HUCKLEBERRY FRIEND

Collected and Edited by BOB BACH
and GINGER MERCER

Designed by Christopher Simon

LYLE STUART, INC.   Secaucus, N.J.

PHOTOS COURTESY OF:
Down Beat Magazine
Charlie Mann
Jules Davis
Frederick C. Baldwin
Bud Selzer
Capitol Records
NBC
Gjon Mili
Bill Durrence
Garrett-Howard Inc.
Seymour Rudolph
The Memory Shop, New York
The Archives Department, Georgia State University
  and
The Mercer family

Cartoon page 63 courtesy of *Playboy* Magazine
Cartoon page 123 courtesy of *Esquire* Magazine

Library of Congress Cataloging in Publication Data

Mercer, Johnny, 1909-
    Johnny Mercer, the life, times and song lyrics of our huckleberry friend

    1. Music, Popular (Songs, etc.)--United Staters--
Texts   2. Mercer, Johnny, 1909-
3. Librettists--United States--Biography.
I. Bach, Bob.   II. Mercer, Ginger.   III. Title.
ML54.6.M4509   1982   784.5'05   82-10503
ISBN 0-8184-0450-7

FOR JEAN

Acknowledgments

Special thanks for help and guidance in the preparation of this book to Jean Bach, Marc Cramer, Walter Rivers, Marshall Robbins, Jim Mahar, Margaret Whiting, Maurice Levine, Dr. William Suttle, Dr. Leslie Hough, Geoff Parker, Bob Dinwiddie, the Department of Archives at Georgia State University, the American Society of Composers, Authors and Publishers, the American Guild of Authors and Composers, and our editor, Arthur Smith.

Contents

From One Singer to Another—A Tribute

Johnny Mercer is a great, great songwriter—and I use that word "great" advisedly because it's thrown around so much. You see, Johnny Mercer—and I go way back with him, when he first came out to R.K.O. and a publishing firm I was associated with published some of his songs—he's not just a lyricist, he's a songwriter, and there's a big difference. He was a singer to begin with (and so was I) and so he knows where words should fall and when to use an open vowel instead of a closed vowel. He has a great feel for words. He had a good education and so he's literate enough to know all those six- and seven-syllable words—but, and this is important, he's smart enough to know when not to use them. He feels things very deeply—as a matter of fact, he's very sentimental and knows how to use tender corn; there's nothing wrong with good corn, believe me.

My favorite Mercer song? Oh my goodness, he's written so many. . . . But I know that all songwriters like their latest hit the best. "Moon River"? Well, that's a great song—I don't know whether the melody came first or what, but it's the perfect combination of words and music; he always knows where to put the right words—sort of like a minister or priest or rabbi who's going to perform the marriage ceremony. Yes, he's a great songwriter and a wonderful person too.

IRVING BERLIN

JOHNNY MERCER

Introduction

"Just Too Very Very"

It was not exactly contrived imagery that for so many years labeled the center of popular music production Tin Pan Alley. The upright, timeworn pianos on which the songs were first banged out *were* tinny, and the side streets surrounding Broadway rarely saw sunshine, thus putting them in the category of what might be called alleys. At the same lengthy period of time—that is, the better part of this century, up until the calamitous arrival of rock 'n' roll and the Beatles—the writers of the nation's song hits were mainly the products of these same citified surroundings. In fact many of the leaders of the Tin Pan Alley fraternity had been born and raised within a subway ride of that musical center. To be even more precise, the overwhelming majority of songwriters and their patrons, the publishers, were not only born and bred New Yorkers but Jewish into the bargain. The oddity, of course, was that these city-born musicians and lyricists wrote lovingly and longingly about country lanes and waterfalls rather than the hustle and bustle of Times Square (the song "Forty-second Street" was the exception rather than the rule) and the song-plugging gang that gathered around Al Jolson, the Elvis of the twenties, knew as much about Jolie's often-sung Dixie as they did about Labrador. The authenticity of regional songwriting had to wait until the arrival in the late twenties of two young men from different rural parts of the country: Hoagy Carmichael from Indiana and Johnny Mercer from Georgia.

Their similarities were quite remarkable: they both sang in a most distinctive, down-home, nasal-tinged style; they both had a great affection for jazz; they both operated from a marvelously sly sense of humor. Where their spiritual predecessor Willard Robison, had been equally authentic and brilliant in a down-home musical way, Carmichael and Mercer were more commercial, and that opened doors. They were a peach of a pair together, sparkling individually, Hoagy slim and saturnine, Johnny "a perfect butterball of a Southerner" as Carmichael describes him in his autobiography. Above all they were twin gusts of fresh air in the troubled days of the early thirties. Together they wrote a whole string of thoroughly distinctive songs, beginning with "Lazybones" in 1933 and ending up with the Academy Award winner of 1951, "In

George Anderson Mercer, grandfather of John Herndon Mercer, our Huckleberry Friend.

the Cool, Cool, Cool of the Evening." Through those years one had an awful time trying to remember which was which in the songs they wrote together and separately: "Small Fry," which Johnny sang many times, sounds as if he wrote it, but it was a solo job by Hoagy; Johnny's famous "Moon River" sounds as if it were written with Hoagy (who wrote "Moon Country") instead of Mancini, and "Jamboree Jones," which Johnny wrote by himself, is somewhat like "The Old Music Master," which he wrote with Hoagy some years before they collaborated on "Skylark," which was written a few years before Hoagy wrote "Baltimore Oriole" without Johnny but several years after Johnny wrote "Mister Meadowlark" without Hoagy. There was a great song they wrote together, "How Little We Know," and a piece of esoterica that probably only Mel Tormé knows, "The Rumba Jumps." There was "Washboard Blues" (Carmichael) and "Blues in the Night" (Mercer), "Stardust" (Carmichael) and "Midnight Sun" (Mercer), "Georgia on My Mind" (Carmichael) and "Pardon My Southern Accent" (Mercer). Between them it seems as if they have contributed the greatest hunk of musical Americana since Stephen Foster and that they may also have laid down the tracks for the current rush of country-flavored blues and ballads.

Luck smiled on Johnny Mercer in other ways than just bringing him to New York at the same time as Hoagy Carmichael's arrival. Mercer was born in Savannah, undoubtedly one of the most aristocratic and languorous cities of the old South. The family, while not of the wealthy land-owning class, was at least well-off, and so young John Mercer was able to be sent to the select Woodbury Academy in North Carolina. One of his major accomplishments at Woodbury was booking the bands for the school's proms. The luck of the Depression (not smiling in this case) brought about Mercer senior's business trouble in the real estate market, and thus John had to forego college, a situation that brought him to New York. The cherub face, the jazz, collegiate clothes, the soft Southern speech and easy-going manner must certainly have set him apart as he went looking for acting jobs and submitting songs around the Broadway area in those bewildering days of 1929 and 1930. There were the usual ups and downs of show business until the first sizable break came in the person of the sizable Paul Whiteman. It was Mercer the "cute" singer with Whiteman who paved the way for Mercer the singing songwriter. With Whiteman, who understood talent better than most, Mercer was able to sing alongside one of his heroes, the great jazz trombonist Jack Teagarden. As with Hoagy, it was a pairing made in jazz heaven—Mercer with the South in his mouth, Teagarden with the rich blues sound of Texas—and they were commercial too! There is much that can be said about Mercer's singing style, almost as much as about his songwriting. He had, of course, an impeccable sense of how a jazz phrase or a blues nuance should sound; all of that came naturally to a man who had spent some of his boyhood years crossing the tracks to the Negro section of town to buy what were then called "race records" (the result may be seen in the postcard from a Black social club shown later in this book which voted him "our favorite colored singer on radio"). The jazz flavor was inherent in him, but he also had a wonderful way with a ballad—for instance, his recorded versions of "Laura," "Tangerine," and "Little Ingenue." It seemed back then in the Whiteman and mid-thirties period that a lot of listeners who became Mercer fans, particularly when Crosby stepped in, were country club types who thought they both sounded like friendly boozers (ho-ho-ho) and there were others who had fun mimicking that devil-may-care singing style in the shower. Johnny Mercer's early following may have been small but it was select, including in it such knowing and well-connected gentlemen as Irving Berlin and Arthur Schwartz

When one begins to consider what were the main influences that made Johnny Mercer tick, two settings come into view: there was the sophisticated East represented by Broadway—still not too far removed by overnight train from the man's true heartland, Savannah; and there was the widespread California arena that stretched from homes in Palm Springs and Newport Beach to the studio of Warner's, Paramount and 20th Century-Fox. Weaving these widely separated and dissimilar influ-

ences together was Mercer's triple strand of talent: the professional singing that came so naturally and contributed so helpfully, as Irving Berlin noted, to his understanding of where the words should fall; the acclaimed songwriting that was often cleverly topical, sometimes universal, and generally touched, as his British show collaborator, Ronnie Harwood, put it, with "the genius of simplicity"; and there was a surprising interest in organization that founded, first, a record company of size (Capitol) in California and then a trade group (the Songwriters Hall of Fame) in New York. On top of all this was a boyish enthusiasm, not necessarily the rah-rah kind of thing, more self-contained, for material and talent he liked. His range of perception was as illuminating and wide ranging as radar. He still liked some Victor Herbert and Rudolf Friml, but he was aware of newcomers and singled out Jimmy Webb, Marvin Hamlisch and Jobim. Whether it was a funny phrase noted in *Time* magazine or a singer heard on the car radio, Mercer picked it up, used the information some way or other, became a booster. He had, as the saying goes, his pores open. Mercer was, particularly in the hectic war years of the forties, a workaholic, an on-top-of-everything guy. But even with such an assembly-line output of jazzy topicality Mercer never strayed too far from

(Here and facing page) Scenes of Savannah during the first two decades of the century.

Scenes from the Mercer family
scrapbook, circa 1910.
Pose number seven—"any place I
hang my hat."

14

his deep South, down-home feelings: birds, meadows, sky, rivers, trains (particularly trains)—these references were with him throughout his life, they were the things he was most comfortable with. The composer and musical guru Alec Wilder put it very well when he said, "Larry Hart was an indoor writer and Johnny was an outdoor writer." One can almost see Mercer sitting on a front porch, watching the fading sunlight—a tall drink (or better still a short one) not far from his side.

While on the subject of drink, it is still somewhat surprising that this true son of the South, while neither a Good Ole Boy nor an out-and-out Bible-smacker, was quite moralistic, even among the heathens of show biz. He did read the Bible often, he never used directly erotic lyrics, and he was openly angered by Tennessee Williams' preoccupation with depravity in bayou country. Johnny Mercer was basically an Ivy Leaguer, much more in the Walker Percy image than Capote, Williams or the current playwrights of off-off-Broadway. He was for progress but not too much of it—and better leave the things at home alone. In California he took on some of the colorations of that sybaritic paradise: golf (briefly), painting (pretty good watercolors), cooking (with a distinctly Southern flavor)—these were a few of the outside interests; that is, after the first fling of cronyism and partying with Bing's crowd wore off. There was also a time for the Mercers with the writing crowd—Nunally Johnson, the Hacketts, etc—where Johnny was a sort of celebrity because he was the only one of his kind in that heady world. In short, he was, to use Duke Ellington's marvelous phrase, Beyond Category.

To take Johnny Mercer through all the ups and downs of his career would consume more space than this volume allows—a full-scale biography is in the works—and so it is best for the moment to let his many wonderful lyrics, such telling visions of time, place and listener as for example, "hear that lonesome whistle blowing cross the trestle" sketch out the portrait. Another song contains a similar hauntingly autobiographically picture:

> *Cross the river,*
> *Round the bend,*
> *Howdy, stranger,*
> *So long, friend.*

To Bob Bach
From Walter Rivers

Bob, as discussed with you on the phone, re "Huckleberry Friend" — John and I and three black boys, Ceasar, Eli and Tommie, in early summer, June or July, went picking these berries. We each had a quart measure, — a small pail from which the hucksters sold a quart of okra, peas, beans, or whatever. John looked forward to these safaris with great pleasure. The black boys knew mainly the best places for finding the berries, and I think now of the brambles, briers and snakes which we encountered. I wouldn't dare go into some of the places now!

We would spend several hours to fill our pails and trudge homeward on the oyster shell roads of Vernon View.

I remember vividly that Walter Mercer, Johns half brother making ice cream for Sunday dinner — Huckleberry Ice Cream — It turned out pretty bad and no one would eat it — I think Huckleberries are the same as blue berries — look and taste the same but grew wild in our area.

Shortly after Moon River became a hit, I called Johnny and told him I loved the line "my Huckleberry friend". He laughed, and said "Hell! you ought to — you were there!"

Another memory was West Broad Street in Savannah. This was totally Black.

Johnny Mercer's cousin, long-time pal, and one-time executive of Capitol Records, Walter Rivers, is now living in retirement in Birmingham, Alabama. He recently wrote this letter when asked for an explanation of the expression "huckleberry friend."

Stores, houses, R.R. Station, Churches, everything for blacks. Just like old time Harlem! John and I frequently slipped off from our families and went over to a record shop, called Mary's Records, or Mamie's Records. There we would listen for hours to Bessie Smith, Armstrong, Joe Pat Sullivan, and many people I can't recall — you would know of many musicians of that era —

John loved to imitate Bessie Smith's Record of "Go Back Where You Stayed Last Night"

We were good customers so we were allowed to listen for hours. A real Victrola, with a horn on top! His Masters Voice —

This, I believe, is where Mercer picked up his beat and phrasing.

I must digress for a moment: The Easter Parade on West Broad St. in Savannah. Black ladies dressed in evening gowns, triple high heels and big flowered hats. Men in everything tuxedos, tails morning formal wear, most with orange shoes, strolling musicians(?) — it seemed that every man in the crowd had a trumpet, banjo, or clarinet.

On this day, Easter, the curb was lined with white people with ancient cars, buggies and wagons, watching the spectacle and it was almost Mardi Gras. I didn't miss one for years and usually went with my mother and some disapproving Aunts — John was there with his father

(Bob. Hope this is sorta what you want)

We lived in the country in the summer. The roads were still unpaved, made of crushed oyster shell, and as they wound their way under the trees covered with Spanish moss, it was a sweet, indolent background for a boy to grow up in. Savannah was smaller then and sleepy, full of trees and azaleas that filled the parks which make it so beautiful and as we drove out to our "place in the country" at Vernon View there was hardly a scene without vistas of marsh grass and long stretches of salt water.

Punctured tires on the Model T made the trips longer at times, but when the family arrived finally to spend the summer there were many things to be done around our summer home. We had to get sawdust to pack the ground bin where we kept the ice, fill the lamps with kerosene, put up the mosquito netting on the beds and have "Man'well" walk the cow out from the commercial dairy farm so we'd have our own milk all summer long.

JOHNNY MERCER

17

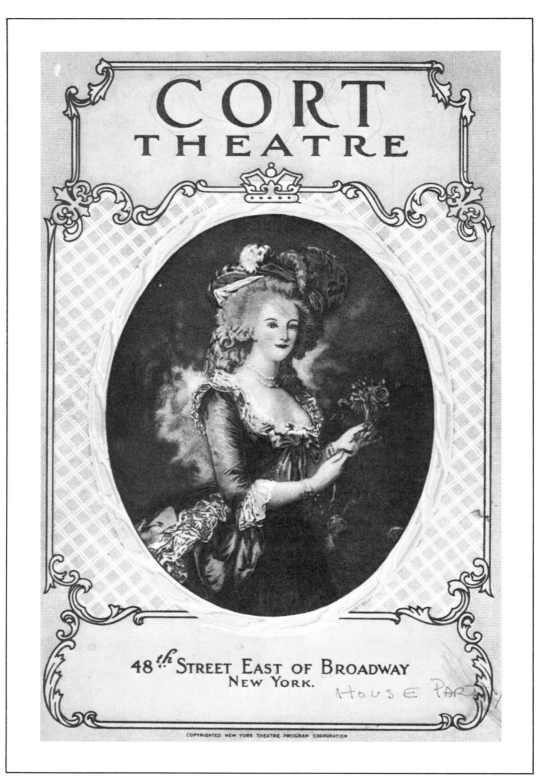

Program cover for *Houseparty*

The Twenties

For a young man, such as Johnny Mercer, whose life centered on music the decade of the 1920s—a breezy time that has since been rather overly-dubbed the Jazz Age—was a period rich in musical delights. The wind-up Victrola and crystal-set radio evolved during that time to the orthophonic phonograph and the three-dial superheterodyne made by Atwater Kent, Zenith or Stromberg Carlson, and these wonders of the communications industry brought with them—certainly reaching all the way to Georgia—such musical novelties as a crazy song called "Yes, We Have No Bananas," a man named Wendell Hall singing "It Ain't Gonna Rain No More No More," and a nimble-fingered pianist named Zez Confrey playing "Kitten on the Keys." There were also the comedy records by Billy Jones and Ernie Hare ("The Happiness Boys"), and The Two Black Crows, Moran and Mack ("Has you ever felt goofer feathers? . . . they is soooooo soft"), "race" records that were rumored to be very naughty, sung by Ma Rainey and Bessie Smith, and records by fellows named Ukelele Ike (Cliff Edwards) and Fuzzy Knight that featured a new way of presenting a song—not so much singing but a sort of gargling sound that seemed "hot," that popular 1920s word appropriated from the colored (no Negro or Black yet) community.

There were also in this flourishing decade, in addition to the passive forms of musical enjoyment, the more active art forms: the banjo, beloved of minstrel shows and dockside revels, now spawned the sprightly ukelele (the uke), which proved so easy to manipulate in a rumble seat or a canoe, and every parlor of any consequence could boast of a piano on whose music rack would be sheet music copies of the latest rage—"Dardanella," "When Day Is Done," "Whispering," "California Here I Come." If all of this remarkable cornucopia didn't prove enough to satisfy the appetite of a music-minded teenager in 1924-25-or-26, there was also a new dance called "The Charleston" to practice in private or in front of the phonograph. At least once a week he could go to a movie in town with a local fellow seated at the upright piano down front, helping the plot along with sentimental surges and agitated rumblings in moments of high passion and peril. And that's how it was in most middle class

American homes during that decade, though a Southern boy had the added advantage of hearing—if even at a distance—the exotic and compelling sounds coming from an occasional tent show or gospel meeting for the colored folk across town. Music was everywhere, in the air, for America was beginning to stretch and feel its oats after the heady business of winning a war for those people "over there."

Then there was the most intoxicating discovery of all—jazz—and Johnny Mercer in Savannah of the mid-twenties plunged into it head over heels. There were two giants of jazz (both of whom would appear in Johnny's later life) that were worth hanging around the local record store and waiting for: Louis Armstrong (and his Hot Five) and Paul Whiteman. Though Paul was mistakenly labelled "King of Jazz," he did nonetheless feature the brilliant jazz cornettist Bix Beiderbecke, and that was enough to pacify the purists of the jazz community. There were countless other recording jazzmen on whom an affluent young man could spend his weekly allowance: Red Nichols and his Five Pennies, McKinney's Cotton Pickers, Miff Mole's Molers, Venuti and Lang, Fletcher Henderson, the California Ramblers, the Wolverines, the Mound City Blue Blowers—the amazingly colorful names ran on and on at the local record store or 5-and-10.

But if young John Mercer knew the names and numbers of all the players in jazz, that was only a part of his ever-growing, knowledgeable attention to the entire world of pop culture in that period: there were the stage plays by Ibsen, O'Neill, Molnar, Golden, and that new fellow Nöel Coward; books by Sherwood Anderson, Irvin S. Cobb, Sinclair Lewis; and various small literary magazines. But mainly there was the element that struck the most responsive chord—the great outpouring of popular songs from a place up north recently named Tin Pan Alley.

His heroes became Victor Herbert, Irving Berlin, George Gershwin, Walter Donaldson, Gus Kahn, Isham Jones.* There were two other songwriters he appreciated perhaps more than that illustrious list, two who came along a few years later and represented the down-home country flavor so dear to Mercer's heart. They were Willard Robison and Hoagy Carmichael.

Johnny Mercer was bursting with the spirit of the age, and so it was inevitable that he come to challenge the tough guys and wise dolls of New York in 1927.

* These were added to his early and continuing passion for the rhymes of W. S. Gilbert.

Houseparty was not quite the disaster that took place farther downtown in Manhattan that October but it might have turned John Mercer's sights in other directions a little.

21

The newlywed Johnny and Ginger heading down the Atlantic City boardwalk to hear Archie Bleyer's band.

The Thirties

Consider for a moment the following list of popular songs:

April in Paris
Brother Can You Spare a Dime
Night and Day
How Deep Is the Ocean
Forty-second Street
I Gotta Right to Sing the Blues
Mimi
Isn't It Romantic
I'm Getting Sentimental Over You
Dancing on the Ceiling

Say It Isn't So
It Don't Mean a Thing if It Ain't Got That Swing
Mad About the Boy
Of Thee I Sing
A Shine on Your Shoes
Shuffle Off to Buffalo
The Song Is You
You're an Old Smoothie
Drums in My Heart
My Silent Love

They were *all* published and became popular within the space of one year—1932. And if the public wanted more of such quality, 1933 wasn't a bad year either, having produced the all-time hit songs "Easter Parade," "Stormy Weather," "Lover," "The Carioca," "Yesterdays" and "Sophisticated Lady." No question about it that, although the Depression had set in grimly, bringing with it the closing of banks, the foreclosing of mortgages, and men selling apples on street corners, the great majority of us who had the good fortune to own radios or phonographs were being offered a banquet of rich musical dishes to brighten up the times. And though "Brother Can You Spare a Dime?" caught the public's imagination in the busy year of 1932, Franklin D. Roosevelt, cigarette holder airily tilted to the sky, had ridden into the White House that same year with a theme song from 1930 titled "Happy Days Are Here Again." There was a lot of good and functional music around.

Movie musicals were also inexplicably thriving in the early thirties: If the rather dull ones of '30-'31, with squares such as Lawrence Tibbett, John Boles and Janet

Gaynor, were hardly lighting up the screens, at least by 1933 there was *Flying Down to Rio* with the beginning of the Astaire-Rogers magic (music by Vincent Youmans); the blockbuster *Forty-Second Street;* Al Jolson, of all people, in a very avant-garde musical by Rodgers and Hart, *Hallelujah I'm a Bum;* Joan Crawford, Clark Gable and Fred Astaire (briefly) in an M-G-M extravaganza called *Dancing Lady;* two jazzy Bing Crosby musicals with the wonderful Jack Oakie in support; and, finally, the successful continuation of the great Maurice Chevalier's Hollywood career which had begun to soar in 1931 with *The Smiling Lieutenant* and in 1932 with *Love Me Tonight.* There were plenty of movies, and many of them were featuring performers lifted from the East, from Broadway and vaudeville: Mae West, W. C. Fields, Burns and Allen, Eddie Cantor, Eddie Foy, Jr., Texas Guinan, Jimmy Durante—even Paul Robeson performing his classic role in *The Emperor Jones.* The music for all these great movies was being written for the most part by other refugees from Broadway, and they constituted the first wave of East to West show tune know-how. There was Ralph Rainger, who had started out as one half of a two-piano team in the pit of several Broadway shows; Dorothy Fields, the brilliant offspring of a distinguished theatrical family; (Weber & Fields) a former dance band pianist, Jimmy McHugh; a chunky ex-Broadwayite named Mack Gordon, who could sell his own lyrics better than most professional crooners; Richard Whiting, a marvelous music man from the Middle West; and—probably without question kings of the heap—the great team of Harry Warren (music) and Al Dubin (words), who were responsible for the success of both *Forty-second Street* and *Gold Diggers of 1933.*

The fun-filled musical movies helped us stave off the Depression-time blues but there was also Broadway, where if you got to Gray's cut-rate ticket office in the basement just off Times Square, you might be lucky enough to pick up a ticket for one of the great musical shows for $1.50—certainly for well under any astronomical five dollars. Between 1932 and 1933 there were many gems to choose from: *Flying Colors* (Schwartz & Dietz) with Clifton Webb and Imogene Coca; *Gay Divorce* (Cole Porter) starring Fred Astaire; the Gershwins' Pulitzer prize-winner *Of Thee I Sing; Music in the Air* (Jerome Kern); *Through the Years* (Vincent Youmans); *As Thousands Cheer* (Irving Berlin) starring Marilyn Miller; *Roberta* (Kern) with Bob Hope and Sydney Greenstreet; *Blackbirds of 1933* with Bill Robinson; *Take a Chance* starring Ethel Merman and Jack Haley; and—who knows?—you might even have wanted to take in *Earl Carroll's Vanities* (Arlen & Koehler) starring Milton Berle. Broadway was swinging then, and it's a safe bet that Johnny Mercer, still in the early thirties a fairly recent arrival on the scene, took in all the shows. One we know he saw—and many times obviously—was 1932's revue *Americana,* for which he collaborated on lyrics with the man he later named "my guru," E. Y. "Yip" Harburg. (Harold Arlen wrote the melodies, and they were called "Whistling for a Kiss" and "Satan's Little Lamb".)

In addition to the "hot" bands that young guys like Johnny Mercer collected in their "frat" houses down south or out west, New York City in 1932-33 was alive with

25

(Facing page)
Well-dressed New York couple returns to Savannah to chaperone a debutante ball.

The skinny kid from Savannah strikes a Joe E. Brown/Martha Raye publicity pose for his first boss "Pops" Whiteman. Johnny's stepping-stone gig with Whiteman's vast Hotel Biltmore band placed him alongside such talented veterans as Ramona, Roy Bargy, Jack Fulton, Peggy Healey and, best of all, Jack Teagarden.

"sweet" or just plain dance bands. They played mainly in the grill rooms and dining places of the town's leading hotels. There was George Olsen (vocals by wife Ethel Shutta) at the Pennsylvania, Vincent Lopez forever at the Taft, Don Bestor at the McAlpin, Guy Lombardo packing them in at the Roosevelt, and a hot new band from Canada via the Midwest, Casa Loma, at the Essex House. Rudy Vallee was no longer at his own Villa Vallee on east Sixtieth Street, but one could still hear him weekly on radio thanks to the Fleischman's Yeast Program. Ben Bernie ("yowsah yowsah"), Horace Heidt and Kay Kyser could all be heard on dance band "remotes" from various places around the country. But still the top man of them all—the King of Jazz, the man who brought you "Rhapsody in Blue" (his theme song too)—was Paul Whiteman, holding court in the Bowman Room of the Hotel Biltmore, in the summer months at The Cascades atop the hotel. Here's how Johnny Mercer describes his meeting with Whiteman, the man most responsible for launching the Mercer career:

"I got to New York in the first place by winning a little theatre contest at the New Amsterdam Roof. Then the next contest was the Pontiac Youth of America contest, which Paul Whiteman held in every city. [Singing a couple of songs] I won the one in New York. Archie Bleyer (later Arthur Godfrey's orchestra leader) was playing piano for me and Paul came out and said, 'Who's that piano player?' I said, 'That's Archie Bleyer, the jazz arranger.' Then he said, 'No wonder.' That's probably why I won the contest. (Mister Modesty.) Anyway, the three songs that sort of constitute my Whiteman career were 'Fare Thee Well to Harlem,' 'Pardon My Southern Accent,' and 'Here Come the British With a Bang Bang.' "

Johnny Mercer's film acting career begins and ends with RKO's *Old Man Rhythm*; Joy
Hodges and Evelyn Poe show that girls wore sweaters before Lana Turner.

Every college boy had to play a ukelele.

Out of Breath

Music by EVERETT MILLER

When tasks superhuman demand such
   acumen
That only a few men possess,
I never have fear to volunteer.
But though others fear me,
Still when you are near me
And willing to hear me express
Such childish delight,
I'm filled with fright.

Mine's a hopeless case,
But there's one saving grace,
Anyone would feel as I do;
Out of breath and scared to death of you.
Love was first divined,
Then explored and defined,
Still the old sensation is new;
Out of breath and scared to death of you.
It takes all the strength that I can call to my
   command,
To hold your hand.
I would speak at length
About the love that should be made,
But I'm afraid.

Hercules and such
Never bothered me much,
All you have to do is say "Boo!"
Out of breath and scared to death of you.

Since you must propose,
Then I'll have to disclose
Secrets that I've hidden from view;
Out of breath and scared to death of you.
When we met, my heart
Gave a queer little start
And the feeling's growing in to
Out of breath and scared to death of you.
Always I've been used
To having my affections spurned
And not returned;
Once my passion's loosed,
Then that's the time to be concerned,
You may be burned.
Think I could be made,
But I'm still so afraid,
Hurry and change my point of view!
Out of breath and scared to death of you.

"Out of Breath" was written for the Theatre Guild's bright young musical revue *Garrick Gaieties* and sung
in that show by Sterling Holloway. It was the first really professional song by John Mercer (as he was
billed) and an attention-getter in the show. One of the dancers in *Garrick Gaieties* was a lady named
Ginger Meehan, who a few years later changed her second name to Mercer.

Words by
JOHN MERCER

OUT OF BREATH
(and Scared To Death Of You)

Music by
EVERETT MILLER

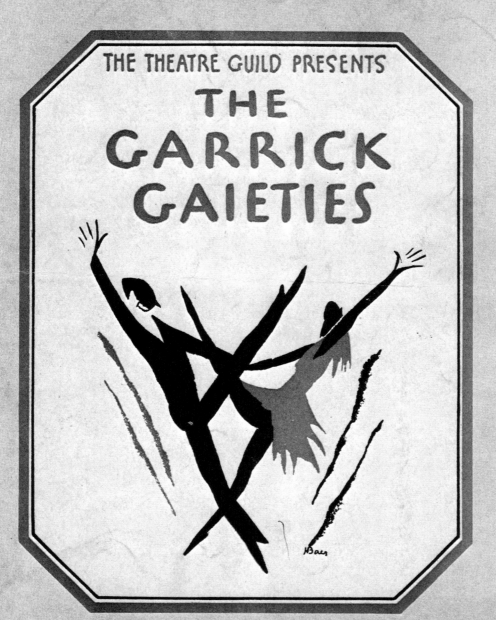

THE THEATRE GUILD PRESENTS

THE GARRICK GAIETIES

PRODUCTION DIRECTED BY
PHILIP LOEB
SETTINGS DESIGNED BY
KATE DRAIN LAWSON
COSTUMES DESIGNED BY
KATE DRAIN LAWSON
AND LOUIS M. SIMON
DANCES ARRANGED BY
OLIN HOLLAND.
ASSISTED BY STELLA BLOCK

MADE IN U.S.A.

I Am Only Human After All
You Lost Your Opportunity
Put It Away Till Spring
Too, Too Divine
Out Of Breath
Ankle Up The Altar With Me
Love Is Like That
I've Got It Again

HARMS
INCORPORATED
62-64 WEST 45TH STREET
NEW YORK
CHAPPELL & CO LTD.
LONDON   SYDNEY

Would'ja for a Big Red Apple?

1932

By HENRY SOUVAINE   EVERETT MILLER
JOHN MERCER

Greater men than I have sought your favor,
But you merely glance at them and grin,
You spurn the vermin,
Who offer ermine and just a bit of sin.

Even though these propositions bore you,
Even though you're weary of the chase,
Let me put a plan before you,
Maybe it will help my case.

Would'ja for a big red apple,
Would'ja for my peace of mind,
Could'ja for a big red apple
Give me what I'm trying to find.

Just imagine you're my teacher,
Teaching me the Golden Rule,
If I had a big red apple,
Would'ja keep me after school?

Cakes and sweets and sugar beets,
May be what a girl deserves,
Choc'late drops and lollipops are sweet on
    the taste
But "H" on the curves.

Would'ja do it just for instance,
Would'ja for my fam'ly tree,
If I had a big red apple,
Would'ja fall in love with me?

The author of "Lazybones" doing what comes naturally.

Buddy Rogers was the star of *Old Man Rhythm* but there was also at far right Lucille Ball (2), under Buddy's left foot Johnny Mercer (4) and under Buddy's right arm Betty Grable (5).

Spring Is in My Heart Again

1932

Music by WILLIAM WOODIN

You've been away so long,
And all the world was wrong
Each little meeting place
Has missed your smiling face;
But now the world is gay
Because you've come to stay,
Those lonely hours
Have passed away.

Spring is in my heart for you are here;
Spring is in my heart and skies are clear.
Life will be the way it used to be
Now that you are back with me.

Ev'ry place I wandered to,
Ev'ry winding street we knew
Brought me memories of you,
Dreaming of the night you said you loved
me.

In our little moonlit rendezvous
I've so many things to say to you;
We will never be apart again.
Spring is in my heart again.

Mercer's co-writer was an interesting partner to have in those Depression days. Banker William Woodin became Franklin Roosevelt's Secretary of the Treasury—which helped not a bit to make this early ballad a money-maker. Fame was still only on its way.

Four music masters: Hoagy Carmichael, Jack Teagarden, Wingy Mannone and J.M.

Mr. Mercer and Mr. Teagarden—they paired off ideally in the Paul Whiteman days and later.

33

Lazybones

1933

Music by HOAGY CARMICHAEL

Long as there is chicken gravy on your rice,
Ev'rything is nice.
Long as there's watermelon on the vine,
Ev'rything is fine.
You got no time to work,
You got no time to play,
Busy doin' nothin' all the live long day.
You won't ever change no matter what I say,
You're just made that way.

Lazybones, Sleepin' in the sun,
How you 'spec' to get your day's work
    done?
Never get your day's work done,
Sleepin' in the noonday sun.

Lazybones, sleepin' in the shade,

How you 'spec' to get your corn meal
    made?
Never get your corn meal made
Sleepin' in the evenin' shade.

When 'taters need sprayin',
I bet you keep prayin'
The bugs fall off of the vine
And when you go fishin'
I bet you keep wishin'
The fish won't grab at your line.

Lazybones, loafin' thru the day,
How you 'spec' to make a dime that way?
Never make a dime that way
(Well looky here,)
He never heared a word I say!

The first real hit for the now newly first-named Johnny Mercer (out with that inappropri-
ately square monicker, John!) It also marks the beginning of a two-peas-in-a-pod musical
partnership and a song that was like home cooking to these relatively new boys in town.
Lazybones took the big city and then the whole country by storm. Mercer and
Carmichael had arrived.

Lazybones

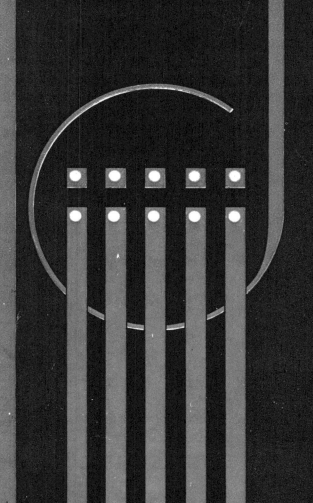

WORDS & MUSIC BY

JOHNNY MERCER

AND

HOAGY CARMICHAEL

Featured by
DO-RE-MI TRIO

WITH GUITAR
AND UKELELE
CHORDS

SOUTHERN MUSIC PUB. CO., INC.
1619 BROADWAY, NEW YORK

Hamilton

The Old Music Master

1933

Music by HOAGY CARMICHAEL

One night long ago by the light of the moon,
An old music master sat composing a tune,
His spirit was soaring and his heart full of
 joy,
When right out of nowhere stepped a little
 colored boy.
You gotta jump it, music master,
You gotta play that rhythm faster,
You're never gonna get it played
On the Happy Cat Hit Parade.
You better tell your friend Beethoven,
And Mister Reginald De Koven
They better do the same as you,
Or they're gonna be corny too.
Long about nineteen seventeen
Jazz'll come upon the scene,
Then about nineteen thirty-five,
You'll begin to hear swing,
Boogie Woogie and Jive,

You gotta show that big broadcaster,
That you're a solid music master,
And you'll achieve posterity,
That's a bit of advice from me.
The old music master simply sat there
 amazed,
As wide-eyed and open-mouthed he gazed,
And he gazed.
How can you be certain, little boy,
Tell me how?
Because I was born, my friend,
A hundred years from now.
He hit a chord that rocked the spinet
And disappeared in "the infinite,"
And up until the present day,
You can take it from me
He's as right as can be,
Ev'rything has happened that-a way.

The team's second outing, but not quite the hit of their first product—(what could be?). Both Hoagy and
Johnny enjoyed writing about jazz, for, after all, the former had been around Bix and the latter was a
dyed-in-the-wool fan who had booked the bands for his prep school's proms. The words "jive" and
"corny" were somewhat avant-garde in 1933, and not many Broadwayites were hip to—who?—"Mister
Reginald DeKoven." But at least "the Happy Cat Hit Parade" could draw a chuckle.

THE OLD MUSIC MASTER

Words by JOHNNY MERCER · Music by HOAGY CARMICHAEL

FAMOUS MUSIC CORPORATION · 1619 Broadway · New York City, N.Y.

When a Woman Loves a Man

1934

Music by BERNARD HANIGHEN

Love to a man is just a thing apart,
To take or leave, according to his whim,
Love to a woman means her very heart,
She only wants to live her life for him.

Maybe he's not much,
Just another man,
Doing what he can,
But what does she care,
When a woman loves a man.

She'll just string along,
All thru' thick and thin,
Till his ship comes in,
It's always that way,
When a woman loves a man.

She'll be the first one to praise him
When he's going strong,
The last one to blame him
When ev'rything's wrong,
It's such a one-sided game that they play,
But women are funny that way.

Tell her she's a fool,
She'll say "Yes, I know,
But I love him so,"
And that's how it goes,
When a woman loves a man.

A great standard among torch songs, recorded by such knowing singers as Billie Holiday, Kay Starr and Jane Harvey. It also marked the beginning of another fruitful alliance, this one with Bernard (soon to be Bernie) Hanighen, a Harvard graduate of *simpatico* musical tastes. Gordon Jenkins went on to achieve great fame for the popular *Manhattan Towers Suite* and Benny Goodman's haunting theme, "Goodbye."

Good songs are like street cars . . . there'll be another one along
in a minute.

Fare-Thee-Well to Harlem

1934

Music by BERNIE HANIGHEN

Mister Jackson, you sho' look cute,
You must have on your trav'lin' suit.
It looks as if you're really gonna go
   somewhere,
Mister Budley, you spoke a book
You just got time for one more look,
'Cause Mister Jackson is leaving you for fair,
For fair, for:

Fare-thee-well to Harlem!
Fare-thee-well to night life!
Goin' back where I can lead the right life
Fare-thee-well to Harlem!

Things is tight in Harlem,
I know how to fix it.

Step aside, I'm gonna Mason Dix it
Fare-thee-well to Harlem!

Lately here my soul is reachin'
For the Bible's kindly teachin'.
Want's to hear the Rev'rund preachin'
"Love each other."
Wants to hear the organ playin'
Wants to hear the folks a prayin'
There's a voice within me sayin'
"Ease off, brother."
So, fare-thee-well to Harlem!
All this sin is "frighteous."
Goin' back where evrybody's righteous.
Fare-thee-well to Harlem!

Mercer had by now found a ready market for his unique and hip (but not too hip) style of song; what was soon added was his stylish way of presenting these songs vocally. This witty and most original specialty number wowed the customers who gathered around the bandstand of New York's Hotel Biltmore when Paul Whiteman (then very popular) presented Mercer and Jack Teagarden as a sort of novelty act. Calling a big, burly jazzman like Teagarden "cute" was way ahead of its time, and the word "frighteous" may be a made-up word but it seems okay for an allowably ethnic song of that time.

FARE-THEE-WELL TO HARLEM

LYRIC BY
JOHNNY MERCER
BY ARRANGEMENT WITH MILLER MUSIC, INC.

MUSIC BY
BERNIE HANIGHEN

Featured by
LEON
BELASCO

SOUTHERN MUSIC PUB. CO. INC. 1619 BROADWAY, N.Y.

Here Come the British

1934

Music by BERNIE HANIGHEN

Children, open up your history,
Turn to lesson twenty-three.
Take a look,
Then close the book,
And I will review it rapidly.

Paul Revere—he took a ride,
Just to look around the countryside.
All at once his horse got skittish;
Here come the British,
Bang! Bang!
Washington—at Valley Forge
Tried to cross the river.
Look out, George!

All at once his boat got skittish;
Here come the British,
Bang! Bang!
Just look around,
No matter where—whoa!
You'll find that
The British are there.
Napoleon at Waterloo
Writin' Josephine a billet doux.
Josie, I've got to close it,
Close this epistle,
There goes the whistle;
Here come the British with a Bang! Bang!

A perfect example of the Mercer wit and originality that caused a stir in professional circles in New York during 1934-35. Broadcasts from the Biltmore spread the Mercer magic, and among those who recognized this new talent on the scene was Irving Berlin. Mr. B's interest led to a working agreement with his major music publishing firm, an important step along the way. Songwriter Arthur Schwartz (& Dietz), big on Broadway in the thirties, also hopped aboard the Mercer bandwagon when he heard Johnny sing this and other originals on the Whiteman broadcasts.

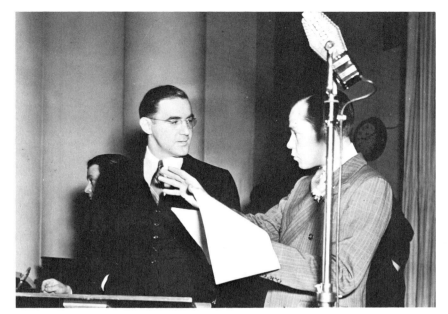

Is the King of Swing giving Johnny his infamous "ray"? J.M. made the Benny Goodman program Camel Caravan a popular tune-in with his very topical "newsy bluesies"

Affable but not yet balding Mercer is shown here obviously song-plugging Benny Goodman's first and best singer, Helen Ward.

Pardon My Southern Accent

1934

Music by MATTY MALNECK

It's a universal moon above you,
Ask the Irish, ask the Greek.
They can always understand "I love you,"
No matter how they speak.

Pardon my Southern accent,
Pardon my Southern drawl;
It may sound funny,
Ah, but honey! I love y'all.

If you don't like my accent,
If you don't like my drawl,
Then just don't listen,
Let's start kissin', bet you'll fall.

Come on, now,
Let me hear you steal my stuff.
When I say,
"Do you love me"
All you gotta say is "Sho'nuff."

Pardon my Southern accent,
Didn't I hear you drawl,
Were you just sighin',
Or replyin'
I love y'all.

Matty Malneck, a violinist in the huge, star-studded Whiteman organization, was another good early partner for Mercer's wonderful way with words. How could anyone from out of Savannah miss with a natural like this? By now even Hollywood was aware of that fresh spring of talent.

Pardon My Southern Accent

Words by
JOHNNY MERCER

Music by
MATT MALNECK

BOURNE INC.
Music Publishers
799 SEVENTH AVENUE · NEW YORK 19, N. Y.

The Dixieland Band

1935

Music by BERNIE HANIGHEN

Dj'ever hear the story of the Dixieland
Band?
Let me tell you, brother,
That the music was grand.
They had piano and a clarinet,
Only think they needed was a second
cornet;
And that's what lead to the ruin;
Ruin of the Dixieland Band.

When the folks would holler for the "Maple
Leaf Rag,"
They would get to swinging,
But the trumpet would drag.
They had to keep him 'cause he played so
sweet,
But they needed someone who could give
them the beat;
Someone who swung with the rhythm,
Rhythm of the Dixieland Band.

He'd play so sweetly.
'Stead of playin' [*musical riff*]
He'd play so sweetly.
They'd be sayin' [*musical riff*]

Sure enough, he got 'em so they couldn't
play right;
Finally he fixed 'em on a Saturday night.
He hit a figure that was off the chord,
Apoplexy got 'em and they went to the
Lord;
And that's the pitiful story,
Story of the Dixieland Band.

Now they're up in heaven and they're
happy at last;
'Cause they found a trumpet man who
really can blast.
The way he swings 'em is an awful shame,
He can really do it, Gabriel is his name.
And now, folks, here is a sample,
Listen to the Dixieland Band.

If you hear a trumpet start to play,
Don't you be afraid, it's the judgment day!
'Cause it's just Mister Gabriel soundin' his
"A."
And the Dixieland Band is fixin' to play.

From Whiteman to Goodman and Mercer is swinging all the way: this is another of the period's hip numbers that not only must have pleased the author's taste but also found a fairly good commercial audience to boot. This one was one of Benny Goodman's first big record hits on the Victor label, helped tremendously by Helen Ward's throbbing vocal. Mercer as usual writes from inside the jazz fraternity with such references as "The Maple Leaf Rag" and a figure that was off the chord. In addition, the song neatly tells a complete little story.

THE DIXIELAND BAND

★

WORDS BY
JOHNNY MERCER

★

MUSIC BY
BERNIE HANIGHEN

PRICE **75**¢ IN U.S.A.

MILLER MUSIC CORPORATION
1540 BROADWAY • NEW YORK 36, N. Y.

On the Nodaway Road

1935

Music by CHARLES BATES

Ploddin,' ploddin,' ol' Betsy's head keeps a
 noddin' noddin'
Ol' Betsy's hoofs are a kickin' up the dust
 along the road,
Haulin' a load down the Nodaway road.
Creakin' creakin'
Ol' wagon wheels keeps a squeakin'
 squeakin'
Groanin' a tune while the crickets sing their
 song,
Go 'long, go 'long
Haulin' a load down the Nodaway road.

Got to get a load o' hay to town,
Hurry back before the sun goes down.
Smoke in the chimney as we climb the hill
'Round evenin' time,

'Round evenin' time.
Ol' Besty hurries goin' past the mill
'Round evenin' time,
'Round evenin' time.
I can hear the dogs bark as I open up the
 gate,
Ain't missed meetin' me yet,
And the lights thru the dark say,
"You'd better not be late, supper table is
 set."
Night is creepin' creepin'
I'll bet ol' Betsy is sleepin' sleepin'
Dreamin' away of another dusty day
To toil away,
Haulin' a load down the Nodaway road,
Haulin' a load down the Nodaway road.

© M. Witmark & Sons

Near the top of the list for thoroughly regional Mercer writing, "Nodaway Road" is a gem of a
song, unfortunately known mainly to the true believers. It is a vignette of heartbreaking
simplicity that Mercer seems to have recreated in the lovely little watercolor that appears in the
front of this book.

48

1937, and another college musical, *Varsity Show,* with Johnnie "Scat" Davis and Fred Waring's Pennsylvanians performing most of the Mercer-Whiting score ("Have You Got Any Castles, Baby?," "Love Is on the Air," "Moonlight on the Campus").

I'm Building Up to an Awful Let-Down

1935   Music by FRED ASTAIRE

I'm like Humpty Dumpty,
Upon the garden wall.
I'm riding high and who can deny,
That whatever goes up must fall.
Poor old Humpty Dumpty,
He got the toughest break,
And yet his fall was nothing at all,
Like the tumble I'm gonna take.

I'm building up to an awful let-down,
By playing around with you.
You're breaking down my terrific buildup,
By treating me as you do.

My castles in the air,
My smile so debonair,
My one big love affair.

Is it just a flash
Will it all go smash,
Like the nineteen twenty-nine market crash?

I'm building up to an awful let-down
By falling in love with you.

© Irving Berlin Inc.

As with so many songwriters and lyricists, the opportunity to have the classy Fred Astaire involved with a song of his was pure joy to Mercer, still new to Hollywood in 1935. Benny Green's book on Astaire quotes Mercer as saying that they met at a recording session that he (Mercer) was doing with Ginger Rogers. They sang "Eeny Meeny Miney Mo," one of Johnny's less illustrious efforts. The idea of their collaborating on a song came about in the casual manner that both men featured so well. The word "debonair" certainly fit at least one of the authors and the reference to the "nineteen twenty-nine market crash" was still a bit of nonchalant bravado in those belt-tightening days.

FRED ASTAIRE'S
I'M BUILDING UP TO AN AWFUL LET-DOWN

Sincerely
Fred Astaire

Music by **FRED ASTAIRE**

Lyrics by **JOHNNY MERCER**

For Sale in the United States and Canada Only

Irving Berlin Inc
MUSIC PUBLISHERS
799 SEVENTH AVE NEW YORK N.Y.

Jamboree Jones

1936

Words and Music by JOHNNY MERCER

I begin my story out in West Virginia
In a little college.
All the student body only cared for football,
Never mind the knowledge.
Never mind the sheepskin,
They preferred the pigskin.
Seemed to have it in their bones.
They knew all about it,
Couldn't live without it,
All except a certain Mister Jamboree Jones.

He played the clarinet with all his might,
He studied night and day,
He practiced day and night;
No running up the field for Mister Jones,
He'd rather run up the scale, what tones.

Even though his buddies
Always cut their studies
To attend a rally,
While they all were rootin'
You could hear him tootin'
"What became of Sally."
How they used to hate him,
Co-eds wouldn't date him,
Thought he was an awful bore.
But he liked his rhythm
More than bein' with 'em,
So he only grinned and went to practice
    some more.

Meanwhile, the team marched on to greater
    fame
Till they were asked to play
The famous Rose Bowl Game;
And on that day of days the students
    beamed,

What did they do when the team marched
    on the field,
They screamed.

Startin' from the kick off
They pulled ev'ry trick off,
But they couldn't win it.
'Stead of goin' forward
They were goin' backward
'Bout a mile a minute.
Seein' their position
They called intermission,
And they heard the ref'ree say,
Seventeen to nothin' ain't exactly nothin'
And you've only got about a minute to play.

Then from the stands there came a distant
    wail
And it was Jamboree
A-swingin' "Hold 'em Yale,"
And then the students all began to yell,
The players marched up the field and down
    the field,
Pell mell.

Rah Rah Rah Rah
Sis Boom Bah Bah
Bop De Oddle-da
Yea Bo Watch'em go.

Now, on a certain West Virginia hill
There stands that college still,
Just as it always will,
And there's a picture in its Hall of Fame.
You'll see the boy in the frame
Who won the game.
Jamboree Jones is the gentleman's name.

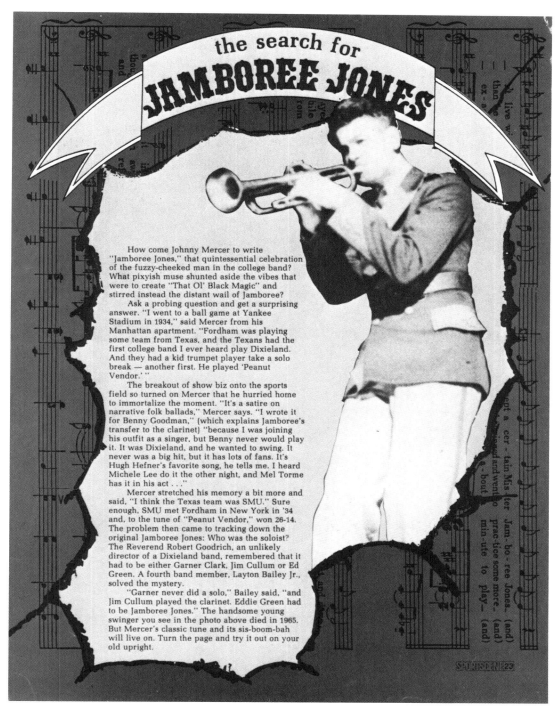

the search for
JAMBOREE JONES

How come Johnny Mercer to write "Jamboree Jones," that quintessential celebration of the fuzzy-cheeked man in the college band? What pixyish muse shunted aside the vibes that were to create "That Ol' Black Magic" and stirred instead the distant wail of Jamboree?

Ask a probing question and get a surprising answer. "I went to a ball game at Yankee Stadium in 1934," said Mercer from his Manhattan apartment. "Fordham was playing some team from Texas, and the Texans had the first college band I ever heard play Dixieland. And they had a kid trumpet player take a solo break — another first. He played 'Peanut Vendor.'"

The breakout of show biz onto the sports field so turned on Mercer that he hurried home to immortalize the moment. "It's a satire on narrative folk ballads," Mercer says. "I wrote it for Benny Goodman," (which explains Jamboree's transfer to the clarinet) "because I was joining his outfit as a singer, but Benny never would play it. It was Dixieland, and he wanted to swing. It never was a big hit, but it has lots of fans. It's Hugh Hefner's favorite song, he tells me. I heard Michele Lee do it the other night, and Mel Torme has it in his act . . ."

Mercer stretched his memory a bit more and said, "I think the Texas team was SMU." Sure enough, SMU met Fordham in New York in '34 and, to the tune of "Peanut Vendor," won 26-14. The problem then came to tracking down the original Jamboree Jones: Who was the soloist? The Reverend Robert Goodrich, an unlikely director of a Dixieland band, remembered that it had to be either Garner Clark, Jim Cullum or Ed Green. A fourth band member, Layton Bailey Jr., solved the mystery.

"Garner never did a solo," Bailey said, "and Jim Cullum played the clarinet. Eddie Green had to be Jamboree Jones." The handsome young swinger you see in the photo above died in 1965. But Mercer's classic tune and its sis-boom-bah will live on. Turn the page and try it out on your old upright.

Here's the way Johnny spoke about this collegiate caper: "I wrote it for Benny Goodman. . . . just a kind of admiration for the way he played. But he didn't play it much, because I don't think he liked it. It's kind of a put-on of 'Casey Jones' and 'Steamboat Bill,' don't you think?"

Mel Tormé, a Mercer buff of the top echelon, does this story-telling novelty often and, of course, is perfect for the performance.

Goody Goody

1936   Music by MATTY MALNECK

You told me that there wasn't a lesson in
   lovin'
You hadn't learned
Oh yeah?
Oh yeah?
You told me that you keep playin' with fire
Without getting burned.
Oh yeah?
Oh yeah?

So you met someone
Who set you back on your heels,
Goody goody!
So you met someone
And now you know how it feels,

Goody Goody!
So you gave her your heart too
Just as I gave mine to you
And you broke it in little pieces,
Now how do you do?
So you lie awake
Just singing the blues all night,
Goody Goody!
So you think that love's
A barrel of dynamite.
Hooray and hallelujah!
You had it comin' to ya.
Goody Goody for him,
Goody Goody for me,
And I hope you're satisfied, you rascal you.

Somebody told us (Malneck?) that Mercer got the idea for this double-word title from the menu of a Chinese restaurant and then stashed it away with other notes in a bureau drawer under some shirts. Several years later he rediscovered it—and *voilà!* Or, ah-so! Helen Ward remembers that she pleaded with Benny Goodman, "Please don't make me sing that damn song." BG knew—it became one of Helen Ward's biggest hits with the Goodman band.

BY AIR MAIL
PAR AVION

Mr. John Mercer
Warners Brothers Studio
Burbank, California
U.S.A. –

---

very pleasant and make good servants.
This is sort of between seasons here
now, so we're getting plenty place
and quiet. Live way out on a point
with fine beach, surf etc.

I spoke to the boys about your
going on the Kraft show, and hope
something definite has been done about
it. Present plans indicate I will
be in Hollywood on the 17th of
October –

Best regards to Ginger. Saw
Bernie in N.Y. He was reeling slightly.
Jack White a riot –

regards
Bing –

I'm an Old Cowhand

(From the Rio Grande)

1936

Words and music by JOHNNY MERCER

Step aside you ornery Tenderfeet
Let a big bad buckeroo past
I'm the toughest hom'bre you'll ever meet
Tho' I may be the last.
Yessirree we're a vanishing race,
Nosirree can't last long.
Step aside you ornery Tenderfeet
While I sing my song.

I'm an old cowhand
From the Rio Grande,
But my legs ain't bowed
And my cheeks ain't tanned,
I'm a cowboy who never saw a cow,
Never roped a steer 'cause I don't know
    how,
And I sho' ain't fixin' to start in now.
Yippy I O Ki Ay,
Yippy I O Ki Ay.

I'm an old cowhand
From the Rio Grande,
And I learned to ride
'Fore I learned to stand,
I'm a ridin' fool who is up to date,

I know ev'ry trail in the Lone Star State,
'Cause I ride the range in a Ford V-Eight.
Yippy I O Ki Ay,
Yippy I O Ki Ay.

I'm an old cowhand
From the Rio Grande,
And I come to town
Just to hear the band,
I know all the songs that the cowboys know,
'Bout the big corral where the doagies go,
'Cause I learned them all on the radio.
Yippy I O Ki Ay,
Yippy I O Ki Ay.

I'm an old cowhand
From the Rio Grande
Where the West is wild
'Round the Border land,
Where the buffalo roam around the Zoo,
And the Indians make you a rug or two,
And the old Bar X is a Bar B Q.
Yippy I O Ki Ay,
Yippy I O Ki Ay.

Mercer told us: "Between movie assignments Ginger and I took a trip down to Savannah in a little car. We took three days out of six just to cross Texas, and I saw all those guys down there in those spurs and ten-gallon hats driving cars around. That struck me as kind of funny and so I thought maybe I should put it all into a song. Bing put the song into a picture, and I really think he saved my Hollywood career, because I began to get more offers after that."

Modest Mercer there. But it was the first of many tie-ups between these two, who had more than just the Hollywood clubbiness in common. Ex-Whiteman vocalist Crosby must certainly have been listening once or twice when Johnny sang later on with that band, and Ginger had had a few dates with Bing before she became Mrs. Mercer.

Skinny Johnny and the old pro, Richard Whiting, who seems to be striking not only a serious chord but a serious pose as well. They made a peach of a productive pair, but who would have thought then that some day the composer of such great hits as "Japanese Sandman" and "Sleepy Time Gal" would be known to millions as the father of little Maggie Whiting.

Too Marvelous for Words

1937

Music by RICHARD A. WHITING

I search for phrases,
To sing your praises,
But there aren't any magic adjectives
To tell you all you are.

You're just too marvelous,
Too marvelous for words,
Like glorious, glamourous
And that old standby, amorous,

It's all too wonderful,
I'll never find the words,
That say enough,
Tell enough,
I mean, they just aren't swell enough,

You're much too much,
And just too very very!
To ever be in Webster's Dictionary,

And so I'm borrowing
A love song from the birds,
To tell you that you're marvelous,
Too marvelous for words.

A solid Mercer standard and a natural song idea for the word-minded author. "Very-very" is a nice idiomatic trick and the brilliant fall-into-place of "Webster's dictionary" adds fun that anyone can dig. The super-chic Bobby Short uses this song as a vehicle for community singing in the best cafés and supper clubs.

1937, and one of Hollywood's classic production numbers. Ruby Keeler and Lee Dixon dance on the keys to the tune of "Too Marvelous for Words," making typists all over the world green with envy. The movie was *Ready, Willing and Able*.

Bob White

(Whatcha Gonna Swing Tonight?)

1937   Music by BERNIE HANIGHEN

Mister Bob, don't you know things have
    changed?
You're behind time with the melody you
    always sing,
All the birds have their songs rearranged,
Better get smart,
Whatcha gotta do today is swing;

I was talkin' to the whippoorwill,
He says you got a corny trill,
Bob White!
Whatcha gonna swing tonight?
I was talkin' to the mocking bird,
He says you are the worst he's heard,
Bob White!
Whatcha gonna swing tonight?

Even the owl
Tells me you're foul,
Singin' those lullaby notes,
Don't be a bring-down
If you can swing down,
Gimme those high notes!
There's a lotta talk about you, Bob,
And they're sayin' you're "off the cob,"
Fake it,
Mister B.
Take it,
Follow me,
Bob White!
(whistle)
We're gonna break it up tonight!

A Crosby-Mercer record classic in the tradition of Gallagher & Shean. Mercer always had
an affinity for the fine feathered friends, and so putting this one onto paper (probably on
assignment for the record date) must have been a breeze. If you can find the record,
you'll hear two pros having a ball.

Hooray for Hollywood

1938

Music by RICHARD A. WHITING

Hooray for Hollywood!
That screwy bally hooey Hollywood,
Where any office boy or young mechanic
Can be a panic,
With just a good looking pan,
And any bar maid
Can be a star maid,
If she dances with or without a fan,

Hooray for Hollywood!
Where you're terrific if you're even good,
Where anyone at all from Shirley Temple
To Aimee Semple
Is equally understood,
Go out and try your luck,
You might be Donald Duck!
Hooray for Hollywood!

Hooray for Hollywood!
That phony super Coney Hollywood,
They come from Chilicothes and Paducahs
With their bazookas
To get their names up in lights,
All armed with photos from local rotos,
With their hair in ribbons and legs in tights,

Hooray for Hollywood!
You may be homely in your neighborhood,
But if you think that you can be an actor,
See Mister Factor,
He'd make a monkey look good.
Within a half an hour,
You'll look like Tyrone Power!
Hooray for Hollywood!

Is there a television special coming from the West Coast that *doesn't* use this song for a theme?
   1938 was a big year in the studios for Mercer. It was the year that found him teamed up with no one, but two, of the very best melody men in Hollywood—Richard Whiting and Harry Warren. This collaboration with Whiting was sung in the movie *Hollywood Hotel* by an effervescent musician, Johnnie "Scat" Davis. Davis seems to have fallen by the wayside, but the song has grown and grown through the years.

You Must Have Been a Beautiful Baby

1938   Music by HARRY WARREN

Does your mother realize,
The stork delivered quite a prize,
The day he left you on the fam'ly tree,

Does your dad appreciate,
That you are merely super great,
The miracle of any century,

If they don't, just send them both to me.

You must have been a beautiful baby,
You must have been a wonderful child,

When you were only startin'
To go to kindergarten,
I bet you drove the little boys wild.

And when it came to winning blue ribbons,
You must have shown the other kids how.
I can see the judges' eyes
As they handed you the prize,
I bet you made the cutest bow.

Oh! You must have been a beautiful baby,
'Cause, baby, look at you now.

Harry Warren was already the seasoned pro and Mercer merely the *wunderkind* around the studios when Warner Bros. paired them up in the busy year of 1938.

Here is Harry Warren's impression of that young partner of long ago: "I called him 'Cloud Boy,' and I'll tell you why. A lot of times when I would play a melody for him . . . particularly if it was after a good lunch . . . he'd stretch out on a couch and just lie there with his eyes closed and his hands folded across his stomach. He was way up there some place in the clouds. Of course, what came out later was just great."

As with many a great pop song, once Mercer found the "then–now" gimmick for this song, the rest might have been quite easy for a master lyricist.

Jeepers Creepers

1938

Music by HARRY WARREN

I don't care what the weather man says,
When the weather man says it's raining,
You'll never hear me complaining,
I'm certain the sun will shine,
I don't care how the weather vane points,
When the weather vane points to gloomy,
It's gotta be sunny to me,
When your eyes look into mine;

Jeepers Creepers!
Where'd ya get those peepers?
Jeepers Creepers!
Where'd ya get those eyes?

Gosh all git up!
How'd they get so lit up?

Gosh all git up!
How'd they get that size?

Golly gee!
When you turn those heaters on,
Woe is me!
Got to put my cheaters on,

Jeepers Creepers!
Where'd ya get those peepers?
Oh! Those weepers!
How they hypnotize!
Where'd ya get those eyes?

"Jeepers creepers, where'd you get those peepers?"

"Jeepers Creepers" brought Mercer's first Academy Award nomination. And here's what he had to say about the song: "I think I heard Henry Fonda say something like 'Jeepers Creepers' in a movie, and I thought it would be a cute idea for a song. I searched around quite a bit and then found that it fit so well as a title for that melody of Harry's. It was lucky casting that we got Louis Armstrong to sing it, although it wasn't written for him."

The Girl Friend of the Whirling Dervish

1938

Lyric by AL DUBIN and JOHNNY MERCER
Music by HARRY WARREN

One fine day I chanced to stray on a little
  side street in old Bombay
And met a sentimental oriental,
She saw me and I saw she had a manner
  too bold and much too free,
Her *eyes were positively detrimental,*

When I asked about this gay coquette,
I discovered much to my regret:

She's the girl friend of the whirling dervish,
She's the sweetest one he's found,
But ev'ry night in the mellow moonlight,
When he's out dervishing with all his might,
She gives him the run around.

All the boy friends of the whirling dervish
  are his best friends to his face,

But there's no doubt, when he isn't about,
They all come hurrying to take her out,
She leads him a dizzy pace,
He dreams of a Hindu honeymoon,
He doesn't dream that ev'ry night when he
  goes out to
Make an honest rupee,
She steps out to make a lotta whoopee.

Oh! The love song of the whirling dervish
Has a sweet and tender sound,
But will he burn if he ever should learn,
That while he's doing her a real good turn,
She gives him the run around.

She's got a nervish, throwin' him a curvish,
Which of course, he doesn't deservish,
Poor old whirling dervish!

A good movie novelty song that utilized the inevitable gag, "a real good turn . . . gives him the
run around." The three-way collaboration of Dubin, Mercer and Warren produced the song for
Garden of the Moon, one of the less than memorable movies that came off the Warner
assembly line in the thirties. Again it was Johnnie "Scat" Davis who sang it on screen (was he
being groomed to be another Jack Oakie or a white Louis Armstrong?).

THE GIRL FRIEND OF THE WHIRLING DERVISH

WARNER BROS.
presents

"GARDEN OF THE MOON"

WITH

PAT O'BRIEN
MARGARET LINDSAY
JOHN PAYNE

JOE VENUTI *and his* SWING CATS

JOHNNIE DAVIS · MELVILLE COOPER

AND

JIMMIE FIDLER

DIRECTED BY BUSBY BERKELEY

Screen Play by Jerry Wald and Richard
Macaulay · From the Saturday Evening Post
Story by H. Bedford-Jones and Barton Browne

Music by

HARRY WARREN

Lyrics by

AL DUBIN
JOHNNY MERCER

CONFIDENTIALLY
GARDEN OF THE MOON
LOVE IS WHERE YOU FIND IT
THE GIRL FRIEND OF THE
WHIRLING DERVISH
THE LADY ON THE TWO CENT
STAMP

HARMS
INC.
NEW YORK

The Weekend of a Private Secretary

1938

Music by BERNIE HANIGHEN

I went to Havana on one of those cruises,
For forty-nine fifty to spend a few days;
I went to Havana, to look at the natives,
To study their customs, their picturesque
  ways.

In searching for some local color,
I ran across a Cuban gent,
And he was such a big sensation,
I forgot the population;
He showed me the city, he taught me the
  customs;
My trip to Havana was quite a success.

We had Bacardi,
I forgot the clock,
So we were tardy
In returning to the dock.
Tho' I delayed it,
Even dropped my shawl,
The Cuban made it,

As they gave the final call.
Darn it all!

I'm back in the office,
I'm punching the time clock,
But you can bet my mind is not on my
  work;
Instead of Bacardis,
I'm ordering Bromos,
Instead of the Cuban,
I'm stuck with a clerk.

The other girls can go to Europe,
And marry into royalty,
And they can get an Earl or Pasha
Or a gent with lots of casha.

But when I get married
And settle in Brooklyn,
He may be a slicker,
He may be a hick or a Reuben,
But you can bet that he'll be Cuban.

Mercer's handiwork with topicality, a couple of mild jokes, and a neat little story-line paid off for the singer but not too much for the song. It was a natural for the sly, soft-swinging Mildred Bailey, who made it into one of her best records that year.

Week End of a Private Secretary

LYRIC BY JOHNNY MERCER ASCAP

MUSIC BY BERNIE HANIGHEN ASCAP

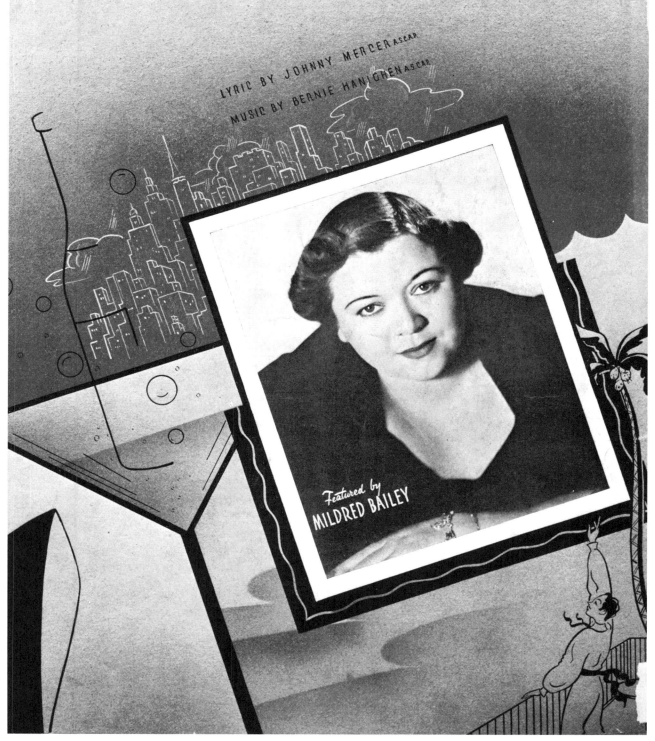

Featured by
MILDRED BAILEY

NORVO
CROSBY

MERCER
GOODMAN

The Rocking Chair Lady, Mildred Bailey, another Whiteman alumna, had the sly singing style for Mercer's satirical cruise song.

Bing Crosby
Hollywood

April 13, 1939

Dear "Verseable":

I thought you would be out this way afore now and was surprised to learn you're not coming for a piece. We all miss your Saturday nite insouciance, but of course you should strike while the iron is hot - and you've got it good and hot right now.

"Angels," to my way of thinking, is your best lyric to date. You're getting practically poetic. It's a hunk of song. Trouble is, by the time Kapp gets them to me, all the good singers have opened many lengths on me.

I hope you kept Drinkable out of the clip joints during his Gotham Sabbatical. Doesn't take but two flagons of Trommers' Lager to send him on the town.

Laughable is a champion now. He's at Palm Springs with his ma, catching a tan and getting well spoiled by all the ladies. He slays the chickadees. Strictly a Crosby, I guess.

"Eastside of Heaven" was good fun under the expansive aegis of D. Wingate Butler. Never engaged in a more pleasant and, I hope, profitable enterprise. The budget was astonishingly low and, if John Public takes to the picture favorably, we're a cinch to make a meg or two.

Now, John, we're expecting you here for the racing and the 'surfin' and turfin', so pack up Ginger et al and summer out this way.

Your friend,

Bing

Mr. John Mercer
111 E. 60th.
New York, New York

This sheet music cover, included only to illustrate the "jolly darkie" image still afoot in some management offices of 1936, despite the European success of such sophisticates as Josephine Baker, Reginald Foresythe and Leslie Hutcheson during the period. If the songs were not too memorable, at least the art work retains a certain period charm.

And the Angels Sing

1939   Music by ZIGGY ELMAN

We meet, and the angels sing.
The angels sing the sweetest song I ever
    heard.
You speak, and the angels sing,
Or am I breathing music into ev'ry word.

Suddenly the setting is strange,
I can see water and moonlight beaming,
Silver waves that break on some
    undiscovered shore;
Then suddenly I see it all change,
Long winter nights with the candles
    gleaming,
Thru it all your face that I adore.

You smile, and the angels sing,
And tho' it's just a gentle murmur at the
    start,
We kiss, and the angels sing
And leave their music ringing in my heart.

Mercer's association with Benny Goodman continued through the 1930s, when he was selected to co-host a radio show called "Camel Caravan" that featured the King of Swing. (The program would often show off Mercer's ingeniousness with almost on-the-spot satires of the day's news called Newsie Bluesies.) The association led to this classic—sung then by Martha Tilton—which is the result of Mercer's adding lyrics to what had been a Ziggy Elman trumpet specialty called "Frälich in Swing."

I Thought About You

1939

Music by JIMMY VAN HEUSEN

Seems that I read, or somebody said
That out of sight is out of mind,
Maybe that' so but I tried to go
And leave you behind,
What did I find?

I took a trip on the train
And I thought about you,
I passed a shadowy lane
And I thought about you,
Two or three cars parked under the stars,
A winding stream,
Moon shining down on some little town,
And with each beam,
Same old dream,

At ev'ry stop that we made
Oh, I thought about you,
But when I pulled down the shade,
Then I really felt blue,
I peeked thru the crack
And looked at the track,
The one going back to you,
And what did I do?
I thought about you!

One of the rare collaborations with the great veteran Jimmy McHugh, this wonderfully sentimental song is placed in the setting that Mercer loved so much and used so often—the train. The brief pictures evoked ("shadowy lane" "cars parked" "some little town") certainly spell out the feeling of a rural countryside at night, and the triple rhyme of "crack, "track" and "back" is train-like too. The composer-musicologist Alec Wilder singled this song out for special praise—but, then, he was another railroad buff.

You Grow Sweeter as the Years Go By

1939

Words and Music by JOHNNY MERCER

When I look at you
Standing there beside me,
I am filled with pride,
I am happy too,
When the winter lies upon the meadow,
I don't mind if summer time is through,
When I look at you;

You grow sweeter as the years go by,
You grow sweeter as the twilights fly,
I need never dream of our first kiss,
When I know our last one is as sweet as this.

Though September takes the place of June
In September there's a harvest moon,
Let the leaves start falling, darling,
What care I
When you grow sweeter as the years go by.

Although there are several photographs of Mercer seated at the keyboard of a piano, that is only photographic license and a cliché as well. He was not a full-fledged musician, although he could read the notes on a piece of sheet music and could obviously pick out a melody single-finger style. This is one example of a nice but unexceptional little song that Mercer wrote by himself.

Day In—Day Out

1939

Music by RUBE BLOOM

Day in—day out,
The same old hoodoo follows me about.
The same old pounding in my heart
Whenever I think of you
And, darling, I think of you
Day in—and day out
Day out—day in,
I needn't tell you how my days begin.
When I awake I awaken with a tingle,
One possibility in view,
That possibility of maybe seeing you.
Come rain, come shine,
I meet you and to me the day is fine,
Then I kiss your lips
And the pounding becomes
The ocean's roar,
A thousand drums,
Can't you see it's love,
Can there by any doubt,
When there it is
Day in—day out.

Always a blockbuster when sung by the magnificent Lena Horne, this lyric strangely presages the title of another even greater Mercer hit—"Come Rain or Come Shine." The co-writer, Rube Bloom, had played piano for many jazz groups through the years and had written the brilliant piano solo "Soliloquy," so Mercer must have admired him greatly. "The ocean's roar . . . a thousand drums"—great for Las Vegas and big rooms with big bands.

Who can compete with Lena's smile? "Day In, Day Out" has been one of her powerhouse numbers for years.

Two very groovey characters do a typical photographer's switch for the camera. Johnny, hippest of all famous songwriters, was the right one to sing "Happy Birthday" to Satchmo for his 50th at the Newport Jazz Festival.

The Rumba Jumps!

1939

Music by HOAGY CARMICHAEL

There's a Harlem band 'way down in San
    Domingo,
A very talented group,
They kicked 'em off of a sloop,
Even tho' the band can't understand the
    lingo,

They're never down in the dumps,
For when the drummer boy thumps,
The Rumba Jumps!

"Hep, hep!" They hollered the moment
    they landed,
"We've got a rumba the King once
    commanded,"
Then they passed a tin and started in to play
The way they learned to play
Back in the U.S.A.

Now they're on the air and San Domingo's
    lappin' it up,

And I do declare those Harlem boys are
    wrappin' it up;
Folks in ev'ry land tune in on San Domingo,
They're never down in the dumps,
For when the drummer boy thumps,
The Rumba Jumps!

"Hep, hep!" they holler,
"Stay right in your villa,
We're on the air for a brand of vanilla."
If you wanna dance and wanna dance in
    style,
You better turn the dial
To San Domingo Isle,

And when you hear "Aye aye,
Hide aye aye,"
You'll know the reason why
The Rumba Jumps!

Hoagy and Johnny, back together in 1939, wrote a few numbers for the stage show *Three After Three*, but despite such talented people as Mitzi Green, Frances Williams and Stepin Fetchit the review limped into New York, where it was re-named *Walk with Music*. This specialty was obviously meant to be the inspiration and background for lots of hot dancing—"hep hep!" was quite hip then.

THE RUMBA JUMPS!

Lyrics by
JOHNNY MERCER

Music by
HOAGY CARMICHAEL

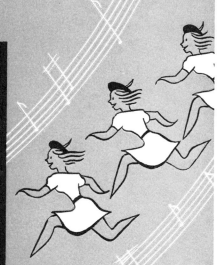

RUTH SELWYN IN ASSOCIATION WITH
MESSRS. SHUBERT

presents

SIMONE SIMON
MITZI GREEN

and

MARY BRIAN

in

'Three After Three'

with

FRANCES WILLIAMS
ART JARRETT
STEPIN FETCHIT

★

From the original play by **GUY BOLTON**
Musical adaptation by
GUY BOLTON, PARKE LEVY and ALAN PRESCOTT
Staged by **CLARKE LILLEY**
Scenery designed by **WATSON BARRAT**
Dances by **BOOTS McKENNA**
Costumes by **LUCINDA BALLARD**

★

MERCER & MORRIS, INC.
1619 BROADWAY NEW YORK, N.Y.

THE RUMBA JUMPS
DARN CLEVER, THESE CHINEE
OOH! WHAT YOU SAID
WAY BACK IN 1939 A.D.
EVERYTHING HAPPENS TO ME
WHAT'LL THEY THINK OF NEXT

Hooray for Spinach

1939

Music by HARRY WARREN

As a kid, I hated spinach and all its ilk,
I abominated cod liver oil and milk,
That was simply that and I'd leave them flat!
Tho' you stuck a gat at my brow,
But I must admit my opinion's different now;

Hooray for spinach!
Hooray for milk!
They put the roses in your cheek soft as silk,
They helped complete you till I could meet
    you, baby!

Hooray for sunshine!
Hooray for air!
They put the permanent in your curly hair,
They helped to raise you till I could praise
    you, baby!

Bless the summer that freckled your nose,
Those galoshes that sheltered your toes,
Bless the fellow who taught you to kiss,
If he taught you to kiss like this.

Hooray for spinach!
It took you far!
Bless all the nourishment in each candy bar,
They helped you grow up till
I could show up and love you as you are.

It has to be tongue in cheek that caused Mercer and Warren to have put in small print on the face of the sheet music "with acknowledgments to Wagner, Lizst, etc." The whole idea of this typically "cute" movie song seems borrowed a bit from the earlier "You Must Have Been a Beautiful Baby," or maybe it was suggested by the tremendously popular *New Yorker* cartoon of that period, "I say it's spinach and I say the hell with it!" At any rate Ronald Reagan might remember it.

Not one of Mercer's greatest efforts but we call your attention to the cast, where even Johnnie (what happened to "Scat"?) Davis takes precedence over the current cowboy from Washington.

Christmas card

BLESSINGS on thee, everyone
Every single mother's son
Blessings, friends of ancient vintage
Blessings, friends of recent mintage
Whomsoever you may be
Merry Christmas unto thee
Old year's gone and we got through it
—though I wouldn't own up to it—
Hope and pray the next one's better
If it ain't we'll make it wetter
Drown our sorrows and our woes
Barkeep, give me one of those!
Let's all drink a toast or toddy
Wishing well to everybody
This is one day hearts have wings
Hark, the Herald Tribune sings!
There is peace in Sunday's chimes
There is—quote—peace in our Times
Brilliant is the Evening Star
Brilliant and somnambular
Let's repeat it once again
Peace on earth—good will to men
Gather neath the mistletoe
A.F.L. and C.I.O.
Wendell Willkie, Gerald Nye
Messers. ASCAP, BMI
With the world hell bent for leather

Now's the time to stick together
Drop the hatchet, stop the fuss
Climb aboard, and come with us
Mr. Kringle drives the sleigh
Don't you hear a reindeer neigh?
Here we go! He cracks his whip
Our imaginary trip
Takes us through the snowy night
—better wrap those blankets tight—
Time for all to go once more
Through the holly-covered door
Down the candle-lighted hall
Merry Christmas to you all!
Things are bad from pole to isthmus
But we still believe in Christmas
Choir, let these guests be carolled!
Annie Arlen, hatless Harold
Johnny Arledge, Fred Astaire
Jane and Squirrel, the Ashcraft pair
Juney Adams, hya, bub?
Ager, Alter, Auto Club
Square and Edith Anderson
Henny Bacchus, Billy Blun
Nora and the kids and Carleton
All of 301 East Charlton
Irving Berlin, Perry Botkin
What's the difference if you're not kin?

For all his sly wit and hip imagery, Johnny Mercer was basically a sentimentalist. Nothing shows this more clearly than the great series of Christmas cards which he began composing and sending to a select list of his friends in the late thirties. He might have been inspired by a similar traditional verse that Frank Sullivan wrote for *The New Yorker* each New Year's, and Johnny's, more California-oriented, were just as eagerly anticipated, as the years went by, for their roll calls of familiar names and their matchless rhymes. Johnny used almost no punctuation in these verses, but so sure was his ear that they read as though carefully copy-edited.

Get together, hug each other
You may be somebody's mother
Berkeley, Bargy, Bleyer, Bloom
This way to the drinking room
Morton Bernstein and his wife
—the first woman in my life—
Gladly did I let her munch on
My first kindergarten luncheon
Johnny Burke, that wine
    should bubble!
Well, poor boy, he's seeing double
I hear Bells—and all the way
From Savannah town, G.A.
Greetings, darling Aunt Nell Blackie
Bless you, and your boys in khaki
Butlers, Burroughs, Mildred Bailey
Try this on your ukelele—
Take this old one off the shelf—
"Love thy neighbor as thyself"
Ronny Burla and his Una
And this summer in Laguna
Henri Blanke, and Miss B
Mr., Mrs., Broccoli
All of A,S,C,A,P
Harry Barris—BVC
Pink and Mary, hey and nonny
Susie, Belle, and killer Johnny
Bing and Dixie and their clan
Barefoot boys with Daddy's pan
And if Daddy's wits are keen
He knows "pan" ain't what I mean
Carol Carol, J. Colonna
All the smudgepots in Pomona
Hattie Clinton, daughter Ann
And the lost Republican
Greetings, Ducky, Bob Carmichael
Hoag and Ruth complete the cycle
Christmas Gift to Chan and Chaplin
Leonard Ross and
    H∗Y∗M∗A∗N K∗A∗P∗L∗A∗N

Bless the Dolans, Mims and Bobby
We the people—Hobby Lobby
Bette Davis, Mary and Mary
And the dwelling of McCarey
Pour the port and fill the chalice
For the Dougalls, Bern and Alice
Tommy Dugan, Buddy Dill
And the folks upon the hill
The DeSylvas—hello, chief!
(When do I go on relief?)
Pass the eggnog, pass the wines
Fill the goblets, fill the steins
William Dozier, Meta Reis
Never let the pouring cease
Drink a cheer to Mr. Dubin
Dorsey brothers, how have you been?
Walter Donaldson, drink hearty
Barney Dean, it's your block party
Jimmy Downey and his mummy
Joseph Dubin and his tummy
E's for Ellfeldt, Emerson
Edelman and everyone
Harry Evans, Eberle
Fill the house with harmony
Skinnay Ennis, have a chair
Everybody, everywhere
Arthur Fishbein, Arthur Franklin
Dwight and Mary, won't you ankl' in?
Shake my writin' hand, Coach Frawley
You still rhyme with Dick MacCauley
Leo Forbstein, start your band
Play for Miss de Havilland
Henry Fonda, Mrs. F
Shout it till the crowd is deaf
O'er the snowy countryside
Happy, happy Xmastide
To the friends too seldom seen
Ira Gershwin, Johnny Green
Close that window—look who blew in
Jack Gordean and Jimmy Gruen

Darling Peggy and their John
Followed by the tribe of Kahn
Benny Goodman, there's Mose Gumble
Won't you help him from the rumble?
Goodwins, get up from the table
Make your bow to Betty Grable
Johnny Galludet and Connie
Looking apple cheeked and bonny
Ring the bells in St. John's steeple
For the Hulls—our favorite people
Here comes Hunter—Christmas calling
Here comes Herzig—ashes falling
Dr. Harris, Byron Harvey
There's the turkey—feeling carvey?
Bob and Peg, and Hanighen
All together once again
Greetings coming—going back
Are you kiddin'?—Murder, Jack!
To the Houstons and the Hitches
And the Hendersons—like Skitch is
Merry Yule and Noel too
Lindsay Howard, Judyroo
Taste the peaches, slice the mutton
For Ray Heindorf, Betty Hutton
—if the madam's glance is wayward
For that dream girl, Susan Hayward
Bob Hope and his bride, Dolores
May I pour a doch-an-dorris?
Footman! Do you hear those klaxons!
Meet the Jenkins and the Jacksons!
Here comes Jarvis and his ballroom
Open up that extra hall room
Irving Kahal and Teddy Koehler
Charlie Chan and Sidney Toler
Hey, toy soldier, hit your cymbals
For Miss Karol down at Gimbels
Hy and Reata, Missy Jill
Holly on your windowsill
I know all you people, but
WHO is Wilhelmina Thutt?

Kaufman, Keyes, and Kuhl and Kress
Everybody—more or less
Even those whom I've forgotten
Jim! My memory is rotten!
And if you think that's a curse
Madam's list is even worse
So if your name is omitted
We both pray to be acquitted
And we love you anyway
If that meets with your okay?
Jimmy Kern, his bairn and mar'm,
Best of luck from madam's arm
Jerry Kern, my circumspect eyes
Say, "Go on and wear those neckties"
Who's that beauty over there?
Gentlemen, meet Annie Lehr
Edgar Leslie, Eddie Lowe
With those cute LaMonts in tow
Jolly, jumping Jerry Lester
John and Mildred Malatester
Lamp Miss Landis' apparel
That's my kind of Christmas Carole
And toujours Lamour toujours
Is my favorite song I'm sure
Who's that in the living room?
Donald Livingston, I presume?
Footman! Bring Priscilla Lane
In out of the frozen rain
Look! We have a pine-cone fire
From the house of McIntire
And some frankincense and myrrh
From the house of Mehlinger
And some old imported vino
Malneck, this is Mannerino
Mayhew, this is Modisett
Have you met the Mitchells yet?
Joseph Wingston (Lawd!) Mannone
Jack, I do not dig your tone!
Miss MacLaughlin . . . Mr. Markey
Always tries that old mullarkey

Here they come—those sailing sharks
Buddy Morris, Albert Marx
Have you met the Mercer tribe?
These cats really can imbibe!
Juliana and Miss Lily
Uncle Robbie—he's a dilly
Hugh and domicile of three
Walter and his family
Mercer, Nancy—best to them
Joseph and Virginia M
Chris and Liz and George and Bess
—Uncle Joe is in distress,
Cousin Mamie's hid the liquor
That just makes a Scotsman sicker—
Uncle Lewis and Uncle Ed
Soiled Aunt Katherine's tablespread!
Pray continue, eat your fill
While we call up Jacksonville
Say hello to Mother there
Ed, and Deborah, and Claire
Goodness how the party grows
Millers, Myers, Monacos
Freddie Martin and Tchaikowsky
Dagmar, I believe, Godowsky
Ray and Eadie Mayer—and Jeanie
Count Oleg and Gene Cassini
Harmon Helson, how's the ham—
Baked and cured by
    Uncle Sam?
Mr. Nobel sound your "A"
Play a simple Christmas lay
To O'Brien, to O'Connell
Out-of-meter John MacDonell
The Orsattis and O'Neills
—Mrs. O's a dream on wheels—
To the Oxnards and the Oakies
O'er the Rockies and the Smokies
Santa brings our heartfelt wish
May your new year be delish!

I could count till I got weary
Playing one, two, three O'Leary
Once again here comes that
    snow man
Fat and smiling faced Phil Ohman
Herb and Midge Polesie, howdy!
Just in time—we're getting rowdy
Hello, Helen Paup and Merle
Whatcha gettin'—boy or girl?
Cheers to Miriam and Jeanette
(If HE calls—I'm on the set)
Really it's too hard to count
All the friends at Paramount
So they'll simply be yclept
Louis Lipstone's Music Dept.
And that goes for Fox and Metro
Warners, R.K.O., etcetro...
And the Pious folk deserve a
Merry Christmas—Hi, Minerva!
Hey, Miss Phillips, talk to Peer
Call him Cuddles—that's a dear
Nina Pape—no teacher's
    topped her
And that goes for Miss Willhopter
Love to Roy and Lucy Potter
Love to all of John Scott Trotter
Dick and Joan, the Powell twain
Walter Rivers—his demesne
We go back in memory
To the old L.B.B.C.
Leo Robin, J.J. Robbins
Park your dog-sleds and your
    dobbins
And that man whose name is spelt
Mr. Franklin Roosevelt
We're 101 percent
With you Mr. President
Mickey Rooney, bring your
    jive in

Greetings to my favorite
  drive-in
Romanoff and Dave and Carl and
David Rose and Judy Garland
Rest your coats and fill your
  glasses
Ere the jolly season passes
—I suppose I'm in a rut
Can't place Wilhelmina Thutt—
Read and Rains, and Smith
  and Shacker
Jimmy Stewart—he's so slacker
Swezey, Schwartz, and Sherwood yet
AND the Navy Blues sextette
Henry Steig bring Artie Shaw in
William Sexton and his squaw in
Silvers, bring both Phil and Sid in
Glad to zee you—we ain't kiddin'!
Footman! Grab that horse's halter
Here's Saroyan—also Salter
Gentlemen, up on your feet
Find Ann Sheridan a seat
(Ha ha, oh boy, that's a hot one—
Just as if she hasn't got one!)
Dave and Libby Shelly, hi!
You're the apple of our eye
Tinturins and Temple too
Gracious, what a varied crew
Square and hip-chick, saint
  and sinner
Lana Turner—"chicken dinner"
Friends and neighbors, love
  you all
Sit thee doon and have a ball
Mighty glad to call your name
Only hope you feel the same

Blessings on you where you are
Glad those wise men saw
  that star
Glad in spite of wars and
  weather
All of us can be together
Rocco Vocco and his cutie
J. Van Heusen, J. Venuti
Jerry Vogel, Rudy Vallee
Come back to our alley, Sally
Come and sit around the tree
Lit without the aid of "tea"
Gangway for the house of Whiting
Still our sweethearts, at this
  writing
Bright red ribbons for Cobina
I mean Juna—also Seena
Brothers Warner, Brothers Barker
Harry Wise and Connie Parker
Sammy Weiss and Vernon Wood
Harry Warren—feeling good
Paul and Margaret Whiteman too
You know what we wish for you!
Double that and add a very
To the "home-folks" at Woodberry
Slicker Warnell, Sambo White
Allie Wrubel—have a bite
Brother, you ain't tasted cakes
Till you've had those mother
  bakes
Choir, sing hello to Young
And your son is almost sung
Now the last guests have been
  kissed
Sam and Maggie Zimbalist
Now the room is really humming

And we thank you all for coming
Eat the food you want to eat
Meet the friends you want
 to meet
This is Christmas—fill your plates
These are these United States
So we won't invent a new toast

We'll propose the tried and true
 toast
We love you and you're our
 friends
And we hope it never ends
So, good neighbors, here's a cheer
Same old

𝔐𝔢𝔯𝔯𝔶 𝔠𝔥𝔯𝔦𝔰𝔱𝔪𝔞𝔰

and a . . . .

𝔍𝔬𝔥𝔫𝔫𝔶, 𝔊𝔦𝔫𝔤𝔢𝔯 and 𝔄𝔪𝔞𝔫𝔡𝔞

P.S. Combed the country over
Under haystacks, deep in clover
Highest snow-cap, lowest cut
Still no Wilhemina Thutt.

From the Desk of
GEORGE A. MERCER, SR.

TO MY FRIENDS AND ALL INTERESTED:

 When I visited Johnny at Rumson, New Jersey, in September, 1939 I had some long confidential and wonderful talks with him. I said to him, "John, tell me how it is that a boy of your age can write over 500 songs and does not know music and cannot play an instrument. How do you account for it?" After pondering and thinking a few minutes, John turned to me and said, "Pop, to tell you the truth I simply get to thinking over the song, pondering over it in my mind and all of a sudden, I get in tune with the Infinite." I believe that he then stated the real truth about his inspiration for his song writing. It comes from the Infinite and very high sources That is why I believe that John's talent is from above and that he is a musical genius.

 Respectfully, his father,

G. A. Mercer Sr.

GAM:R   Age 72.

A couple of cut-ups who both got their start with Pops Whiteman. Johnny must have learned that announcer's ear-shielding pose when they did broadcasts from the Hotel Biltmore.

The whole Mercer family, including faithful dog, in the days when convertibles were popular. The towhead is Jeff and the one in the skimmer far right is Amanda, also known as Mandy.

The Forties

The 1940s were a roller coaster of ups and downs for most Americans, and Johnny Mercer was riding well up in front. The forties were also an interesting time for people in the various branches of the arts and communications.

As the era began, there was some experimentation with the sending of sound *and* pictures through the air, an exciting idea called television that had been shown tentatively to the public at New York's World's Fair in 1939. But with the war in Europe drawing ever closer, the television idea was shelved and the entertainment-hungry public remained true to their radios and phonographs. Popular music—"pop music"—was a common denominator to both. On radio there was "Your Hit Parade," "The Chesterfield Supper Club," "The Camel Caravan" (no anti-smoking campaigns yet!), Kay Kyser's "Kollege of Musical Knowledge," Andre Kostelanetz, Bing Crosby on "The Kraft Music Hall," and dozens of dance band "remotes" later in the evenings, with marvelous musicians and singers performing marvelous songs. Almost any night of the week you might hear Tommy Dorsey's band with Frank Sinatra, Jo Stafford, Connie Haines and the Pied Pipers; or Glenn Miller's band with Tex Beneke and Marion Hutton; Eddy Duchin's piano or Artie Shaw's clarinet; powerhouse jazz by Jimmy Lunceford's band or mickey mouse music from Orrin Tucker. But you had to listen fast, because by 1942, no thanks to Pearl Harbor, most of it was gone.

As for the music that was supposed to go 'round and 'round, 1942 brought an unfortunate and certainly most untimely moratorium on recording because of a contractual dispute between the Petrillo-led musicians' union and the record manufacturers. There followed—necessity (and ingenuity) being the mother of invention—a rather dreary period during which America listened to records made without musical instruments. Singers would sing all right, but the backgrounds were something to boggle the mind. Groups of singers would make up what was intended to sound like sections of horns, reeds or rhythm instruments but sounded instead sappy, syrupy and completely synthetic. Adding to the confusion of the period was the simultaneous flourishing of a mechanical wonder with a tremendous appetite—the jukebox. It was a time for both "Jukebox Saturday Night" *and* "Saturday Night Is the Loneliest Night of the Week" ("Sing it, Frankie!"). There was a crying need for red, white and blue American popular music.

Hollywood, its ear ever to the ground, was particularly sensitive to such a simple demand. So it was full steam ahead for songs and pretty girls. There were Betty Grable, Betty Hutton and Rita Hayworth for starters and plenty more where they came from. There were Hope and Crosby with their put-it-there-pal, regular-guy clowning. Hollywood ground out musicals like clockwork, and so it was a time made to order for Johnny Mercer's wise and sentimental songs. Where Mercer had always had his ear to the streets and country byways, he was now, in the war years of 1942–45, plugged in to the sounds and descriptiveness of wartime gadgetry, to the Jeeps and bombers and blues-seekers of the U.S.A. He was also by this time an accepted member of the Hollywood elite. In 1941 Mercer and his ideal partner, Harold Arlen, wrote what many experts believe to be the greatest blues song of all time, after the classic "St. Louis Blues." It is, of course, "Blues in the Night" with its unbelievably evocative "a-whooooeee da-whooeeeeee" (Irving Berlin was bowled over by that invention) and the great piece of luck (and genius) that prompted Arlen to suggest to Mercer that they move the line "my momma done told me" up from some place farther down and open the song with it. It may be apocryphal, but the story is that when Oscar Hammerstein won his 1941 Academy Award (with Jerome Kern) for "The Last Time I Saw Paris," he told a friend who was returning to the Coast, "If you see Johnny Mercer, just tell him I think he was robbed." Of course the Hammerstein lyric did have the help of that sad period going for it, and Johnny Mercer did get many other Oscars as time went on. But "Blues in the Night" was surely worthy of an award, and its failure to get one was a forerunner of another bitter pill that Mercer and Arlen were to swallow before the forties were over.

But first there was another success for Mercer—this time in a whole new field. With the financial assistance of Buddy DeSylva, onetime member of the Broadway songwriting team of DeSylva, Brown & Henderson, but then producer at Paramount Pictures, Mercer and Glen Wallichs, the owner of a successful Hollywood music store, decided to start their own record company. They named it Capitol Records, based it in the center of things on Vine Street, a short stroll from the famous Brown Derby Restaurant, and proceded to line up an interesting and hip lineup of talent. They had Ella Mae Morse, Freddy Slack, Bobby Sherwood, and Stan Kenton for beginners, and shortly thereafter Peggy Lee and Nat "King" Cole. Capitol also offered its co-founder and part-time guiding light a chance to record too, and he quickly came up with a couple of jukebox winners—"Strip Polka" and "G.I.Jive." Johnny Mercer was now a household name. At one point during this super-productive period Mercer had four of his tunes among the top ten of the weekly radio show "Your Hit Parade." Buoyed by all this success, in 1946 Arlen and Mercer struck out into the more difficult and prestigious field of the Broadway musical theatre; struck out was what they indeed did. Despite a great score ("Come Rain or Come Shine," "Any Place I Hang My Hat," etc.) *St. Louis Woman*, directed by the brilliant Rouben Mamoulian and featuring Pearl Bailey and the Nicholas Brothers, was a resounding flop. Thoroughly disappointed and chastened, the hot songwriting team chugged on back to the warmth of California and the easy life of the movie studios. Mercer was never able to scale the heights of Broadway (a climb he wanted badly), and the 1946 debacle should have warned him of future disappointments. California was where he belonged, and he closed out the forties with a few more good songs and some diminishing attention to the affairs of Capitol Records.

Fellow southerners. Dinah Shore was one of the earliest to do "Blues in the Night," and she's kept it in her books ever since.

Mercer also "takes it off." Not many songwriters have been as much at home in front of a microphone.

Ruby Elzy and Mary Martin upstage Bing's *Birth of the Blues* combo in this shot, but one can still discover trumpet man Brian Donlevy, trombonist Jack Teagarden and bass player Harry Barris.

On Behalf of the Visiting Firemen

1940

Music by WALTER DONALDSON

Well, blow me down,
Look who's in town,
Pull up a chair,
There's one over there.
How've you been?
How's the next of kin?
Fellas, look who just blew in!

On behalf of the visiting firemen from
   Kansas City,
Let's have a "smile" on me,
On behalf of the gentlemen slicked up and
   lookin' pretty,
Let's make it two or three.
Like the governor of Carolina North,
Told the governor of Carolina South,
On behalf of the firemen from any city,
Let's have a "smile" on me.

[Repeat first 16 bars]

We're all gathered here on this auspicious
   day
And we'd . . . Bless my soul there's Elmer
   Whatcha say?

[Repeat last 8 bars]

On behalf of the visiting firemen from
   Minnesota,
Let's have a "smile" on me,
On behalf of the citizen just in from North
   Dakota,
Let's make it two or three.
Just as our forefathers always tried to show
"Give us liberty or give us . . ." well, let it
   go,
On behalf of the visiting firemen who filled
   their quota
Let's have a "smile" on me

By this time it was no longer a case of the mighty King Bing extending a helping hand to a chum on the way up. Mercer had arrived, and this outing was an effort to repeat the unexpected success of "Bob White." It was not quite the hit of the earlier record, but one can hear the fun these two cats (that was the word in 1940) obviously had in the studio. Mercer always enjoyed using place names, not to mention things bibulous.

No, he didn't play piano, but of course photographers love to get a little action into their shots. He looks a little like the late actor Myron McCormick in this one.

The dude on the left is obviously glad to see an old pal like Jimmy Dorsey, even though they seem not to be joining the crowd heading for the next hole.

One double-A ASCAP member welcomes another aboard. *(Left to right)* Frank Loesser, Betty Downey, Ginger Mercer, Jimmy Downey, Lynn Loesser and J.M.

Mister Meadowlark

1940

Music by WALTER DONALDSON

I'm in the country but I dunno why,
'Cause I am strictly a city lovin' guy,
I'm sittin' there when
A little bird flies my way one day.
I look at him and he's lookin' at me,
Both satisfyin' our curiosity,
Quick like a rabbit,
I get me a thought,
So I up to him and say,
Hey!

Mister Meadowlark,
We've got an awful lot of serenadin' to do,
Mister Meadowlark,
I'm just a city slicker and I'm counting on
    you,
She's got a country guy who whistles,

My whistle is thin,
So when I begin,
[Whistle]
That's where you come in.
[Whistle]

Mister Meadowlark,
If you should cop a gander
When I'm kissin' my chick,
Needless to remark,
I hope you'll have the decency to exit,
But quick!
And if Missus M. thinks you're out steppin',
I'll make it all right,
Mister Meadowlark,
Meet me in the dark
Tonight.

Walter Donaldson was a hero to Mercer. Not only was he an established melody man—good meat-and-potatoes tunes his forte—but he had his name on such successful regional songs as "Georgia," "Carolina in the Morning," "Down South," and (wow!) "How Ya Gonna Keep 'Em Down on the Farm?" The aviary was in use again and Mercer was bringing Donaldson right up to the moment with the line, "If you should cop a gander when I'm kissing my chick." Bing and Johnny relished such tough guy—racetrack lingo mixed with jazz and so they recorded this one too.

Fools Rush In

Music by RUBE BLOOM

"Romance is a game for fools,"
I used to say;
A game I thought I'd never play.
"Romance is a game for fools,"
I said and grinned;
Then you passed by,
And here am I
Throwing caution to the wind.

Fools rush in
Where angels fear to tread,
And so I come to you, my love,
My heart above my head.
Though I see
The danger there,
If there's a chance for me
Then I don't care.
Fools rush in
Where wise men never go,
But wise men never fall in love
So how are they to know?
When we met
I felt my life begin;
So open up your heart,
And let this fool rush in.

"Wise men never fall in love. . . ." An unusually cynical line for the ever-romantic Johnny Mercer. The big record of this ballad was made by Tommy Dorsey's band with an exceptionally silken vocal by Frank Sinatra. The record and many air plays propelled this song onto radio's "Hit Parade," and that was a good change from the Hollywood soundtrack songs of the years before.

```
Oh, Mr. Crosby,
Oh, Mr. Crosby,
All the orchestras are swinging it today.
And I wanted to find out
What the noise is all about.
Do you really think that swing is here to stay?

Oh, Mr. Mercer,
Oh, Mr. Mercer,
Swing is really much too ancient to condemn.
In the jungles they would play
In that same abandoned way.
On the level, Mr. Crosby?
On the down beat, Mr. "M".
```

```
Oh, Mr. Crosby,
Oh, Mr. Crosby,
I've been reading in the latest magazine
That a jivin' jitter bug
Blew his top and cut a rug.
Will you tell me what that language really means?

Oh, Mr. Mercer,
Oh, Mr. Mercer,
As a student of the slang they use pro-tem,
That just means a solid gait
Cut a murderistic plate.
That's amazin', Mr. Crosby,
Elementary, Mr. "M".
```

Still another go at the back and forth jiving that Gallagher & Shean began and Bing then continued well into the forties with Bob Hope. These are the actual cards that the two guys carried into the studio, since the longish lyric was too busy to commit to memory. "Allegretto—Alligators," "retardo—Lombardo" are Mercer's always successful music-biz jokes.

```
Oh, Mr. Crosby,
Oh, Mr. Crosby,
Is it true that swing's another name for jazz?
And the first place it was played
Was in New Orleans parade?
And the southern negro gave it all it has?

Oh, Mr. Mercer,
Oh, Mr. Mercer,
I believe that its foundation came from then.
They just slowed the tempo down
And they really went to town.
Allegretto, Mr. Crosby.
Alligators, Mr. "M".
```

```
Mr. Mercer,
Well, I trust that I have made the matter clear.
So, when someone plays a thing,
You will understand it's swing,
And appreciate the rhythm that you hear.


Oh, Mr. Crosby,
Oh, Mr. Crosby,
I'm afraid that type of rhythm's not for me.
I prefer my music plain
A la Shubert's Serenade.
Sort of retardo, Mr. Mercer.
Sort of Lombardo, Mr. "C".
```

The Happiness Boys of 1940 listen to
a playback, but it can't be all that bad.

Blues in the Night

Music by HAROLD ARLEN

My mama done tol' me
When I was in knee pants (knee pants
                              (pigtails
My mama done tol' me—(son
                              (hon'
A woman'll sweet talk,
   (man's gonna sweet talk,
And give ya the big eye,
But when the sweet talkin's done
A woman's a two-face
   (man is a two-face
A worrisome thing who'll leave ya t'sing
The blues in the night,

Now the rain's a-fallin',
Hear the train a-callin',
Whooee,
(My mama done tol' me)
Hear that lonesome whistle
Blowin' 'cross the trestle,
Whooee,
(My mama done tol' me)
A whooee-duh-whooee,
Ol' clickety clack's
A-echoin' back
The blues in the night,

The evenin' breeze'll start
The trees to cryin'
And the moon'll hide its light,
When you get the blues in the night.

Take my word, the mocking bird'll
Sing the saddest kind of song,
He knows things are wrong
And he's right. [whistle]

From Natchez to Mobile,
From Memphis to St. Jo,
Where ever the four winds blow;
I been in some big towns
An' heard me some big talk,
But there is one thing I know,
A woman's a two-face,
   (man is a two-face,
A worrisome thing
Who'll leave ya t'sing
The blues in the night.
[hum]
My mama was right,
There's blues in the night.

Arthur Schwartz: "Probably the greatest blues song ever written—and that includes 'St. Louis Blues.' "
Robert Emmett Dolan: "I was in New York, and Kern & Hammerstein's "The Last Time I Saw Paris" had just won the Academy Award over "Blues in the Night." Oscar said to me, 'When you get back to Hollywood, tell Johnny he was robbed.' "

Harold Arlen: "It was a jail sequence in the movie, and I wanted to write it as authentic as possible. It took a day and a half to write and I couldn't wait to get over to Johnny's house to play it for him. He's not much of a reactor and so we fussed around with it for quite awhile. I remember he had lots of phrases and lines written down but none of them seemed to fit that opening phrase right. But then I saw those words, 'my momma done tol' me,' way down at the bottom of the pile and I said, 'Why don't we move them up to the top?' It sure worked.

BLUES IN THE NIGHT

Whenever the night comes
I'm heavy in my heart
I'm heavy in my mind - Lawd!
A woman'll sweet talk
A woman'll glad eye
But pretty soon you'll find
A woman's a two-face
A changeable thing
Who leaves you to sing the blues
In the night
Hear the rain a-fallin'
Hear the train a-callin' --- whoooeee
(whoooeee whoooeee whoooeee)
Hear that lonesome whistle
Blowin' 'cross the trestle --- whoooeee
(I'm heavy in my heart)
A-whoooeee -duh- whoooeee
That clickety-clack
A-echoin' back the blues
In the night
The evenin' breeze'll start the trees to cryin'
And the moon'll hide its light
When you've got the blues in the night
Take my word, the mockin'-bird'll sing the saddest kinda song
He knows things are wrong
And he's right
(Whistle)
From Natchez to Mobile
From Memphis to St. Joe
Don' nobody yet know why
A woman'll sweet talk
A woman'll glad eye
Then leave you high an' dry

The original work sheet for the classic "Blues in the Night."
Note how the captivating opening line was moved up—
at Arlen's suggestion.

99

The Waiter and the Porter and the Upstairs Maid

1941

Music and Words by JOHNNY MERCER

As your genial host,
May I offer a toast,
To the wine buying guest on my right.
May his bank account grow,
Heavy laden with dough,
May he spend it in here ev'ry night.
Seeing this night in its glory,
You people so loyal, so true,
Puts me in mind of a story
It might have happened to you.

The people in the ballroom were stuffy and
arty,
So I began to get just a little afraid,
I sneaked into the kitchen and found me a
party;
The waiter and the porter and the second
story maid.

I peeked into the parlor to see what was
hatchin',
In time to hear the hostess suggest a
charade,
But who was in the pantry a-laughin' and
scratchin';
The waiter and the porter and the upstairs
maid.

When they heard the music that the
orchestra played,
The waiter and the porter grabbed ahold of
the maid,
Then they all proceeded to go into a clog,
Hot diggety dog!

If ever I'm invited to some fuddy duddys;
I ain't a gonna watch any harlequinade,

You'll find me in the kitchen
Applaudin' my buddies;
The waiter and the porter and the upstairs
maid.

I went and got a dishpan to use as a cymbal,
The porter found a regular glass that he
played,
The fingers of the waiter were each in a
thimble,
You should of heard the music that the
combination made.

Of course we had to stop for a short
intermission,
When anybody rang for a pink lemonade,
But soon as it was done we were back in
position,
The waiter and the porter and the upstairs
maid.

Marchin' through the kitchen to the party
and back,
Why, man, you should a seen us, we were
ballin' the jack.
Once a half an hour passed without any call,
Jack, we had a ball.

The waltzes and mazurkas, we hate 'em, we
spurn 'em,
We got a lotta rhythms we wanna hear
played,
And we know who to go to if we want to
learn 'em;
The waiter and the porter and the upstairs
maid.

©Famous Music Corporation

100

The Air-minded Executive

1941   By BERNIE HANIGHEN

Life, Look, Pic, Peek,
Always print a beautiful calf,
And another thing they love
Is a certain photograph.
Over a beer, they agree
The man of the year was

The air-minded executive,
He dearly loved to fly.
He was an up-to-date go getter,
His lady friend was even better,
She went along to take a letter,
Way up in the sky.

The air-minded executive
Would take off on the sly,
He was a most romantic feller,
And oh the things he used to tell her

Above the roar of his propeller.
Somewhere in the sky,
Foggy or fair,
They would be there
Lightin' a flare at the airport.

Fillin' the tanks,
Callin' the banks,
Tellin' 'em,
"Hold up the contract . . . contact!"

The air-minded executive
Became a wealthy guy.
And so he wed his secretary,
They settled down in Waterbury,
And they commute by stratosferry.
My, they love to fly
Even as you and I.

Mercer was a great reader of magazines and newspapers, hence the opening line which may have been the impetus for the rest of this unusual song idea. In retrospect he seems to have been quite prescient about today's glut of executive jets. In this day of space shuttles, the made-up "stratosferry" isn't at all far out. Try and find Mercer's record of this—as always he's the best salesman of his own great material.

(Facing page) Mercer trying his wings solo once again was lucky enough to have the powerhouse trio of Crosby–Mary Martin–Jack Teagarden romping through the lyrics in the movie *Birth of the Blues* (which comes first in chicken and egg style, the song or the spot and the stars?). Good show-stopping lyrics here, the line "I ain't a-gonna watch any harlequinade" pure Mercer.

Skylark

1941

Music by HOAGY CARMICHAEL

Skylark,
Have you anything to say to me?
Won't you tell me where my love can be?
Is there a meadow in the mist,
Where someone's waiting to be kissed?
Skylark,
Have you seen a valley green with Spring
Where my heart can go a-journeying,
Over the shadows and the rain
To a blossom covered lane?
And in your lonely flight,
Haven't you heard the music in the night,
Wonderful music,
Faint as a "will-o-the-wisp,"
Crazy as a loon,
Sad as a gypsy serenading the moon (Oh)
Skylark,
I don't know if you can find these things,
But my heart is riding on your wings,
So if you see them anywhere,
Won't you lead me there?

Move over, Mr. Keats. Mercer's affinity for all the winged creatures of the world served him well, though this complete set of lyrics took him the better part of a year to complete. All the great singers—Sinatra, Ella, Tormé, Tony Bennett—have had a go at this gem.

Christmas Card

THIS modern age we're going through
    has got me in a spin
I ain't too bright to start with—now here's
    the shape I'm in

With everything and anything—there's
    stamps you gotta use
The Bs and Cs are groceries—I think the T's
    are shoes
You have to be a F.B.I. man to figure out all
    the clues
And that's the situation when you get the
    duration blues

The Army and the draft board gets me kinda
    mixed up too
You're in if you are 1A—but if you ain't then
    who are you

The 2As are essential—and the 4F's
    probably have asthma
The 3B gents are in defense—or else they're
    giving plasma
But if you ain't got nothin' then you are
    somebody that nobody at all can use
And that's the situation—when you get those
    duration blues

Now food will win the war they say, and
    that's okay with me
But I went to the corner store—what did I
    see?

There's Spam and wham and deviled ham
    and somepin new called zoom

Just take it home and cook it to the
    temperature of the room
And you can bake it—cake it—flake
    it—make it—take it anyway you choose
And that's the situation—when you got
    those duration blues

And then on top of everything the taxes
    roll around
I went to see the income man and this is
    what I found
You multiplies the profits and incorporates
    the loss
Deducting all expenditures business fees
    you come across
Then if you satisfy the government—it's
    ten to one the little lady sues
And that's the situation when you get the
    duration blues

Howdy do, Mr. Crosby, I would—like
    to say
Happy New Year to you in the—good old
    way

Well, thank you, Mr. Mercer, that is—
    mighty fine
And the same to you from me and mine
And while I'm passin' those—words your
    way
Let's extend 'em to the whole wide—
    U.S.A.

Every city and village and farm and town
And every front door from the—White

House down
To the boys in khaki—and the boys in blue
To the generals and the admirals and the
    company and crew

Let the whistles whistle and the bells all ring
For General Marshall, General Arnold and
    Cominch King

Red, white and blue confetti in a veritable
    shower
For Messrs, MacArthur and Eisenhower

To the fightin' Marines on Guadalcanal
Wherever you are, Happy New Year, pal
To the ship-yard workers and the swing-shift
    crowd
We can't sing good but we sure sing loud

So we send our heartiest felicitations
To all our allies—the United Nations

Get out the brightest-colored paper hats
For Nimitz and Hadley—Doolittle and
    Spaatz

Mr. Nelson, Mr. Jeffers, Mr. Morgenthau
Had the busiest year we ever saw

And an even busier one comin' in
Well, the harder we work—the quicker we'll
    win

Happy New Year, everybody, near and far
From John Q. Public to F.D.R.
To the New New Jersey, and all her crew
To Birmingham Bertha and Suzy Q.

That's our 1943 wish for you
And thanks for all you did in '42
Around this time in forty four
We hope you'll be with us in person once
    more
But till that time be of good cheer
And to everybody—Happy New Year

Strip Polka

1942

By JOHNNY MERCER

There's a burlesque theatre where the gang
   loves to go,
To see Queenie the cutie of the burlesque
   show,
And the thrill of the evening is when out
   Queenie skips,
And the band plays the Polka while she
   strips!

"Take it off," "Take it off" Cries a voice
   from the rear,
"Take it off," "Take it off," soon it's all you
   can hear,
But she's always a lady even in pantomine,
So she stops! And always just in time.

She's as fresh and as wholesome as the
   flowers in May,
And she hopes to retire to the farm some
   day,
But you can't buy a farm until you're up in
   the chips,
So the band plays the Polka while she strips!

"Take it off," "Take it off," all the customers
   shout,
"Down in front" "Down in front," while the
   band beats it out,

But she's always a lady even in pantomine,
So she stops! And always just in time.

Oh! she hates corny waltzes and she hates
   the gavotte,
And there's one big advantage if the
   music's hot,
It's a fast moving exit just in case
   something r-r-rips,
So the band plays the Polka while she strips!

Drop around, take it in, it's the best in the
   west,
Take it off, "Take it off," you can yell like
   the rest,
Take her out when it's over, she's a peach
   when she's dressed,
But she stops! And always just in time.

Queenie, Queen of them all,
Queenie, some day you'll fall,
Some day churchbells will chime,
In Strip Polka Time.

It's the Polka time,
Churchbells will chime,
It's the Polka time.

The war was on, and Mercer was doing his bit in triplicate: He wrote words and music, sang it with the proper amount of humor, and produced it on his new Capitol Records. The song became a solid hit on jukeboxes, particularly those around army bases and GI hangouts. The number was just sexy enough for the guys without being dirty.

Dearly Beloved

1942

Music by JEROME KERN

Tell me that it's true,
Tell me you agree,
I was meant for you,
You were meant for me.

Dearly beloved, how clearly I see,
Somewhere in Heaven you were fashioned
   for me,
Angel eyes knew you,
Angel voices led me to you;

Nothing could save me, Fate gave me a
   sign;
I know that I'll be yours come shower or
   shine;
So I say merely,
Dearly beloved, be mine.

The publisher's subtitle "Suitable For Weddings" is hardly necessary for this fine song, in which Mercer's directness of romantic lyric matches the beauty of Kern's melody. A standard among movie love songs.

DEARLY BELOVED

Song Suitable for Weddings

Words by

JOHNNY MERCER

Music by

JEROME KERN

PRICE 75 CENTS

T. B. HARMS
— COMPANY —
NEW YORK

MADE IN U.S.A.

You Were Never Lovelier

1942   Music by JEROME KERN

I was never able
To recite a fable
That would make the party bright,

Sitting at the table
I was never able
To become the host's delight;

But now you've given me my after dinner
    story,
I'll just describe you as you are in all your
    glory.

You were never lovelier,
You were never so fair;
Dreams were never lovelier,

Pardon me if I stare.

Down the sky the moonbeams fly to light
    your face;
I can only say they chase the proper place.

You were never lovelier,
And to coin a new phrase;
I was never luckier
In my palmiest days.

Make a note, and you can quote me, honor
    bright,
You were never lovelier than you are
    tonight.

A great assignment—writing with the master, Jerome Kern, and for Fred Astaire!
One can imagine the keen sense of pride this musical relationship brought to
Mercer, but at the same time caution, since Kern had a reputation of sometimes
being difficult. Fred sang this dreamy title song to the gorgeous Rita Hayworth,
then did a hip dance number that Mercer titled "The Shorty George" after an
actual dance step of the day and one that was a little removed from the Alt Wien
realm of Kern.

YOU WERE NEVER LOVELIER

Music by JEROME KERN
Lyric by JOHNNY MERCER

★

FRED ASTAIRE AND RITA HAYWORTH
IN THE NEW COLUMBIA MUSICAL PRODUCTION
"YOU WERE NEVER LOVELIER"
WITH
ADOLPHE MENJOU
AND
XAVIER CUGAT
AND HIS ORCHESTRA

★

PRICE
75c

T. B. HARMS
COMPANY
NEW YORK

I'm Old Fashioned

1942

Music by JEROME KERN

I am not such a clever one
About the latest fads.
I admit I was never one
Adored by local lads;
Not that I ever try to be saint,
I'm the type that they classify as quaint.

I'm old fashioned,
I love the moonlight,
I love the old fashioned things—
The sound of rain
Upon a window pane,
The starry song that April sings.
This year's fancies
Are passing fancies,
But sighing sighs, holding hands
These my heart understands.
I'm old fashioned,
But I don't mind it,
That's how I want to be,
As long as you agree
To stay old fashioned with me.

More to the Kern taste than "Shorty George." We've been told that when Mercer brought the completed lyric to Kern's home, the composer, generally a rather laconic gentleman, rushed to the staircase and summoned his wife to come hear it—a rare display of enthusiasm. Kern's kudos were warranted, since this is one of Mercer's most sincerely romantic works.

I'M OLD FASHIONED

Music by JEROME KERN
Lyric by JOHNNY MERCER

★

FRED ASTAIRE AND RITA HAYWORTH

IN THE NEW COLUMBIA MUSICAL PRODUCTION

"YOU WERE NEVER LOVELIER"

WITH

ADOLPHE MENJOU

AND

XAVIER CUGAT

AND HIS ORCHESTRA

★

DEARLY BELOVED
I'M OLD FASHIONED
YOU WERE NEVER LOVELIER
WEDDING IN THE SPRING
THE SHORTY GEORGE
ON THE BEAM

★

75 cents

CHAPPELL

That Old Black Magic

1942

Music by HAROLD ARIEN

That old black magic has me in its spell.
That old back magic that you weave so well.
Those icy fingers up and down my spine.
The same old witchcraft when your eyes
   meet mine.

The same old tingle that I feel inside
And then that elevator starts its ride
And down and down I go,
'Round and 'round I go
Like a leaf that's caught in the tide.

I should stay away,
But what can I do?

I hear your name
And I'm aflame,
Aflame with such a burning desire
That only your kiss
Can put out the fire.

For you're the lover I have waited for.
The mate that fate had me created for,
And ev'ry time your lips meet mine
Darling, down and down I go,
'Round and 'round I go
In a spin,
Loving the spin I'm in
Under that old black magic called love!

Another all-time winner from that ideal pair, Arlen and Mercer. (It had been ten years earlier that they first met, during preparations for the Broadway revue *Americana*.) Most people associate this standard with that well known hand-against-ear singer, Billy Daniels. But no, it was a fellow named Johnnie Johnston, who made a bit of a reputation for himself by announcing to the executives of Paramount Pictures, "This lot isn't big enough for him [Bing Crosby] and me—you better get rid of him." That threat must have been made after the movie *Star Spangled Rhythm*, in which Johnston sang this elongated torch song while most of the footage was given over to the dancing of Vera Zorina.

Typical wartime movie plot paired Navy man Eddie Bracken with girl friend Betty Hutton, who showed her loyalty by working in a defense plant. She belted out two good Mercer numbers.

On the Swing Shift

1942

Music by HAROLD ARLEN

Like some old tom cat out like a light
I dream all day of the previous night.
Not that we frequent the same habitat
But in a way I'm a cat.

Life is fine with my baby on the swing shift
On the line with my baby on the swing shift
It's the nuts
There among the nuts and bolts
Plus a hundred thousand volts
Shining from her eyes.
She's a beautiful bomber!
What care I if they put me on the wing shift?
She's near by in the fuselage
Overtime?
Here's why I'm
Doin' it free—
Baby's with me on the swing shift jamboree!

Another bright Arlen-Mercer number from Paramount's all-star wartime musical, *Star Spangled Rhythm*. Betty Hutton, a big movie name in 1942, gave this topical song the required "pizzazz" and also swung another upbeat number called "I'm Doin' It for Defense," in which there was the wonderful couplet, "If you think you're Cary Grant, brother, relax, you're just a rebate on my income tax" Mercer had a ball with all the defense industry and air force verbiage of the day.

Hit the Road to Dreamland

1942

Music by HAROLD ARLEN

Twinkle, twinkle, twinkle goes the star,
Twinkle, twinkle, twinkle, there you are.
Time for all good children to hit the hay.
Cock-a-doodle, doodle, doodle, brother,
It's another day,
We should be on our way!

Bye bye, baby
Time to hit the road to dreamland,
You're my baby
Dig you in the land of Nod.
Hold tight, baby,
We'll be swinging up in dreamland,
All night, baby,
Where the little cherubs trod.
Look at that knocked-out moon,
Been a-blowin' his top in the blue,
Never saw the likes of you;
     (What an angel)

Bye, bye, baby,
Time to hit the road to dreamland,
Don't cry, baby,
It was divine
But the rooster has finally crowed,
Time to hit the road.

©Famous Music Corp.

Still another interesting song from *Star Spangled Rhythm*. Mercer, with his great attachment to rail rather than air travel, enjoyed the setting of this song in the dining car of an overnight train and it also gave the director an opportunity to introduce the fine Golden Gate Quartet dressed as Pullman porters to sing counterpoint (the NAACP hadn't gained its clout yet). The main lyrics of the song were sung by the always-serviceable Dick Powell in the direction of his tablemate, Mary Martin.

Tangerine

1942

Music by VICTOR SCHERTZINGER

South American stories
Tell of a girl who's quite a dream,
The beauty of her race.

Though you doubt all the stories
And think the tales
Are just a bit extreme,
Wait till you see her face.

Tangerine,
She is all they claim,
With her eyes of night
And lips as bright as flame.

Tangerine,
When she dances by,
Senoritas stare
And caballeros sigh.

And I've seen
Toasts to Tangerine
Raised in ev'ry bar
Across the Argentine,
Yes, she has them all on the run,
But her heart belongs to just one.
Her heart belongs to Tangerine.

An all-time hit song that most people will always associate with Bob Eberle and Helen O'Connell. Their brilliantly conceived two-tempos duet on Jimmy Dorsey's record is a pop classic. Mercer told George Simon that he got the title from Broadway show he had liked way back in the twenties. Mercer's career was really skyrocketing at this point, what with two movie scores, Capitol Records starting to turn out hit records, and the radio "Lucky Strike Hit Parade" often presenting three or four Mercer songs among the honored Top Ten of the week.

Arthur Murray Taught Me Dancing in a Hurry

1942   Music by VICTOR SCHERTZINGER

Life was so peaceful at the drive-in,
Life was so calm and serene,
Life was trés gay
Till that unlucky day
I happened to read that magazine.
Why did I read that advertisement
Where it said . . .
"Since I rhumba, Jim thinks I'm sublime."
Why, oh why,
Did I ever try
When I didn't have the talent,
Didn't have the money,
And teacher did not have the time.

Arthur Murray taught me dancing in a hurry.
I had a week to spare,
He showed me the ground work,
The walkin' around work,

And told me to take it from there.
Arthur Murray then advised me not to
    worry.
It'd come out all right.
To my way of thinkin',
It came out stinkin,'
I don't know my left from my right.
The people around me can all sing
A-one and a-two and a-three,
But any resemblance to waltzing
Is just coincidental with me,
'Cause Arthur Murray taught me dancing in
    a hurry.
And so I take a chance.
To me it resembles
The nine-day trembles,
But he guarantees
It's a dance.

Rarely does a public figure show up in a popular song title, but this one worked awfully well. It was Helen O'Connell's personal property on the Dorsey record this time. An extra set of lyrics was written for radio performance so that the word "stinkin'" wouldn't offend the dancing master. Ginger tells us that the Mercers had to make peace with Arthur and Kathryn by taking an actual lesson, and, she adds, Arthur was no great shakes on the dance floor (as ex-Broadway hoofer Ginger ought to know).

Helen O'Connell, dressed to the nines, has the mike all to herself, as she did on the great Arthur Murray number.

AMERICAN SOCIETY OF COMPOSERS, AUTHORS AND PUBLISHERS
THIRTY ROCKEFELLER PLAZA
NEW YORK CITY

DEEMS TAYLOR
PRESIDENT

June 17, 1942.

Mr. John Mercer,
c/o Vernon D. Wood,
2018 N. Vine Street,
Hollywood, Calif.

Dear Johnny:

It gives me great pleasure to inform you that at a meeting of the Writers' Classification Committee held on June 15th, your rating was changed from Class A to Class AA.

This advancement will take effect the Third Quarter of 1942.

With all good wishes,

Sincerely yours,

Deems

DT:SR

Deems Taylor,
President.

and you didn't have to ask.

119

Mandy Is Two

1942

Music by FULTON McGRATH

Look at the ribbon and look at the curl,
Look at the pinafore.
Here's to the beautiful birthday girl,
May she have many more.

Mandy is Two,
You ought to see her eyes of cornflower
    blue;
They really look as if they actually knew
That she's a big girl now.

Mandy is Two,
You ought to see how many things she can
    do,
She knows her alphabet and ties her own
    shoe
And no one showed her how.

If you could see her majesty with braids in
    her hair;
Almost as though her Sunday beau came
    around and
            brought her an orchid to wear.

Mommy is blue
Because her little girl is going on three,
But Miss Amanda's just as proud as can be
That she's a big girl now.

There really is a Mandy (Amanda)—now past forty and a parent herself. Mercer was always a proud father, and this loving lyric certainly tells how he felt in those growing-up years. The music came from a musician pal, Fulton "Fidgey" McGrath.

Mandy is Two

Lyric by
JOHNNY MERCER

Music by
FULTON McGRATH

BVC
BREGMAN, VOCCO and CONN, Inc.
1619 BROADWAY · NEW YORK, N.Y.

Greetings

121

One for My Baby

(And One More for the Road)

1943

Music by HAROLD ARLEN

It's quarter to three,
There's no one in the place except you and
  me,
So, set 'em up, Joe,
I've got a little story you oughta know,
We're drinking, my friend,
To the end of a brief episode,
Make it one for my baby
And one more for the road.

I got the routine,
So drop another nickel in the machine,
I'm feelin' so bad,
I wish you'd make the music dreamy and
  sad,
Could tell you a lot,
But you've got to be true to your code,
Make it one for my baby
And one more for the road.

You'd never know it,
But, buddy, I'm kind of poet
And I've gotta lotta things to say,
And when I'm gloomy,
You simply gotta listen to me,
Until it's talked away.

Well, that's how it goes
And Joe, I know you're anxious to close,
So thanks for the cheer,
I hope you didn't mind my bending your
  ear,
This torch I've found,
Must be drowned or it soon might explode,
Make it one for my baby
And one more for the road.

Another quintessential Arlen-Mercer "late night" song (strong ideas seemed to flow from the two of them in those days). Although the story line was sung with his usual grace, the mood of it doesn't seem to fit Fred Astaire too well in the movie *The Sky's the Limit*. It does suit Sinatra down to his dress shoes and he gives it the full treatment—spoken preamble, spotlight, deep drag of a cigarette—as he so often performs it on concert stages. Mercer knew about bars (uh-huh), and the line, "But, buddy, I'm a kind of poet" is brilliantly on target.

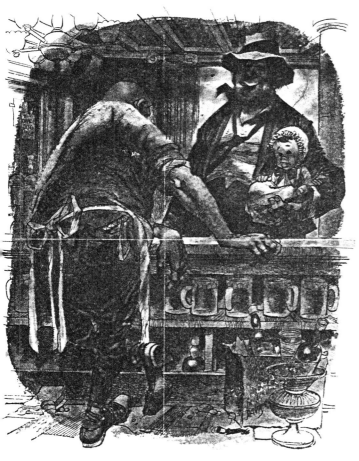

"Make it one for my baby and one more for the road."

Mercer replaced Bob Hope on the Pepsodent radio show for the summer of 1943 ("Poor Miriam . . . forgot to use her irium"), and his hip singing style certainly fooled some people as this postcard plainly shows.

THIS SIDE OF CARD IS FOR ADDRESS

Johnny Mercer,
Chesterfield Program,
National Broadcasting Co.,
Radio City,
Hollywood, California.

The Abraham Lincoln Junior Club of this city has this date voted you the most popular young colored singer on the radio.

Harris Owens,
Secretary.

123

My Shining Hour

1943

Music by HAROLD ARLEN

This moment, this minute
And each second in it,
Will leave a glow upon the sky,
And as time goes by,
It will never die.

This will be my shining hour,
Calm and happy and bright,
In my dreams, your face will flower,
Through the darkness of the night.

Like the lights of home before me,
Or an angel watching o'er me,

This will be my shining hour,
Till I'm with you again.

Fred Astaire was a test pilot (topical theme in 1943) in *The Sky's the Limit* and sang this lofty ballad to Joan Leslie. It is a no-frills, straightaway singer's song and it's therefore not surprising that it appeals to Sinatra, Margaret Whiting, Mel Tormé and other discriminating stars of the music world. As brief as the song appears to be on the page, it packs a wallop when sung thoughtfully.

124

MY SHINING HOUR

Lyrics by Johnny Mercer

Music by Harold Arlen

"MY SHINING HOUR"
"I'VE GOT A LOT IN COMMON WITH YOU"
"ONE FOR MY BABY"
"HARVEY, THE VICTORY GARDEN MAN"

EDWIN H. MORRIS & COMPANY
INC.
music publishers
1619 BROADWAY . NEW YORK, N. Y.

BUY
WAR BONDS
AND STAMPS
FOR
VICTORY!

Trav'lin' Light

1943

Music by JIMMY MUNDY and TRUMMY YOUNG

I'm trav'lin' light
Because my man has gone
And from now on
I'm trav'lin' light.

He said "goodbye"
And took my heart away.
So from today
I'm trav'lin' light.

No one to see,
I'm free as the breeze,
No one but me
And my memories.

Some lucky night
He may come back again,
But until then
I'm trav'lin light.

An unusual combination of writers, produced "Trav'lin' Light," and the lyric is not Mercer at his most inspired. Nevertheless, it served as a good vehicle for Billie Holiday and for one of the rare records she made on the Capitol label. It *does* have a good title.

Lady Day with two good saxophonists, Vido Musso and Dave Mathews. No one else could approach her singing of "Trav'lin' Light"

Accentuate the Positive

1944   Music by HAROLD ARLEN

[For verse, sheet music suggests "Slowly . . .
sermon-like"]

Gather 'round me,
Ev'ry body,
Gather 'round me
While I preach some,
Feel a sermon
Comin' on me.
The topic will be sin
And that's what I'm agin.'
If you wanna
Hear my story,
Then settle back
And just sit tight
While I start reviewin'
The attitude of doin' right.
 You've got to
 Accent-tchu-ate the positive,
 E-lim-my-nate the negative,
 Latch on to the affirmative,

Don't mess with Mister In-between.
You've got to spread joy
Up to the maximum,
Bring gloom down to the minimum,
Have faith, or pandemonium
Li'ble to walk upon the scene.
To illustrate my last remark,
Jonah in the whale, Noah in the Ark,
What did they do
Just when everything looked so dark?
"Man," they said,
"We better
Accent-tchu-ate the positive,
E-lim-my-nate the negative,
Latch on
To the affirmative,
Don't mess with Mister In-between."
No, don't mess with Mister In-between.

The preacher man spirit of this song was ideal for Bing Crosby, who always enjoyed clowning around with a minstrel show dialect. The title came about, according to one story, from a newspaper clipping that quoted the Harlem revivalist preacher Father Divine using the phrase. A friend sent the clipping along to Mercer, who kept it among his many scribbled notes for a long time. It fell into place one day when they were driving in Arlen's car and Harold sang one of his typically provocative strains. It was an Academy Award nominee, but not a winner that year.

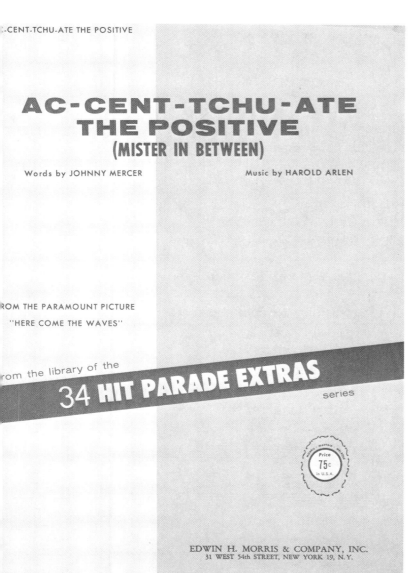

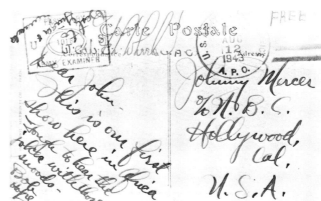

Bob Hope, the perennial gagster, kept in touch with the folks back home from one of his many U.S.O. stops.

How Little We Know

1944

Music by HOAGY CARMICHAEL

Maybe it happens this way,
Maybe we really belong together,
But after all, how little we know.

Maybe it's just for a day,
Love is as changeable as the weather,
And after all, how little we know.

Who knows why an April breeze never
    remains?
Why stars in the trees hide when it rains?
Love comes along casting a spell,
Will it sing you a song,
Will it say a farewell?
Who can tell!
Maybe you're meant to be mine,
Maybe I'm only supposed to stay in your
    arms awhile,
As others have done.
Is that what I've waited for?
Am I the one?
Oh, I hope in my heart that it's so,
In spite of how little we know.

Which is the first team—Arlen & Mercer or Carmichael & Mercer? It's hard to tell when such a marvelously "right" song such as this one comes along to interrupt the flow of the other collaboration. Hoagy Carmichael also appeared on screen in this movie *(To Have and Have Not)* singing "Baltimore Oriole," one of those solo contributions that sounds as if Mercer were looking over his shoulder. This one, however, sounds a little like both of them and therefore has a nice, easygoing feeling to it.

G.I. Jive

1944   Words and music by JOHNNY MERCER

This is the G.I. Jive,
Man alive.
It starts with the bugler
Blowin' reveille over your head
When you arrive.
Jack, that's the G.I. Jive
Root-tie-tee toot
Jump in your suit
Make a salute (Voot!)
After you wash and dress,
More or less,
You go get your breakfast
In a beautiful little café they call the mess.
Jack, when you convalesce,
Out of your seat
Into the street,
Make with the feet (Reet!)

If you're a P.V.T. your duty
Is to salute the L.I.E.U.T.;
But if you brush the L.I.E.U.T.,
The M.P. makes you K.P. on the Q.T.
This is the G.I. Jive
Man alive,
They give you a private tank
That features a little device called fluid drive.
Jack, after you revive,
Chuck all your junk,
Back in the trunk
Fall on your bunk (Clunk!)
Soon you're countin' Jeeps,
But before you count to five,
Seems you're right back diggin' that
G. I. Jive!

This breezy wartime favorite was written in practically no time flat, according to Dave Dexter, who was then Capitol Records' publicity director—a & r man—jazz expert—general scout and utility outfielder. Says Dave: "Mercer got the idea for 'G.I. Jive' while waiting for the traffic light at the corner of Sunset and Vine. He noticed all the servicemen on the streets around that busy intersection. So he drove that one block to where our offices were, came upstairs, sat down at the typewriter and dashed the whole thing off in a couple of minutes. It was one of our biggest hits that year."

Dream

1944

Words and music by JOHNNY MERCER

Get in touch with that sundown fellow,
As he tiptoes across the sand.
He's got a million kinds of stardust,
Pick your fav'rite brand, and:

Dream when you're feelin' blue,
Dream, that's the thing to do.

Just watch the smoke rings rise in the air,
You'll find your share
Of memories there.

So dream when the day is thru,
Dream and they might come true,

Things never are as bad as they seem,
So dream, dream, dream.

This proves that Mercer could write a "big" melody. And here's the way he told us about it back in the sixties: "I was just fooling around at the piano and I got a series of chords that attracted me. I played it for Paul Weston and he said, 'Why don't we use it for the theme song on the show?' We were doing the Chesterfield Show on radio—Paul had the band—and I was on it for six months. Then along came Perry Como and did the show for twelve years! I guess that shows something about me as a performer." (Wrong.) And it doesn't show us too much more about the construction of a fine song; we can leave more up to Paul Weston, who added: "Johnny seemed dissatisfied with the sixth note, the one that falls on the word 'blue' but I think that almost 'makes' the song and I convinced him to let it stay."

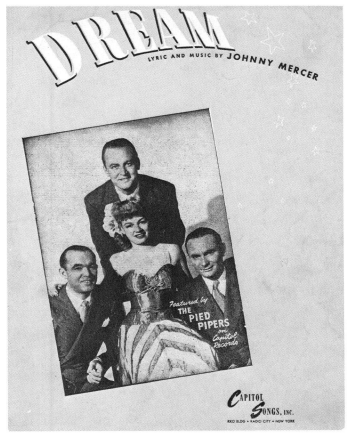

On the Atchison, Topeka and The Santa Fe

1946

Music by HARRY WARREN

Do yuh hear that whistle down the line?
I figure that it's engine number forty-nine,
She's the only one that'll sound that way.
On the Atchison, Topeka and the Santa Fe.

See the ol' smoke risin' 'round the bend,
I reckon that she knows she's gonna meet a
   friend,
Folks around these parts get the time o' day
From the Atchison, Topeka and the Santa
   Fe.

Here she comes!
Ooh, Ooh, Ooh,
Hey, Jim! yuh better git the rig!
Ooh, Ooh, Ooh,
She's got a list o' passengers that's pretty
   big,

And they'll all want lifts to Brown's Hotel,
'Cause lots 'o them been travelin' for quite a
   spell,
All the way from Philadelphiay,
On the Atchison, Topeka and the Santa Fe.

A blockbuster of a song that helped make Judy Garland's big production number in *The Harvey Girls* a Hollywood classic. It was a natural for Academy Award honors, and win it did for Mercer's first and somewhat overdue Oscar. (Harry Warren once said to Harold Arlen as they went into a party in Palm Springs, "Walk two Oscars behind me.") Once again a favorite subject—this one a daytime train—was running right on time.

"On the Atchison, Topeka and Santa Fe" recently was Johnny Mercer who boarded the Super Chief at Chicago November 2 along with Mrs. Mercer bound for home in Los Angeles via their favorite railroad. President John S. Reed was on hand to wish happy traveling to the well-known couple. This year marks the 25th birthday of that ever-popular song by Johnny Mercer and Harry Warren, which was used in the musical score of "The Harvey Girls." Here, aboard the Super Chief, President Reed appropriately presents an "Award of Appreciation to Johnny Mercer on the 25th Anniversary of the introduction of the song 'On The Atchison, Topeka and Santa Fe' with best wishes."

Judy Garland made any song worth hearing, but "Atchison, Topeka" was a triumph.

Laura

1945

Music by DAVID RAKSIN

You know the feeling
Of something half remembered,
Of something that never happened
Yet you recall it well.

You know the feeling
Of recognizing someone
That you've never met
As far as you could tell; well:

Laura is the face in the misty light
Footsteps that you hear down the hall,
The laugh that floats on a summer night
That you can never quite recall.
And you see Laura
On the train that is passing thru,
Those eyes, how familiar they seem,
She gave your very first kiss to you.
That was Laura,
But she's only a dream.

This song is unquestionably among the top three or four of Mercer's all-time greats, and rightly so: the wispy, mysterious quality that was necessary to match the film holds up well, the haunting "those eyes how familiar they seem," the flash-moment we've all experienced, "Laura on the train [again] that is passing thru" all contribute to this song's universal appeal. Amazingly, Mercer wrote the lyrics some time after the release and subsequent popularity of the movie, thus making it more of a challenge than putting words to a melody usually is.

Out of This World

Music by HAROLD ARLEN

You're clear out of this world.
When I'm looking at you
I hear out of this world
The music that no mortal ever knew.

You're right out of a book.
The fairy tale I read when I was so high.
No armored knight out of a book
Was more enchanted by a Lorelei
Than I

After waiting so long for the right time
After reaching so long for a star,
All at once, from the long and lonely
    nighttime
And despite time
Here you are.

I'd cry out of this world
If you said we were through,
So, let me fly out of this world
And spend the next eternity or two
With you.

©Edwin H. Morris & Company, Inc.

The title song of an undistinguished movie that starred Eddie Bracken, Veronica Lake and Diana Lynn
and that is remembered, if at all, for the fact that when Eddie Bracken began to sing it was Bing Crosby's
voice that one heard. The phrase "out of this world" was somewhat ahead of its time here. T. Dorsey and
Bing both had popular records of the tune.

Come Rain or Come Shine

1946

Music by HAROLD ARLEN

I'm gonna love you
Like nobody's loved you,
Come rain or come shine.
High as a mountain
And deep as a river,
Come rain or come shine.
I guess when you met me
It was just one of those things,
But don't ever bet me,
'Cause I'm gonna be true if you let me.
You're gonna love me
Like nobody's loved me,
Come rain or come shine.
Happy together,
Unhappy together
And won't it be fine.
Days may be cloudy or sunny,
We're in or we're out of the money,
But I'm with you always,
I'm with you rain or shine!

A rarity for Mercer because it's probably his only Broadway hit song. "Don't ever bet me"
underlines the show's theme, which was the racetrack at the turn of the century and the black
jockeys popular at the time. Interestingly, there's no verse to this song.

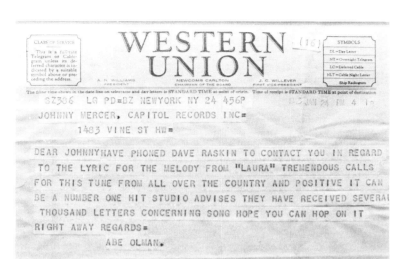

The filing time shown in the date line on telegrams and day letters is STANDARD TIME at point of origin. Time of receipt is STANDARD TIME at point of destination

SZ306 LG PD=BZ NEWYORK NY 24 456P

JOHNNY MERCER, CAPITOL RECORDS INC=
    1483 VINE ST HW=

DEAR JOHNNYHAVE PHONED DAVE RASKIN TO CONTACT YOU IN REGARD
TO THE LYRIC FOR THE MELODY FROM "LAURA" TREMENDOUS CALLS
FOR THIS TUNE FROM ALL OVER THE COUNTRY AND POSITIVE IT CAN
BE A NUMBER ONE HIT STUDIO ADVISES THEY HAVE RECEIVED SEVERAL
THOUSAND LETTERS CONCERNING SONG HOPE YOU CAN HOP ON IT
RIGHT AWAY REGARDS=
        ABE OLMAN.

Pearl Bailey was the main show stopper in *St. Louis Woman*. She and Mercer were simpatico souls as the show struggled along.

The original manuscript of one of the lesser songs from Arlen and Mercer's finest score.

The Capitol Records tower on Vine Street. The name Capitol was suggested by the ever-resourceful Ginger M.

Mercer as executive of Capitol Records sits in on a record session with Dave Dexter (left) and co-founder Glenn Wallichs.

The sheet music cover is more interesting than the song, for photogenic reasons alone.

Arlen and Mercer in a marvelously posed shot. They were at their best when this was taken.

I Wonder What Became of Me

1946   Music by HAROLD ARLEN

Lights are bright,
Pianos making music all the night
And they pour champagne just like it was
   rain.

It's a sight to see,
But I wonder what became of me.

Crowds go by,
That merrymaking laughter in their eye
And the laughter's fine,
But I wonder what became of mine.

Life's sweet as honey
And yet it's funny
I get a feeling that I can't analyze,
It's like, well, maybe,

Like when a baby
Sees a bubble burst before its eyes.

Oh, I've had my fling,
I've been around and seen most ev'rything,

Oh, I've had my thrills,
They've lit my cigarettes with dollar bills,

But I can't be gay,
For along the way
Something went astray.

And I can't explain,
It's the same champagne,
It's a sight to see
But I wonder what became of me.

It was a great score, but as so often happens, the music didn't save the show, and *St. Louis Woman* proved a major disappointment to everyone. This song is an unappreciated beauty—like so many others in the score—and could be one of those special favorites, pride of the litter, for the authors. We find the first three lines of this one wonderful.

Any Place I Hang My Hat Is Home

1946

Music by HAROLD ARLEN

Free an' easy, that's my style,
Howdy do me, watch me smile,
Fare thee well me after while
'Cause I gotta roam
An' any place I hang my hat is home!

Sweetnin' water, cherry wine,
Thank you kindly, suits me fine.
Kansas City, Caroline,
That's my honeycomb.
'Cause any place I hang my hat is home.

Birds roostin' in the tree
Pick up an' go,
An' the goin' proves
That's how it ought to be,
I pick up too
When the spirit moves me.

Cross the river, round the bend,
Howdy stranger, so long friend,
There's a voice in the lonesome win'
That keeps whisperin' roam!
I'm goin' where a welcome mat is,
No matter where that is
'Cause any place I hang my hat is home.

Anyone who knew Mercer at all would agree that this is a definitive song of his. In Otis Guernsey's book on *Lyricists and the Broadway Theatre*, writer Jerome Lawrence says, "The line 'Howdy stranger, so long friend' is one that I can't get out of my head." Second the motion. Barbra Streisand has made a fine record of this gem.

It's a Woman's Prerogative

1946

Music by HAROLD ARLEN

I don't know who it was wrote it,
Or by whose pen it was signed
Someone once said, and I quote it,
It's a woman's prerogative to change her
   mind.
He may have you in a halter
Harnessed before and behind,
But till you kneel at that altar
It's a woman's prerogative to change her
   mind.
Promise anything,
Anything at all,
Promise everything,
Everything, honey—don't swerve,
Throw him a curve
String 'em along
Till they show you what they've got in
   reserve.
Though his bank shows a big balance
And he seems heaven designed,
If the boy's short on his talents,
It's a woman's prerogative to change her
   mind.

Any fruit, even a lemon,
Should have a beautiful rind,
But if that lemon's a lemon,
It's a woman's prerogative to change her
   mind.
If he won't bow from the center,
And you're politely inclined,
If he won't rise when you enter,
It's a woman's prerogative to change her
   mind.
They say precedent
Makes a thing a law,
Hooray precedent,
I can say yes
When I mean no.

Hard to believe,
But they tell me that it's legally so.
So don't fret how much you kissed 'em,
If on their couch you're reclined,
Don't forget we've got a system,
It'a a woman's prerogative to change her
   mind.

This was meant to be a show-stopper and succeeded to the extent that it helped Pearl Bailey along on her rise to stardom. Mercer was a great fan of Pearlie-Mae's and so he gave her a lot of good comedy lines here. The theme of female twisting male around her little finger is always surefire, particularly in the theatre.

Harlem Butterfly

1948

Words and Music by JOHNNY MERCER

Harlem butterfly, the moon got in your eye
The night you were born.
Harlem butterfly, you listen'd to the cry
Of some lonely horn.
And that combination left you a mark
That you'll never, never lose.
While you chase some will o' the wisp in the
    dark,
Your heart keeps on singin' the blues.

Oh, Harlem butterfly, the writin's in the sky,
You'll come to no good.
But I'm not blamin' you,
I'm certain I would do the same if I could.
For even though a candle burn'd at both
    ends
Can never last out the night
Harlem butterfly, it really makes a lovely
    light.

It was still possible in 1948 to write a lyric with the word Harlem in it, despite the beginnings of postwar race troubles, and Mercer was one of the few major songwriters who had an understanding of what the Black world and its mores were. He often wrote about Blacks, but never in a patronizing way. Though Julie London's picture peps up the sheet music, it was Maxine Sullivan who did (and still does) the song best. Showing his literary interests, the last three lines are a paraphrase of Edna St. Vincent Millay's famous verse.

The lyricist of "Any Place I Hang My Hat," age six.

Though she may always be known as "The Loch Lomond Girl" Maxine Sullivan is closely identified with Mercer's lovely "Harlem Butterfly." This jazzy pose came from the Warner Brothers set of *Going Places*

146

Lazy Mood

(Love's Got Me in a)

1947

Music by EDDIE MILLER

I'll tell you why
The days go by,
Like caterpillars do,
And clouds are cotton blossoms
In a field of blue,
Love's got me in a lazy mood,

I'll tell you why,
Stars in the sky,
Pick ev'ry night to shine.
And why the moon's a watermelon on the
    vine,
Love's got me in a lazy mood.

When a bright and early sun begins to steam
    it up,
You'll find me underneath the nearest tree,
While I dream it up. Pickin' petals off a
    daisy,
Just the absentminded kid, that's me.
I'll tell you why,
I don't reply
    To mail that's overdue.
And why I never answer when I'm spoken
    to,
It isn't that I'm really rude,
Love's got me in a lazy mood.

After the Benny Goodman period, Mercer was hired again to do a weekly radio show that featured commercialized jazz. This time the band was Bob Crosby's Dixieland Band, a happy sounding outfit that was right down Mercer's alley. The tenor saxophonist Eddie Miller played a pretty solo that captured Mercer's ear and the result was this pretty piece.

Early Autumn

1949

Music by RALPH BURNS and WOODY HERMAN

When an early autumn walks the land
And chills the breeze
And touches with her hand
The summer trees,
Perhaps you'll understand
What memories I own.

There's a dance pavilion in the rain
All shuttered down,
A winding country lane all russet brown,
A frosty window pane shows me a town
    grown lonely.

That spring of ours that started
So April hearted
Seemed made for just a boy and girl.
I never dreamed, did you,
Any fall could come in view so early, early?

Darling, if you care,
Please let me know,
I'll meet you anywhere,
I miss you so.
Let's never have to share
Another early autumn.

Who else but Mercer could conjure up such a marvelously nostalgic picture as "a dance pavilion in the rain all shuttered down"? Here are the author's comments on the song: "That's by Ralph Burns—a superior tune—and I've never even met Ralph yet. I think it's one of my best lyrics. [Unusual for him to say] Not a big hit, but you can't tell the public what they like—they usually pick the right ones."

Johnny may be thanking Woody Herman for making possible the great song "Early Autumn." The kid on the right, Woody's grandson, has enough hair for Johnny, Woody, Artie Shaw and George Simon.

Sidney Zion

This, That

BING. When he got away last week, disconnected melodies jumped all over me, and I'll bet over millions of people all over the world Not only his songs, though of course his songs, but fragments like so: the phone number of a girl I haven't seen in 25 years; my great little red Rambler; the attic where the victrola lived and so did I for hours each day against walls festooned with DiMaggio, Keller, Luckman, Bertelli, Grable and Durante; a sign over a place in Passaic saying Weddings, Banquets, Sandwiches; a high school fraternity dance in *Albany,* where I saw the girl whose number I remembered on Friday afternoon when Bing Crosby . . .

Of course, he changed the whole course of pop singing, and yet in his duos with Jolson and Armstrong, he flowed perfectly, moving the old stuff around like a great control pitcher, and always managing, in that casual way, to take the center and hold it. When he went one-on-one with Sinatra, particularly in the movie "High Society," he simply wiped out Sinatra, took him with the first glance, though Frank was at his peak and Bing supposedly over the hill. Of all the great stars he sang with — it's funny how few of the ladies come to mind — the only one he didn't shade was Johnny Mercer, but then nobody could touch up Johnny Mercer, who broke the mold himself. They did a TV show together years back, and if some tasteful, enterprising producer would only do a replay we'd see the best musical evening television ever made. But is there such an animal as an enterprising producer with taste? There must have been once, but where are they now?

And now, alas, where is Bing and Al and Johnny and Louis?

Christmas Card

**oel**

Yule and Christmastide
To everybody—every side
Best of fortune, health, and cheer
In everybody's atmosphere
Let foe kiss friend—and friend kiss foe
Beneath a common mistletoe
Republicans! Be Democratic
Drag the tinsel from the attic
Light the tree and fill the bowl
(You won the Lit'ry Digest poll)
Step right up and love thy neighbor
Capital! Shake hands with Labor
Hurry and unlatch the door
For Santa Claus is here once more
Despite a million annual beatings
Here he is—dispensing greetings
Bringing them from us to you
From who knows, Lord, to Lord
  knows who
To all the people on our list
To everyone we may have missed
To those who'll say to us, "I see—
You didn't send a card to me!"
To those who'll say, "Of all the gall!"
A Merry Christmas to you All!
A Happy Yule to all of you
Who should have sent us something too
Season when the heart has wings
Hark! The Herald Tribune sings!
Have a pretzel, have a beer
Christmas comes but once a year
Greetings Harold, Anya Arlen
Buddy Morris, you too, Carlin
Johnny Arledge, Fred Astaire
Edith Anderson and "Square"

Greetings Ashcrafts, Jane and "Squirrel"
Milton Ager and his girl
Greetings Mr., Mrs. Alter
Billy Blun and Lawrence Salter
All the guys on Bull and Broughton
Messrs. Arco and MacNaughton
Botkin, Borut, Brewster, Blum
Come and make yourselves "to hum"
Drink with Bacchus, ring up Bell
Charles, Ed, Mac and Muriel
Mrs. Baldwin, bring your Earl in
Where's a chair for Irving Berlin
Mr. Bargy, Mr. Bloom
Let's have music in the room
Archie Bleyer, Johnny Burke
Busby Berkeley go to work
Show the Burroughs and the Blowes
How the anvil chorus goes
Merry Christmas—sing it gaily
Ronny Burla, Mildred Bailey
Bacon, Lloyd, and Aunt Nell Blackie
Call time out on "Nagasaki"
Sing a simple Christmas lay
Barris Harry, Bregman J.
So we go from B to C
Greetings Cochran, Charlie B.
Prosit Pink and Mary Cavett
'S only schnapps, but you can have it
Philip Charig, prosit too
Carol Carol—both of you
Greetings Crosbys, Bing and Larry
Dixie, Coop, and Lin and Gary
Philip, Dennis, Everett, Bob
What do you Crosbys hear—from the mob?
Happy New Year—fide bona

Clinton, Clark, and chez Colonna
May the Carmichaels be lucky
Hoagy, Ruth, and Bob and Ducky
Ken Carpenter, Sidney Clare
Everybody—Everywhere
To the Davis clans, hey nonny
Marvin, Mary, Bette, Johnny
Tommy Dugan, Buddy Dill
Buddy (now B. G.) De Syl-
Dorsey J. and Dorsey T.
Dubin Al and Douglas P.
Dubin J. and A. Devine
Hello Oscar Hammerstein
Here's a crimson wreath of holly
For Walter Donaldson and Wally
P. De Rose—May Singhi Breen
Jimmy Downey, how've you been?
And Margot de la Falaise
You wear that name—no matter what any
    says
Ere the jolly season pass
Happy, Happy Michaelmas!
Turkey stuffing, hot cross buns
Edelmans and Emersons
William Ellfeldt, Skinnay Ennis
Johnny Faunce (and how's your tennis?)
Fishbeins, Franklins, how you all?
Dave, Dwight, Mary (neé McCall)
Wishes can't be Fonda, Hank
Just like money in the bank
Then there's F for Families
Christmas Gif' to both of these
Mother, Mother, Father too
Walter, Big and Little Hugh
Ed and Deborah and Claire
Polish up the silverware
Lay the snowy tablespread
Uncles Lewis and Rob and Ed
Gather 'round and all get clubby

Meet Elizabeth's new hubby
George and Bess and George the third
Cousin Mamie, cut the bird
Mercer, Adeline, Aunt K.
Polish off the egg frappé
Dorothy and Mary Lou
Joseph and Virginia too
Every oldster—every sprout
Mustn't leave a person out
Uncle Joe will mix the toddy
Happy headaches everybody!
Ira Gershwins, Johnny Greens
Elliott Grennards, Jack Gordeans
Here's a package tied in ribbons
For the Gruens and the Gibbons
While the Goffs and L. Wolfe Gilberts
Get a box of chocolate filberts
And to Goldie, mon chou chou
The remaining nuts to you
Mr. Gumble, Mrs. Geary
Hope your Xmas comes on cheery
While B. Goodman's—Krupa's too
Comes on like Gangbusters do
Farmer or sophisticate
Happy New Year to you, Gate
Galludets and Crooner Frawley
Allie Wrubel, Dick MacCauley
Dr. Joe and Mrs. Harris
Happy, happy plaster paris
Harry Arthur, Harris Jane
Charlotte, Jack, long may you reign
Blessings on your domiciles
Here and in the British Isles
May a goodly batch of manna
Find the Hull home in Savannah
Laughter in the Herzig den
Love to Bernie Hanighen
And may Joe and Mrs. Helbock
Open up a keg of swell bock

To the Harveys—Bob and Peg
Goes the biggest turkey leg
And the Hawkins, Houstons, Herts
May they get their just desserts
Greetings Bob, Dolores Hope
Here's a present—do not ope
Lindsay Howard and Seabiscuit
Here's a fin—or should I risk it?
Sonny Hitch and Margery
Willie Horowitz—how be?
Isaccs, Jarvis, how do you be?
And the Jolsons, Al and Ruby?
Babo Jackson, Poppa Bill
Your socks would be hard to fill
Gordon Jenkins, Georgie Joy
Mrs. Johnston's little boy
Irving Kahal—tap the barrel
Miriam, sing a Christmas Karol
Blessings Margaret Keyes and Zipper
Teddy Koehler—Hi ya, Dipper?
Hiram Kraft and daughter Jill
You too, Reata—now, be still!
I know all you people, but—
Who is *Wilhemina Thutt?*
Lots of Noels, lots of Yules
To the Cal and Mandy Kuhls
Love to Grace and Gus (the Kahns)
"Kosty" Ianetz, Lily Pons
C. and E. Kress—by the way—
Have you ever thought of writing a play?
Harry Kaufman wants to know
Harry, we can't do that show.
Guy Lombardo, Harry Link
Carmen, Leibert, have a drink!
Eddie Lowe and Bonnie Lake,
Have a slice of angel cake!
Hello Fud and hello Don!
In the name of Livingston
Mr. Leslie, Mrs. Lehr

Here's a rather tough affair
How's a guy to rhyme La Mont
Maybe Nash can, but I cawn't
Greetings, greetings, greetings all
Hallelujah! Have a ball!
Have a party and we'll pay
If we get the bank's okay
Put the taper to the fire
In the house of McIntire
Bring the frankincense and myrrh
To the house of Mehlinger
Ralph Malone and Una Merkel
Gather 'round the family circle
Jeeves, get out more firewater
Toast McDonough's wife and daughter
Jeeves, go fetch the old Bacardi
Comes the Malnecks and Mienardi
Comes the Mitchells and Marcels
From the land where King George dwells
Mrs. Mannerino (Mary)
Jno. Mayhew, Leo McCarey
Modisetts and Monacos
Have you tasted some of those?
Have you tried the seven layer?
Have some, Ray and Edith Mayer
Mr. Rothmere, have some too
Really, there's enough for you
I know all you people, but—
Who is *Wilhemina Thutt?*
Greetings Millers—Everett, Charlie
Bless your hearts particularly
Here, you minstrels! Tune your lyres
Sing to Zi and Betty Myers
Mr. Norvo, taste the jam
Mr. Nelson, how's the Ham?
Nolan, Joe and Noble, Ray
Merry, merry Xmas day
Mr. Gordon Oliver
May you get what you prefer

Though the censors find it shocking
May a brunette fill your stocking
Keep the sweets from Oakie, Jack
Or the poundage may come back
To the Tommy Oxnards, hey!
To the Bennys, watcha say?
Greetings, Temple, Dot, not Shirley
Just because her teeth are pearly
Rocco Vocco and his Dolly
Joe Venuti and his Sally
Jerry Vogel's smiling pan
Emmerita Vanneman
Who's that singing in the alley?
Let him in—why, Rudy Vallee!
Hang the geese and stuff the pheasants
Almost time to open presents
Comes the late guest through the yard
To present his calling card
Hang his off'ring on the bough
Jeeves, there goes the doorbell now
In the late arrivals float
Mrs. Whiting, rest your coat?
Margaret, Barbara and Blossom
Cut yourselves a slice o'possum
Look who's here! It's Harry Wise
Christmas spirit in his eyes
Here's the Warner Music Staffs
(Can I have your autographs?)
Kenny, Hazel, Sandy, Sammy

Polished up with soap and chamois
Jack and Ruth and Norman Foley
Harold, Mack, both roly-poly
Love to all the Warner house
Look out, ladies, there's a Mouse
And his brother, Harry Warren
Back with Jo from travels foreign
Hal B. Wallis, J. L. Warner
Sorry I ain't in your corner
But it's nice to have a day off
Knowing that it's not a lay off
Margaret Whiteman! Hello, Paul—
Still the Daddy of them all
Will you say how-do for me
To the Big and Little T?
Vernon Wood, it's time you came!
Mrs. Willingham, the same!
Harold Warnell!—listen, "Slicker"
Don't expect that pre-war liquor
Close the door and lock it tight
Wait a second—something White
All the brothers and their wives
See! the troupe of Young arrives
Youngs from Lincoln St. and Hall
Youngs from N.Y. Enter all!
Everybody's here again
Did I hear a footstep then?
Who's that in the snowy mist?
Sam and Maggie Zimbalist!

154

Ginger and Johnny at home in Palm Springs (beer or Scotch?).

The Fifties

If phonographs were the big influence on young people in the twenties and radio broadcasting in the thirties and forties, the full-scale arrival of television in the early fifties was equally influential on young and old alike—for awhile. The postwar young would soon become captivated by another phenomenon—a Southern singer with the sex appeal of a Valentino and the unique name of Elvis. As for the rest of the music world, television was not the bonanza that the earlier wonders of American communications had proved: TV producers discovered that pointing their cameras into the bell of a trumpet or into the larynx of, say, Julius LaRosa of "The Arthur Godfrey Show" wasn't nearly as exciting to home viewers as seeing Soupy Sales get a pie pushed into his face or Jackie Robinson sliding safely into second base. The new box in the corner of the living room (not yet called "the boob tube") was causing still another problem for people like Johnny Mercer and other creative fellows: the production of movies— particularly lavish musicals—was being cut back considerably. In the year 1938 Hollywood had produced fifty-nine musical films of one quality or another, but by 1950 the output was reduced to a paltry twenty-one. The sad omens were in the air, particularly with that guitar-playing kid from Tennessee gyrating around so successfully in the middle of the bland Eisenhower years.

The decade of the 1950s was a time of paradox too: there were Dave Garroway and Uncle Miltie, Pat Boone and "Rock 'Round the Clock," *Hellzapoppin* and Rodgers and Hammerstein. For the man we're principally concerned with, however, the time, while not as productive as the previous two decades, saw him now a member of the Hollywood elite. Capitol Records was moving into the big leagues, challenging Victor, Columbia and Decca, Mercer's second Oscar ("In the Cool, Cool, Cool of the Evening"–1951) was resting on the mantel shelf of his Newport Beach home, and the story of an amazing piece of family business had leaked out to make his name known beyond just the music business. The story concerned Mercer's father, a well-known real estate broker in Savannah, who had gone bankrupt in the troublesome times of the late twenties. Johnny Mercer, honorable son of the old, *old* south, decided more than twenty years later to repay his father's debts, and so he tracked down all the original investors or their heirs and sent off a check of $300,000 to a local bank for the complete repayment. This story hit the wire services and, typically of Mercer's quiet, private ways, was a surprise to his wife of so many years, who had to hear about it first from the newspaper reporters. Quiet and private he was, also a bit vague and absentminded at times—the Savannah bank phoned to call to Johnny's attention the fact that he had forgotten to sign the gentlemanly check.

Movie scores were not coming around as often, now that Hollywood was slowing down, and Capitol Records was losing its original flavor as it moved into the world of big sales and big business. "Johnny said, 'There's no fun there any more,'" says Ginger Mercer. "He thought it had become a bit of a bore." Dave Dexter and Margaret Whiting, who were both very much involved with the company, agree that the disenchantment of Capitol's guru was total. "He'd come back from New York, walk in the office and the receptionist wouldn't know who he was," says Margaret. So Johnny Mercer bowed out of the one big business venture he ever became involved with (money and art rarely mix, said some sage) and even though he left Capitol a little resentfully, there was a great deal of financial recompense. It was time to turn his attentions elsewhere.

Undaunted by the total disappointments of both the brilliantly scored *St. Louis Woman* in 1946 and the not-so-brilliant 1949 *Texas, L'il Darlin'*, on which he collaborated with Robert Emmet Dolan, in the fifties Mercer indulged a great deal in one of his favorite sports—riding the trains from coast to coast (and occasionally south to refresh himself in Savannah). Broadway was becoming a tougher mountain to scale, with such strong competition as Frank Loesser's *Guys and Dolls*, Leonard Bernstein's *West Side Story*, and Rodgers and Hammerstein's *Carousel* and *The King and I*, but Mercer kept trying. In the space of ten years that some wits have retrospectfully dubbed the Fabulous Fifties (J. McCarthy fabulous?) he gave the Broadway arena three more tries. In 1951 *Top Banana*, for which he wrote both words and music and which starred Phil Silvers, who, though hot on TV as "Sergeant Bilko," couldn't make it into a real hit; in 1956 *L'il Abner*, based on the Al Capp cartoon strip, with music by a good musician friend from Hollywood, Gene DePaul; and finally, in 1959, *Saratoga*, which had the greatest of ingredients—book by Edna Ferber, costumes and sets by Cecil Beaton, songs by Harold Arlen—and the worst of reviews. But of course the trains could always take him back to California.

And back there where the sun always made it so easy to play a little golf, shoot the breeze on the Vine Street sidewalk outside the Brown Derby, or just laze about in the backyard, Johnny Mercer forgot about the New York rat race. Even though the music he loved so much was changing radically in the late fifties—rock 'n' roll and bebop were never his cup of tea—the Mercer touch continued for awhile, and just ahead were two of his biggest hit songs, bringing in two more Oscars.

Great impromptu shot of two musical greats—J.M. and Nat "King" Cole at a Capitol Records gathering.

The Big Movie Show in the Sky

1950   Music by ROBERT EMMETT DOLAN

A fella can get lonesome when he is all
    alone,
Out there in the Pacific with no friends to
    call his own.
A fella gits to thinkin' if he's gittin'
    anywhere,
A fella gits to wond'rin' how it's gonna
    be up there.

When your final chip is cashed
And the pearly gates swing wide,
And there is old Saint Peter
Askin' you to come inside.
He whispers "Son, go find a seat,
I hope you like the show,"
And then you see a picture of the life you
    led below!

Imagine you are one of that great celestial
    crowd,

A settin' back relaxin' with your feet upon a
    cloud.
You're pourin' buttered sunshine on your
    popcorn
White as fleece
And waitin' for the latest inter-hemisphere
    release.
The stars spell out the title and the cast
Before your eye.
The show commences on the silver screen
They call the sky.
The past begins unfoldin' and you see it
    takin' place,
And pretty soon you're lookin' at your own
    big, ugly face!

Bye and bye, bye and bye,
Can you look your self in the eye,
When you come on the screen "up yonder,"
At the big movie show in the sky?

© Chappell & Co., Inc.

Mercer's second outing on Broadway was in tandem with a pal, Robert Emmet (Bobby) Dolan, whom Mercer had met on the Paramount lot where Dolan was a conductor/musical director. *Texas L'il Darlin'* never quite got off the ground, which was not surprising considering the competition at the time: *South Pacific, Kiss Me Kate* and *Guys and Dolls.* Dolan and Mercer put together a pleasant but rather undistinguished score which featured a toe-tapper "It's Great to Be Alive" and this hunk of down-home philosophy.

Autumn Leaves

1950

English lyric by JOHNNY MERCER
Music by JOSEPH KOSMA

The falling leaves
Drift by the window,
The Autumn leaves
Of red and gold.

I see your lips,
The summer kisses,
The sunburned hands
I used to hold.

Since you went away
The days grow long,
And soon I'll hear
Old winter's song.

But I miss you most of all, my darling,
When Autumn leaves start to fall.

This, the first of Mercer's three big adaptations of French songs, remains one of the most performed of ballads in nightclubs, piano bars and lounges. It can probably best be categorized as something of a tearjerker and Mel Tormé, a songwriter's best friend, says that the image "old winter's song" knocks him out.

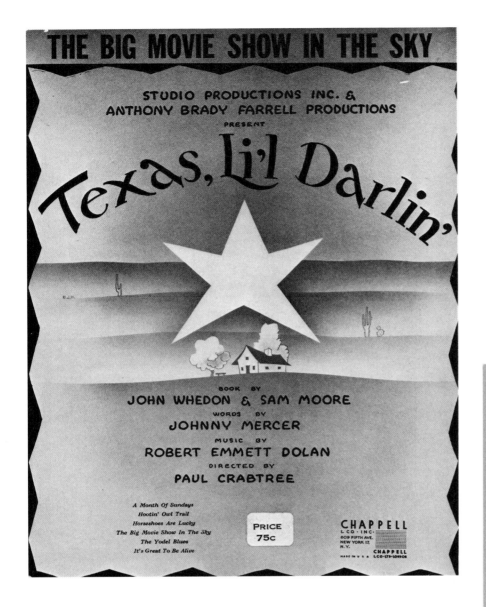

Epicurean Dining at its Smartest

Tally-Ho

(formerly Old Canterbury)

Westport Center

Open Every Day
From 11 A.M. to 1 A.M.

Telephone for Reservations
Westport 2-8987

Entertainment Nightly by EDDIE FURMAN, Dean of Piano Humor

WEEK OF AUGUST 29 - SEPTEMBER 3, 1949

The Westport Season of 1949, Inc.

Lawrence Langner, Armina Marshall, John C. Wilson — Directors
Martin Manulis, Managing Director

Boston Post Road, Westport   Tel. Westport 2-4179

presents

Prior To Broadway!
A New Musical Comedy

"TEXAS, LI'L DARLIN'"

Book by	Lyrics by
JOHN WHEDON and SAM MOORE	JOHNNY MERCER
Music by	Special Choreography by
ROBERT EMMETT DOLAN	EMY ST. JUST
Staged by	Settings & Lighting by
PAUL CRABTREE	Edward T. Cooper

featuring

KENNY DELMAR	ELAINE STRITCH
DANNY SCHOLL	HARRY BANNISTER

A Home As Charming

as the owner. Choice location, walk to Westport shops, churches, schools. 4 bedrooms, 2 baths, 5 fire places, 2 open porches, commodious library. Colorful garden, flowering shrubs. See this for convenient, gracious living.

W. B. HAWLEY
Real Estate

1024 Unquowa Road, Fairfield, Conn.
Phone 9-0455

Miss Weld's

To those who enjoy home-cooked food served in a delightful atmosphere, Miss Weld opens her home at

27 Elm Street   Westport

Luncheon 11:30-2:30   Buffet Lunch
Dinner 6:00 to 8:30
a la carte and regular

Thursdays — Buffet Supper — $3.50

Closed Wednesdays   Westport 2-4037

COUNTRY PLAYHOUSE, INC., LESSORS

Here's to My Lady

1951

Music by RUBE BLOOM

Although it lies outside of my dominion
If you should ask me for my opinion,
When out with good companions and voices
   ring.
There comes a time before the party's
   closing,
Perhaps the old ones have started dozing,
When one toast needs proposing,
I raise my glass and sing:

Here's to my lady,
Here's a toast to my lady
And all that my lady means to me.

Like a hearth in the Winter,
A breeze in the Summer,
A Spring to remember is she.

Though the years may grow colder
As people grow older,
It's shoulder to shoulder we'll be.

But be it sunshine or shady,
Here's my love to my lady.
I pray, may she always love me.

Another collaboration with a pal—they hadn't worked together since "Fools Rush In" in 1940—and, though Rube Bloom was an old jazzman, this song is both musically and lyrically romantic. It was never a big hit, but this song meant a lot to both Mercers, since Johnny announced that it was dedicated to Ginger. "My lady" is a nice way of saying it.

In the Cool, Cool, Cool of the Evening

1951

Music by HOAGY CARMICHAEL

Sue wants a barbecue,
Sam wants to boil a ham,
Grace votes for Bouillabaisse stew.
Jake wants a weeny bake,
Steak and a layer cake,
He'll get a tummy ache too.
We'll rent a tent or teepee.
Let the town crier cry.
And if it's R.S.V.P.
This is what I'll reply:

In the cool, cool, cool of the evenin',
Tell 'em I'll be there.
In the cool, cool, cool of the evenin',
Better save a chair.
When the party's gettin' a glow on,
'N' singin' fills the air,
In the shank o' the night,
When the doin's are right,
You can tell 'em I'll be there.

"Whee!" said the bumblebee,
"Let's have a jubilee!"
"When?" said the prairie hen, "Soon?"
"Shore!" said the dinosaur.
"Where?" said the grizzly bear,
"Under the light of the moon?"
"How 'bout ya, brother jackass?"
Ev'ryone gaily cried,
"You comin' to the fracas?"
Over his specs he sighed;

In the cool, cool, cool of the evenin',
Tell 'em I'll be there.
In the cool, cool, cool of the evenin',
Slickum on my hair.
When the party's gettin' a glow on,
'N' singin' fills the air,
If I ain't in the clink,
And there's sumpin' to drink,
You can tell 'em I'll be there.

The verse is just as swinging and happy as the chorus on this, another Carmichael-Mercer all-timer and the second Mercer Academy Award winner. The movie, *Here Comes the Groom*, was hardly an all-timer but Bing's recording saved the day. The ending phrase, "sumpin' to drink," is sho-'nuff Mercer.

162

When the World Was Young

1951

Music by M. PHILIPPE-GERARD

It isn't by chance I happen to be,
A boulevardier, the toast of Paris,
For over the noise, the talk and the smoke,
I'm good for a laugh, a drink or a joke.
I walk in a room, a party or ball,
"Come sit over here" somebody will call.

"A drink for M'sieur!
A drink for us all!"
But how many times I stop and recall.

Ah, the apple trees,
Blossoms in the breeze,
That we walked among,
Lying in the hay,
Games we used to play,
While the rounds were sung,
Only yesterday
When the world was young.

Wherever I go they mention my name,
And that in itself, is some sort of fame
"Come by for a drink, we've having a
    game,"
Wherever I go I'm glad that I came.
The talk is quite gay, the company fine,
There's laughter and lights, and glamour
    and wine,

And beautiful girls and some of them mine,

But often my eyes see a diff'rent shine.

Ah, the apple trees,
Sunlit memories,
Where the hammock swung,
On our backs we'd lie,
Looking at the sky.
Till the stars were strung,
Only last July
When the world was young.

While sitting around, we often recall.
The laugh of the year, the night of them all.
The blonde who was so attractive that year,
Some opening night that made us all cheer.
Remember that time we all got so tight,
And Jacques and Antoine got into a fight.

The gendarmes who came, passed out like a
    light,
I laugh with the rest, it's all very bright.

Ah, the apple trees,
And the hive of bees
Where we once got stung,
Summers at Bordeaux,
Rowing the bateau,
Where the willow hung,
Just a dream ago,
When the world was young.

A great story-telling lyric that many people still refer to as "Ah, the apple tree." This fine adaptation from a lovely French *chanson* surprised fellow lyricist and Mercer devotee Gene Lees (writing in *High Fidelity* magazine) when he found out that Johnny never learned to speak French. A big record of this song was made by Peggy Lee, another fan and *simpatico* soul. Just consider this picture-book couplet: "Summers at Bordeaux, Rowing the bateau."

Top Banana

1951   Words and music by JOHNNY MERCER

Your big timers and small timers
Don't happen the easy way.
The star comes first,
Then the leading man,
Then the actors in the play.
There are no comics like low comics,
Who finally make the grade.
But recall, sweethearts,
All the phony starts,
And the lousy parts they played!

If you wanna be the top banana,
You gotta start at the bottom of the bunch.
You gotta know the joke about the farmer's
  daughter,
Then take it in the kisser with the soda
  water,
If you wanna be a burlesque comic,
It's basic trainin' for you to take a punch.
You gotta roll your eyes and make a funny
  face,

'N' do a take and holler,
"Dis must be duh place!"
If you wanna be the top banana,
You gotta start from the bottom up.

If you wanna be the top banana,
You gotta start at the bottom of the bunch.
It doesn't matter if the jokes are clean or
  shady,
Make fun of anybody, even your old lady.
What's the diff'rence if she's someone's
  mother?
She's a straight man who oughta know her
  part.
She raised you from an infant
And she's kind and sweet,
But does she know the way to get to Flugel
  street?
If you wanna be the top banana,
You gotta start from the bottom up.

There could only be one pal at a time—Hy Kraft wrote the book—so Mercer took on both words and music for this good idea of a Broadway musical. Unfortunately, even the lovable clown Phil Silvers, then at the height of his "Sergeant Bilko" TV fame, couldn't save *Top Banana*, which rattled around in the huge Winter Garden Theatre. In this breezy title song, notice how hip and on-target Mercer is with his reference to "Dis must be duh place!" and "Flugel Street." Deservedly or not, the show is getting a second life in summer stock and places like Las Vegas.

At least the sign was a big splash on Broadway—even Irving Berlin's offices next door are overshadowed.

165

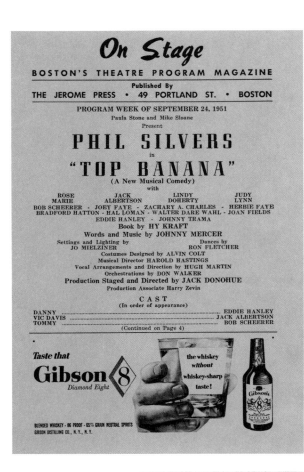

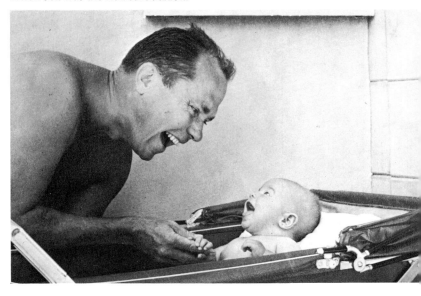

"Whatcha say, Dipper?"
When Jeff was the newest addition.

The great Mills Brothers, who helped the "Glow Worm" revival—and vice versa.

Glow-Worm

1952

Music by PAUL LINCKE (1902)

Glow, little glow-worm, fly of fire,
Glow like an incandescent wire,
Glow for the female of the specie,
Turn on the A-C and the D-C;
This night could use a little brightnin',
Light up, you li'l ol' bug of lightnin',
When you gotta glow, you gotta glow,
Glow, little glow-worm, glow

Glow, little glow-worm, glow and glimmer,
Swim through the sea of night, little
    swimmer,
Thou aer-o-nau-tic-al boll weevil,
Il-lu-mi-nate yon woods primeval;
See how the shadows deep and darken,
You and your chick should get to sparkin',
I got a gal that I love so,
Glow, little glow-worm, glow.

Glow, little glow-worm, turn the key on,
You are equipped with tail light neon;
You got a cute vest pocket Mazda
Which you can make both slow or "Fazda";
I don't know who you took a shine to,
Or who you're out to make a sign to,
I got a gal that I love so,
Glow, little glow-worm, glow.

One can only imagine what a ball Mercer had writing this great updating ("tail-light neon," "vest pocket Mazda") and how stunned the original lyricist, Lilla Cayley Robinson, might have been could she have heard it. The Mills Brothers made such a famous record of the modern "Glow-Worm" that they still have to sing it wherever they go (even on American Express commercials) thirty years after its introduction.

Song of India

1953

Text and adaptation by JOHNNY MERCER
From the original by N. RIMSKY-KORSAKOW

And still the snowy Himalayas rise
In ancient majesty before our eyes,
Beyond the plains, Above the pines,
While thru the ever, never changing land,
As silently as any native band
That moves at night, the Ganges shines;

Then I hear the song that only India can
   sing,
Softer than the plumage on a black raven's
   wing;
High upon a minaret I stand
And gaze across the desert sand
Upon an old enchanted land,
There's the maharajah's caravan,
Unfolding like a painted fan,
How small the little race of Man!

See them all parade across the ages,

Armies, kings and slaves from hist'ry's
   pages,
Played on one of Nature's vastest stages.
The turbanned Sikhs and fakirs line the
   streets,
While holy men in shadowed calm retreats
Pray thru the night and watch the stars,
A lonely plane flies off to meet the dawn,
While down below the busy life goes on,
And women crowd the old bazaars;

All are in the song that only India can sing,
Softer than the plumage on a black raven's
   wing;
Tune the ageless moon and stars were
   strung by,
Timeless song that only could be sung by
   India,
The jewel of the East!

©Criterion Music Corp.

During the Mercer memorial at the Music Box Theatre (Irving Berlin had donated the use of it) in 1976, Mel Tormé singled this lyric out from among the hundreds of Mercers that had been published. Mel said he had heard a Mario Lanza recording of the song on the radio, had phoned the station to inquire about its modern lyrics, and had been amazed when told they were by Mercer. Even as astute a musician as Tormé is impressed by Mercer's all-round adaptability, represented here by beautifully high-flown, appropriate imagery.

Spring, Spring, Spring

1953
Music by GENE de PAUL

Oh, the barnyard is busy
In a regular tizzy,
And the obvious reason
Is because of the season.
Ma Nature's lyrical
With her yearly miracle,
Spring, Spring, Spring!

All the henfolk are hatchin'
While their menfolk are scratchin'
To insure the survival
Of each brand new arrival.
Each nest is twittering,
They're all baby sittering,
Spring, Spring, Spring!

It's a beehive of budding son and daughter
    life,
Ev'ry family has plans in view.
Even down in the brook the underwater life
Is forever blowing bubbles too.
Ev'ry field wears a bonnet
With some spring daisies on it,
Even birds of a feather
Show their clothes off together.
Sun's gettin' shinery
To spotlight the finery,
Spring, Spring, Spring!

In his hole, though the gopher
Seems a bit of a loafer,
The industrious beaver
Puts it down to spring fever.
While there's no antelope
Who feels that he can't elope,
It's Spring, Spring, Spring!

Slow but surely the turtle
Who's enormously fertile
Lays her eggs by the dozens,
Maybe some are her cousins.
Even the catamount
Is nonplussed at that amount,
It's Spring, Spring, Spring!

Even out in Australia the kangeroos
Lay off butter fat and all French fries.
If their offspring are large it might be
    dangerous,
They've just gotta keep 'em pocket size.
Even though to each rabbit
Spring is more like a habit,
Notwithstanding, the fact is
They indulge in the practice
Each day is mother's day,
The next day some other's day,
It's Spring, Spring, Spring!

To itself each amoeba
Softly croons, "Ach du lieber,"
While the proud little termite
Feels as large as a worm might.
Old poppa dragon fly
Is making the wagon fly,
It's Spring, Spring, Spring!

Ev'ry bug's snuggled snuggy
In its own baby buggy,
And in spite of policing
Seems the tribe is increasing.
'Cause Missus Katydid
Once did what her matey did,
It's Spring, Spring, Spring!

Daddy Long Legs is stretching out his
   creaking joints,
And how busy can a bumble bee?
Flitting hither and thither she keeps seeking
   joints
With a spare room and a nursery.
Each cocoon has a tenant

So they hung out a pennant
"Don't disturb, please keep waiting;
We are evacuating.
This home's my momma's,
I'll soon have my own domicile,"
It's Spring, Spring, Spring!

A natural rhyming trip for Mercer with his long-standing affinity for the animal world (he should have worked for Disney) and things homespun and rural. The movie *Seven Brides for Seven Brothers,* in which this song appeared, has become a classic principally because of Michael Kidd's brilliant choreography. Mercer and his new writing partner Gene de Paul later teamed up again with Kidd for the Broadway show *L'il Abner;* obviously they all worked well together.

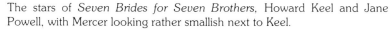

The stars of *Seven Brides for Seven Brothers,* Howard Keel and Jane Powell, with Mercer looking rather smallish next to Keel.

170

Capitol Decade

More than a decade ago Johnny Mercer and Glenn Wallichs used to talk about the record business in Wallich's big music store at Sunset and Vine in Hollywood. As one of the nation's leading songwriters ("Lazybones," "Goody Goody," "Jeepers Creepers," etc.), Mercer had many faults to find. Recording artists, he felt, were seldom presented at their best, and arrangements too often did not do justice to his own, or fellow composer's, compositions. And the major companies generally ignored budding talent.

Wallichs, as owner of the Music City, one of the country's largest music emporiums, had his complaints, too. As a record dealer, he disagreed fundamentally with the merchandising and distribution policies of the "big" companies.

The result of their discussions was inevitable: Why not form a record company of their own? At this point, the late B.G. (Buddy) DeSylva, executive producer of Paramount Pictures, endorsed their enterprise and put up $10,000 to get them going. On April 8, 1942, Capitol Records was formed. On April 18 the War Production Board reduced the shellac available to record companies by about 70 per cent. By July 1, Capitol had sold its first records—only to be faced with a curt note from James C. Petrillo, president of the American Federation of Musicians, to the effect that no more records could be made after Aug. 1.

Big Four: It was hardly an auspicious birth, and few except Wallichs, Mercer & Co. saw how Capitol could survive, let alone be a threat to the "Big Three"—RCA Victor, Columbia, and Decca. But survive it did, and last week, as Capitol was in full swing celebrating its tenth birthday, the company had not only be-

come a threat to the "Big Three," but forced the industry to recognize there was now a "Big Four" in the business.

In 1942, Capitol grossed $195,000. Last year, total sales exceeded $13,000,000, a gain of more than $1,000,000 over 1950. The company has still to match its all-time high in 1948, when it grossed $16,800,000. But that it bounced back from the horrors of 1949, when the firm netted only $60,000 after taxes, all concerned feel is a miracle made possible only by Capitol's young and aggressive leadership. For 1949 found Capitol caught short in the "Battle of the Speeds," when the record industry was forced to face—and convert to—the new 33⅓ and 45 rpm. The nightmares of this fight for survival were enough to make Wallichs, already a camera enthusiast, take up miniature railroading as an antidote for sleepless nights and worried days.

Camera-bug Wallichs focuses on . . .

When Capitol began, it had nine artists, and its first hits were Ella Mae Morse's "Cow-Cow Boogie" and Johnny Mercer's "Strip Polka." As the years passed there came Mercer's "GI Jive" and "Accentuate the Positive," Betty Hutton's "Doctor, Lawyer, Indian Chief," Peggy Lee's "Golden Earrings" and "Mañana," Nat King Cole's "Mona Lisa" and "Too Young," Tex Williams's "Smoke, Smoke, Smoke, That Cigarette," Les Paul and Mary Ford's "How High the Moon," "Mockin' Bird Hill," "The World Is Waiting for the Sunrise," "Tennessee Waltz," and "Tiger Rag," Kay Starr's "Wheel of Fortune," and, to round out the tenth year, Ella Mae Morse again with "Blacksmith Blues."

Kids and Classics: In addition to its extraordinarily strong popular catalogue, Capitol also boasts a kiddie list (the "Bozo the Clown" series as its leader) which accounts for about 20 per cent of the firm's business. And its classical catalogue, initiated with prewar German Telefunken masters, has now increased to include such domestic organizations and artists as the Pittsburgh Symphony, the Hollywood String Quartet, and the young pianist Leonard Pennario.

The aims which Wallichs and Mercer set up in the beginning have been adhered to as far as possible. Wallichs, elected president in 1947, has borne most of the administrative burdens and has seen to it that Capitol's merchandising and distributing policies have followed his progressive ideas.

And Mercer's aims for greater artistic integrity have also been respected. Most major firms supervise—and even dictate—the repertoire and arrangements of their artists. Capitol let Peggy Lee gamble on "Mañana," and it sold 1,500,000 records. Les Paul and his wife Mary Ford last year sold 6,000,000 records.

. . . Capitol recording stars (l. to r.) Les Paul and Mary Ford, and Nat King Cole

Two very successful and musically compatible California gentlemen. Mercer is probably scratching his head over the idea of Arthur Godfrey being on the cover of *Down Beat*.

Something's Gotta Give

1954   Words and music by JOHNNY MERCER

When an irresistible force such as you
Meets an old immovable object like me,
You can bet as sure as you live,
Something's gotta give, something's gotta
  give,
Something's gotta give.

When an irrepressible smile such as yours
Warms an old implacable heart such as
  mine,
Don't say no because I insist
Somewhere, somehow, someone's gonna
  be kissed.

So, en garde, who knows what the fates
  have in store,
From their vast mysterious sky?
I'll try hard ignoring those lips I adore,
But how long can anyone try?

Fight, fight, fight, fight, fight it with all of our
  might,
Chances are some heavenly star spangled
  night,
We'll find out as sure as we live,
Something's gotta give, something's gotta
  give,
Something's gotta give.

Bobby Dolan told us how this hit song came about, which in his professional opinion underlined Mercer's great talent for discovering the clever, original approach to music. There had been a long, stymied script conference in the preparation of *Daddy Long Legs* at 20th Century-Fox. The problem—which might not be a problem today—was what to do about the older man (Astaire) being in love with a much younger woman (Leslie Caron). Mercer solved the impasse, said Dolan, with this sensible but unsensual lyric.

Midnight Sun

1954   Music by SONNY BURKE and LIONEL HAMPTON

Your lips were like a red and ruby chalice,
Warmer than the summer night,
The clouds were like an alabaster palace
Rising to a snowy height.
Each star its own aurora borealis,
Suddenly you held me tight,
I could see the midnight sun.

I can't explain the silver rain that found me,
Or was that a moonlight veil?
The music of the universe around me,
Or was that a nightingale?
And then your arms miraculously found me,
Suddenly the sky turned pale,
I could see the midnight sun.

Was there such a night,
It's a thrill I still don't quite believe,
But after you were gone,
There was still some stardust on my sleeve.

The flame of it may dwindle to an ember,
And the stars forget to shine,
And we may see the meadow in December,
Icy white and crystalline.
But, oh, my darling, always I'll remember,
When your lips were close to mine,
And I saw the midnight sun.

Without question a Mercer tour de force: "Red and ruby chalice" "alabaster palace" "aurora borealis"—who else could put together such rhymes without making it sound contrived? To add to the wonder of this brilliant lyric, Mercer told us that he wrote almost the entire lyric in his head while driving from Palm Springs to Hollywood (two hours) after hearing Lionel Hampton's record on the car radio. That handy modern-day gadget, the car radio, was always one of Mercer's greatest sources of inspiration—and we know how much time Californians spend in their cars, for which hallelujah!

The romantic coupling that caused concern at 20th Century-Fox. Fred Astaire and Leslie Caron in a scene from *Daddy Long Legs*. Mercer's idea for a song pulled them out of the bind.

Lionel Hampton might be telling Johnny a story about their former boss Benny. Mercer's lyrics were a big boost for Hamp's tune "Midnight Sun."

A television interview for Stan Kenton,
Henry Mancini, J.M.

Love in the Afternoon

1957

Music by MATTY MALNECK

Love in the afternoon
Was as sly as a wink and as gay as a pink
   balloon;
We walked along in a kind of trance
And the very streets began to dance.

To think that love nearly passed us by,
Then I happened to be where you
   happened to catch my eye.
And now both our lonely hearts are filled
   with June,
Because of love in the afternoon.

Another title song (movies with full scores of many songs were becoming fewer) with that great chum from the Whiteman days, Matty Malneck. Despite such heavyweights as Gary Cooper, Audrey Hepburn and Maurice Chevalier, with direction by Billy Wilder, this film refused to fly, and the Mercer-Malneck contribution was unusually second rate. (We include it here merely to remind us of the ups and downs in the studios.)

If I Had My Druthers

1956

Lyric by JOHNNY MERCER
Music by GENE de PAUL

If I had my druthers,
I'd druther have my druthers
Than anything else I know
While you'd druther hustle, accumulatin'
    muscle,
I'd druther watch daisies grow.
While they're growing' slow'n
The summer breeze is blowin'
My heart is overflowin' 'n so;
If I had my druthers
I'd druther have my druthers
Than anything else I know.

If I had my druthers,
I'd druther have my druthers
Than work anywheres at all.
It ain't that I hates it, I often contemplates it
While watchin' the raindrops fall.
I sits there for hours,
Developin' my powers
A-figurin' how flowers gets tall.
If I had my druthers
I'd druther have my druthers
Than anything else at all.

Undaunted, Mercer agreed to give Broadway another shot: the company was good (Panama & Frank, Michael Kidd, Gene de Paul) and Hollywood's studios weren't calling as much as they did in the thirties and forties. Then too, the back-country flavor of Al Capp's looney characters was right in Mercer's ballpark. The score, while not up to the high standard of *St. Louis Woman*, has been somewhat unappreciated. The two lyrics we take from it are fun throughout.

Giselle MacKenzie and Stubby Kaye rehearse for the *L'il Abner* recording, but Mercer seems slightly skeptical.

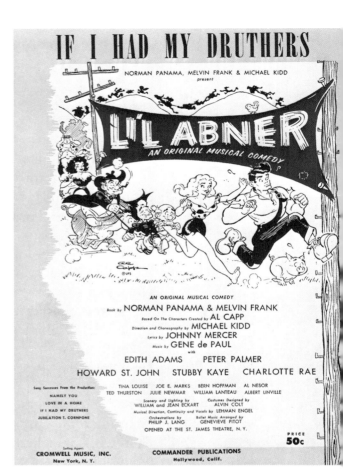

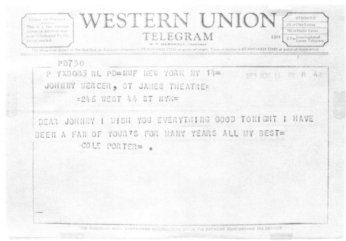

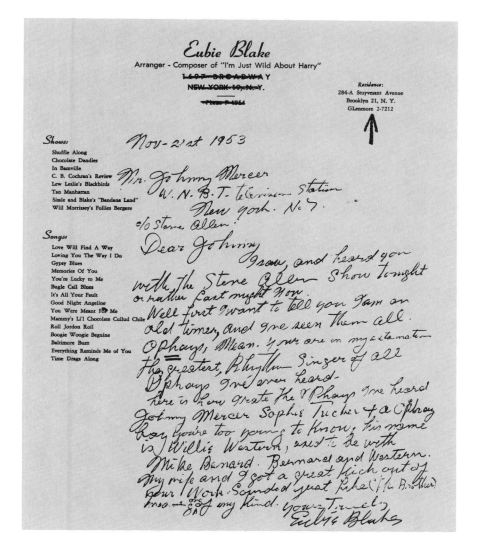

Eubie Blake
Arranger - Composer of "I'm Just Wild About Harry"
~~1607 BROADWAY~~
~~NEW YORK 19, N.Y.~~
~~PLaza 7-1954~~

Residence:
284-A Stuyvesant Avenue
Brooklyn 21, N. Y.
GLenmore 2-7212

Shows:
Shuffle Along
Chocolate Dandies
In Bamville
C. B. Cochran's Review
Lew Leslie's Blackbirds
Tan Manhattan
Sissle and Blake's "Bandana Land"
Will Morrissey's Follies Bergere

Songs:
Love Will Find A Way
Loving You The Way I Do
Gypsy Blues
Memories Of You
You're Lucky to Me
Bugle Call Blues
It's All Your Fault
Good Night Angeline
You Were Meant For Me
Mammy's Li'l Chocolate Cullud Chile
Roll Jordon Roll
Boogie Woogie Beguine
Baltimore Buzz
Everything Reminds Me of You
Time Drags Along

Nov-21st 1953

Mr. Johnny Mercer
W. N. B. T. television station
New York. N.Y.
c/o Steve Allen.

Dear Johnny

I saw, and heard you
with the Steve Allen show tonight
or rather last night Now.
Well first I want to tell you I am an
old timer, and I've seen them all.
Ofhays, Mean. You are in my estamation
the greatest, Rhythm Singer of all
Ofhays I've ever heard.
here is how grate the Ofhays I've heard
Johnny Mercer Sophie Tucher & a Ofhay
Boy you're too young to know, his name
is Willie Western, used to be with
Mike Bernard. Bernard and Western.
My wife and I got a great kick out of
your Work. Sounded just like(the Brother)
mean of my kind. Yours Truely
Eubie Blake

It goes like this (and they ought to know).
Noble Sissle, standing, and the remarkable Eubie Blake at the keyboard.

The Country's in the Very Best of Hands

1956

Music by GENE de PAUL

The country's in the very best of hands,
The best of hands, the best of hands.
The treasury says the national debt
Is climbing to the sky.
The government expenditures
Have never been so high.
It makes a fella get
A gleam of pride within his eye.
To see how our economy expands,
The country's in the very best of hands.

The country's in the very best of hands,
The best of hands, the best of hands.
You oughta hear the Senate
When they're drawing up a bill.
Whereas's and to wit's
Are crowded in each codicil.
Such legal terminology
Would give your heart a thrill.
There's phrases there
That no one understands.
The country's in the very best of hands.

Satin Doll

1958

JOHNNY MERCER
DUKE ELLINGTON
BILLY STRAYHORN

Cigarette holder
Which wigs me
Over her shoulder
She digs me
Out cattin'
That satin doll

Baby, shall we go
Out skippin'
Careful, amigo,
You're flippin'
Speaks latin
That satin doll

She's nobody's fool,
So I'm playin' it cool as can be
I'll give it a whirl
But I ain't for no girl catchin' me
Telephone numbers
Well, you know'
Doin' my rhumbas
With uno,
And that's my satin doll.

An alliance of three greats—and their product is becoming more of a pop hit every year (lately, of course, because of the Broadway show *Sophisticated Ladies* and in New York at least because of an incessant TV commercial). Mercer always gets the flavor of both the tune and the subject matter he's writing about (the melody was around awhile without words) and in this case he does it with his usual ease and skill. "Doin' my rhumbas with uno"—Duke must have loved that! Would that they had hooked up more.

Portrait of Mr. Ellington, one third of the "Satin Doll" triumvirate, taken by one of his biggest fans.

1952 TV—"Harry Warren. . . . this is your life!" (Mercer and Warren had just completed *Belle of New York.*)

If this shows up on a TV late show, see how Mercer's word juggling can compete with both Danny Kaye and a chimp.

Sketched in a California restaurant by an unknown admirer. "Crazy Oscar" probably refers to a performer known as Crazy Otto, who was then the rage.

A marvelous Gjon Mili study of Mercer waiting out a rehearsal.

JOHNNY MERCER

April 23, 1958

Dear Bob:

Many thanks for the clipping with the complimentary write up of my singing-(?). I guess even an old jazz singer can dig up an old friend or two.

I saw the Benny Goodman show; thought it was very groovy. He is as set in his ways about music as I am. But I thought it really swung when Jo and Ella sang and when Teddy Wilson played. Also thought Norvo was, as usual —— marvelous! All in all a great show. I don't believe you can convince broadcasters that jazz is as big as westerns.

I hope to see you soon, but in any event my love to all. Thanks again for the letter.

Dipper

JM/gw
Mr. Bob Bach
41 East 57th Street
New York 22, New York

A Game of Poker

1959

Music by HAROLD ARLEN

Love is a game of poker
Ev'rything's wild and the chips are down;
One night you may draw the joker,
Next night you may own the town.

One look at the cards they've tossed you,
One look at her you decide to play.
You stay, but they've double-crossed you
And your hunch has cost you more than
    you can pay.
You've won, but oh,
You've lost your heart along the way.

So here goes you and I,
Win or lose, do or die!
But it's sure worth a try
If it's love.

Another opening, another blow: *Saratoga* seemed ready for (finally) an Arlen-Mercer Broadway success, having all the necessary ingredients—Edna Ferber's story, the colorful spa setting, costumes by Cecil Beaton, direction by Morton Da Costa. But, alas, the critics destroyed it, passing quite perfunctorily over the score, which did contain one or two noteworthy items: "Goose Never Be a Peacock" (sung with great depth by concert artist Carol Brice), "One Step Two Step" and the would-be hit "A Game of Poker," the worksheets for which we include to show how diligently Mercer applied himself to the search for the right combination of words.

An Original Cast Recording

RCA VICTOR
LOC-1051
A "New Orthophonic" High Fidelity Recording

ROBERT FRYER
presents

HOWARD KEEL   CAROL LAWRENCE

in

The MORTON DA COSTA Productiom

SARATOGA

Based on the novel "SARATOGA TRUNK"
by EDNA FERBER
with
ODETTE MYRTIL

WARDE DONOVAN   CAROL BRICE   TUN TUN   JAMES MILLHOLLIN   RICHARD GRAHAM   TRUMAN GAIGE

and

EDITH KING

Music by
HAROLD ARLEN
Lyrics by
JOHNNY MERCER
Settings & Costumes Designed by
CECIL BEATON
Choreography by
RALPH BEAUMONT
Lighting by
JEAN ROSENTHAL

Musical Direction by   Vocal Arrangements by
JERRY ARLEN   HERBERT GREENE

Orchestrations by   Music for Dances by
PHILIP J. LANG   GENEVIEVE PITOT

Dramatized and Directed by
MR. DA COSTA

185

Love

Is a game of poker

Some is a hand of chemin de fer

One night

                The poker

Next night

          It a love affair

             draw a pair

this/love — as I roam & ramble

This life is a lucky gamble

    On

You never knows where good fortune

            where your luck may starts

               begin

Each kiss is a sweet preamble

           to the greatest gamble

            of the blackest art —

              oldest

Any man can win

     cannot choose   win or lose

Making the most of each shining day

   That ever   magical night

       a gamble when you can lose your heart

Any two cards play

   hearts can ..

             is the biggest gamble

               of them all

Everything wild— and the stakes are high

One night all you folds the poker
    You're a lonely poker

Next night — You can bet the sky

Love is a turn on the wheel of fate

One night — You may hold the poker —

Next night — You're at heaven's gate

You hope — that you'll throw a seven
    for a great big seven

You're home — if you roll a

If anyone thinks that writing lyrics for a musical comedy song is easy, a look at these three handwritten worksheets of Mercer's should dispell that notion. There were a good dozen more pages for "A Game of Poker", which proved only moderately successful in the hapless show *Saratoga*.

CLINT   ~~LOVE IS A GAMBLE~~ Love's a game of Poker

Love is a game of poker
Everything's wild - and the stakes are high
You lose ....
So you go for broke, or
You win ...
And you own the sky!
You'd swear - that the fates were cheating
Dealing you hands - only fools would play
You raise- and your heart stops beating
But you keep repeating
It's your lucky day .....
You win!
~~But love is a gamble all the way~~
But Love's a game of poker all the way —

CLIO -CLINT
So here goes!
You and I
Win or lose
Do or die
But it's sure - worth a try - if it's love!!!

CLIO

Love is a game of poker
Anything goes - and the chips are down
One night
You may draw the joker
Next night
You may own the town
etc.   ...

188

Posed by the fine Savannah photographer Fred Baldwin
in front of the historic Owens-Thomas house.

The Sixties and the Seventies

Does anyone need to be reminded for the hundredth time of what travails the sixties brought us? Probably as great an influence as anything in those turbulent times was the arrival in America of records by four long-haired kids from Liverpool, England—the Beatles. They were British, and that was different. They were kind of clean-cut, even though shaggy-haired, and that was different too. They were not as threatening as some of the scroungy, home-grown rock 'n' rollers, and their songs had some sweetness and charm to them. Thus their success was phenomenal. The Beatles were, thanks to the expanding avenues of communication, many times more powerful in popularity and earnings than had been Rudy Vallee in the twenties, Bing Crosby in the thirties, Frank Sinatra in the forties, and even Elvis Presley in the recent fifties, for they were international in scope and their influence spilled over into areas that changed many life styles of the young. Learned sociologists and musical pundits (Leonard Bernstein among them) gave the Beatles serious consideration, and one can only imagine the feelings of men such as Ira Gershwin, sitting in quiet retirement alongside his Beverly Hills swimming pool, or Jule Styne, pacing around a crowded office in New York's Mark Hellinger Theatre—men who had spent years and years getting to their position of importance in the music world.

But there was some cheer to the situation. Where Elvis and his fellow travellers of the fifties—Chubby Checker, Jerry Lee Lewis, Fats Domino, James Brown—were anathema to ASCAP's songwriting elite because of their remove from the world of Kern and Gershwin, the Beatles got qualified approval from these elders because of their respect for the 32-bar form and for recognizable melody. The Beatles were also miles apart from the yeh-yeh-baby lyrics (lyrics!) of their forerunners in the world of rock. Johnny Mercer, among other survivors, was not ready to throw in the towel.

Throughout America there were the new sounds of stereo in millions of homes and so the record/music business of the sixties held its own against television, movies, paperback books, and the relaxed censorship of both Broadway and Hollywood. In the small nightclubs there were protestors like Lenny Bruce and folksingers in dungarees with guitars. On Broadway there was a musical called *Hair* and another called *Oh Calcutta!* It was a long way indeed from Paul Whiteman at the Biltmore and the *Garrick Gaieties*. And just as Bing had bowed with his usual ease to the changing tastes of audiences, so too did time play a little rough with another pal, Bob Hope, as the sixties saw Mort Sahl, Shelley Berman and the Smothers Brothers moving ahead in popularity.

Song-filled movies such as the ones that kept the writers busy in the thirties were no longer in vogue, but the producers still liked a theme melody to play under the titles, and Johnny Mercer easily tailored his art to those demands. There were two Mercer homeruns right at the beginning of the decade. In 1961 he collaborated with Henry Mancini on a song that Audrey Hepburn was supposed to look as if she were singing while seated on a fire escape and strumming a guitar. The movie was *Breakfast at Tiffany's,* the song was "Moon River," and it was a runaway Oscar winner at the 1962 Academy Awards. The following year it was another Mercer-Mancini success—the title song for a Jack Lemmon movie, *The Days of Wine and Roses*—and Oscar #4 for Johnny Mercer.

By the early sixties the Mercer children, Jeff and Mandy, had grown out of adolescence, California friends were disappearing, and Ginger had found a small apartment, a long-sought pied-à-terre, in New York. The cross-country trains were not as great as they once had been, but for a guy who liked to read so much and jot down ideas so much it was still a kick to travel from coast to coast in a leisurely fashion. In 1963 there was the last attempt at a Broadway show—a Broadway show that opened far, far out of town, in Dawson City, Alaska. The show was titled *Foxy,* based on Ben Jonson's *Volpone,* and it starred the great clown Bert Lahr, with Larry Blyden in a supporting role. The music was again by Mercer's close friend Bobby Dolan (remember *Texas, L'il Darlin'*), and one would be hard pressed today to find any one of the show's songs. Mercer did, however, provide Lahr with a perfect vehicle called "Bon Vivant," in which there is the line, "sailing on the Firth of Forth. . . . or was it Forth of Firth?" Even the clever David Merrick can guess wrong—*Foxy* finally reached New York's Ziegfeld Theatre and closed shortly thereafter.

The New York scene, particularly its swank, never really interested Johnny Mercer much anyway, nor did he care to get involved in the heated political talk of the sixties and early seventies. However, a line here and there in his beautiful Christmas cards of that period show that he cared about the country's plight in Vietnam, about the growth of violence on all sides, and, as a southern country boy, about the ruination of the environment. Margaret Whiting tells of a moment in the early 1970s that seems quite typical of the man: "We were on a train going to Philadelphia for the 'Mike Douglas Show,' and it was a gray, dreary day. As we came out of the tunnel leaving New York—you know those ugly auto graveyards filled with junk that are alongside the tracks just before Newark?—well, Johnny was staring out of the train window and he suddenly said to me, 'Kid, you see that? That's what they're doing to America.' " He rarely let those thoughts out—or at most he kept them wrapped in the gentler philosophy of his song lyrics.

Came the seventies, with so many old friends and collaborators gone, the music business in a completely new bag, and the call for Mercer's services diminished considerably. Therefore the four-time Oscar winner turned to an adjunct of songwriting that had been on his mind for some time—the establishment of a Songwriters' Hall of Fame, an equivalent of the Cooperstown place of honor for the all-time great baseball players. As with the formation of Capitol Records, Mercer's spirit moved things along with class, and before long the organization was housed in a building on New York's Times Square. Old friends Abe Olman and Howie Richmond helped Johnny launch the Hall of Fame. Mercer was immediately elected President, and the first inductees included Irving Berlin, Duke Ellington, Richard Rodgers, Dorothy Fields and Hoagy Carmichael. It was a most impressive beginning, yet Mercer was wise enough and open-minded enough to tell those who would listen how much he liked some of the newer writers—Jimmy Webb was one of the favorites he mentioned.

In 1973 Johnny Mercer embarked on his last full-scale venture. The Mercers moved to London for a year to work on a musical version of J. B. Priestley's *The Good Companions*, with John Mills in the starring role. The music was by André Previn, who was not easy to work with because of his heavy schedule as conductor of the London Symphony Orchestra. But there were frequent visits to the lovely Sussex home of the Previns, where Johnny could also enjoy the company of Previn's pretty wife, Mia Farrow, and their several small children. Despite his bon vivant tastes, Mercer always was a dedicated family man. Things didn't go too well with *The Good Companions* (the London critics singled out Mercer's lyrics as not being English enough), and the ill health that had plagued him for a few years finally took its toll. Johnny Mercer died on June 25, 1976, and people from former maids to the President of the United States sent messages of sadness to Ginger Mercer. Many great tributes were offered at the memorial services in New York and Hollywood—from old friends such as Fred Astaire, Bing Crosby and Dinah Shore—but the collaborators on this book feel that the most moving and accurate estimate of all was written by the columnist Carl Rowan. (See page 231.)

JIMMY McHUGH

February 27, 1968

Dear John Boy,

I would so much appreciate having an
autographed photo of yourself, and a copy
of BLACK MAGIC. They would both be among
my most treasured possessions, I assure you.

As always, it is a real pleasure being with
you. Take care and God Bless You.

Love,

JFM:m   JIMMY McHUGH

Mr. Johnny Mercer
10972 Chalon Road
Los Angeles, Calif. 90024

*Please autograph the
copy of Black Magic too.
J.*

Richard Rodgers

598 MADISON AVENUE • NEW YORK 22, N. Y.

Telephone MUrray Hill 8-3640

AUGUST 8, 1968

DEAR JOHNNY:

I HAD SEEN THE NEW YORK TIMES PIECE ON THE
CONCERT AT CITY HALL BUT I PROMISE YOU IT
GAVE ME NO MORE PLEASURE THAN YOUR THOUGHT-
FULNESS IN SENDING IT TO ME AND THE KIND
THINGS YOU SAID ALONG WITH IT. THERE SEEMS
TO BE LITTLE DOUBT THAT YOU AND I BELONG TO
A MUTUAL-ADMIRATION SOCIETY. MY REGARD FOR
YOU AND YOUR WORK IS SURELY NO LESS THAN
YOUR FEELING ABOUT MINE.

HAVE YOU PLANS TO COME EAST? DO LET ME KNOW
BECAUSE I WOULD LIKE VERY MUCH TO SEE YOU AND
TALK TO YOU.

THANKS SO MUCH FOR YOUR THOUGHTFULNESS AND
ALL KINDEST REGARDS.

YOURS SINCERELY,

Dick.

RICHARD RODGERS

MR. JOHNNY MERCER
10972 CHALON ROAD
LOS ANGELES,
CALIFORNIA 90024

RR:NS

Bobby Darin, bandleader Billy May and J.M. during the recording session of their "Two of a Kind" duet in 1963.

Christmas Card

*T*HIS blessed time of Jesus' birth
May there be really Peace on Earth
Around the tree—amongst our friends
Let's pray this season never ends
And show the way—for all to see
How brave and good mankind can be
The way the world is whirling on
I wonder where the years have gone
But when I think . . . . don't laugh . . . . I do
What pleasant vistas come in view!
Leave it to Beaver—Dan'l Boone . . . . .
How many years of Twilight Zone?
Jack Paar, Jack Benny, Newhart, Hope
Have flashed across our TV-scope
While Ozzie Nelson—how time flies!
Has raised two boys before our eyes
The Smothers Brothers, heads unbowed
Were fired (for speaking up too loud)
Ah, well, we'll have to find the touch
To straighten out this rabbit hutch
The Moon and Mars are now next door
But we're more distant than before
Let's hope, in God's great scheme of things
We find why we've been given wings
So huge and vast the infinite
We must be just a speck in it
So let us all raise humble eyes
To God's immeasurable skies
Then each one pray—"in his own way"
To do the right thing every day
Who wields the knife—who hurls the stone

The risk be his—the neck his own
Let retribution—fast and sure
Revenge the innocent—the pure
(I hope you wiser heads don't find
I tilt at Windmills of the Mind)
Then may we lift the flowing glass
Invite the strangers in who pass
And drink a toast—and have a pause
And spend a while with Santa Claus
We'll take the children on our knee
And tell them how it used to be
And let them know it's really love
That's kept us humans on the move
Then say to God—and mean it too
Thanks for today—and all year through
Thanks for the good things we've all had
Now—help us overcome the bad
Teach us, like children still in school
The facts of life—the Golden Rule
Teach us to know what Jesus meant
Why we are here—why He was sent
With brimming hearts, teach us to say
A Merry, Merry Christmas Day!
And may this Happy New Year too
Be filled with joy the twelve-month through
For goodness, kindness, peace and love
Beats Anybody's treasure trove
So God Bless YOU—and everyone!

THE MERCERS
(GINGER, JEFF AND JOHN).

193

Moon River

1961

Music by HENRY MANCINI

Moon River,
Wider than a mile:
I'm crossin' you in style
Some day.
Old dream maker,
You heart breaker,
Wherever you're goin',
I'm goin' your way:

Two drifters,
Off to see the world,
There's such a lot of world
To see.
We're after the same
Rainbow's end
Waitin' round the bend,
My huckleberry friend,
Moon River
And me.

Probably his most famous song of all. Even Irving Berlin picked this one out as one of the great American popular songs. He was also curious, in the manner of a complete outsider, as to which came first, the music or the lyrics. Audrey Hepburn, seated on a fire escape, mimed singing this song while strumming a guitar in the movie *Breakfast at Tiffany's* and so it was a shoo-in for Mercer's third Oscar. "Huckleberry friend" is so properly descriptive of our songwriting hero that no one quarreled with the choice of it for the title of this book.

Mancini, Mercer and Miss Reynolds all smile on cue for the battalion of
photographers backstage at the Academy Awards.

The Bilbao Song

1961

English words by JOHNNY MERCER
Music by KURT WEILL

That old Bilbao moon,
I won't forget it soon,
That old Bilbao moon,
Just like a big balloon,
That old Bilbao moon,
Would rise above the dune,
While Tony's beach saloon
Rocked with an old time tune.

We'd sing a song the whole night long
And I can still recall
Those were the greatest,
Those were the greatest,
Those were the greatest nights of them all.

No paint was on the door,
The grass grew through the floor,
Of Tony's two by four
On the Bilbao shore,
But there were friends galore
And there was beer to pour
And moonlight on the shore,
That old Bilbao shore.

We'd sing all night with all our might
And I can still recall
Those were the greatest,
Those were the greatest,
Those were the greatest nights of them all.

Those old Bilbao guys,
They loved to harmonize,
Who stopped to realize
How fast the summer flies!
The moon was on the rise,
We'd catch the ladies' eyes
And whisper Spanish lies,
They never did get wise.

We'd sing a song the whole night long
And I can still recall
Those were the greatest,
Those were the greatest,
Those were the greatest days of them all.

Another Americanized version of an already accepted foreign hit song shows once again Mercer's versatility. The Middle European flavor of Kurt Weill's music and the Brecht background didn't throw the boy from Savannah a bit. "We'd sing a song the whole night long" and "those were the greatest . . . etc . . . etc." are just as beery lines in Chicago or Cincinatti as they might be in Berlin. Bobby Darin was just the right tough-guy singer to make this into a modest native hit.

Days of Wine and Roses

1962

Music by HENRY MANCINI

The days of wine and roses
Laugh and run away
Like a child at play,
Through the meadowland
Toward a closing door,
A door marked "Nevermore,"
That wasn't there before.

The lonely night discloses
Just a passing breeze
Filled with memories
Of the golden smile that introduced me to
The days of wine and roses and you.

© M. Witmark & Sons

This was J.M.'s fourth Oscar winner, and it is unique in that the entire song is encompassed in just two sentences. It was, of course, helped consideraly by the strength of Jack Lemmon's award-winning performance in the movie of the same name. Jack told us that when Mercer first sang this for him and the director it was in a darkened studio under a single spotlight, and the effect was so dramatic that the easygoing Lemmon found tears streaming down his face at the end. Mercer was unquestionably a powerful singer of certain lyrics.

I Wanna Be Around

1962

Words and music by JOHNNY MERCER
SADIE VIMMERSTEDT

I wanna be around
To pick up the pieces,
When somebody breaks your heart;
Some somebody twice as smart as I,
A somebody who will swear to be true,
Like you used to do with me.
Who'll leave you to learn
That mis'ry loves company,
Wait and see!

I wanna be around,
To see how he does it
When he breaks your heart to bits;
Let's see if the puzzle fits so fine.
And that's when I'll discover that revenge is
    sweet;
As I sit there applauding from a front row
    seat,
When somebody breaks your heart
Like you broke mine.

© Commander Publications and Zeller Music Co.

A great human interest story and most revealing (as was the repayment of his father's debts) of Mercer's Southern gentlemanly character. The idea for the song—and certainly a good one—was sent to him in the mail (see illustrations) by the proverbial "little old lady" from Youngstown, Ohio. The very name Sadie Vimmerstedt probably helped a little. Mercer arranged for her to receive a nice 50% of the royalties, made her, by her own account, "a star" around Youngstown, and got his publishing company to line up Tony Bennett for a terrific record.

Johnny Mercer
Song Writer
New York, N.Y.

c/o ASCAP
575 Madison Ave
N.Y. N.Y.

Johnny Mercer Splits Royalties On New Song With 'Cinderella'

Press 3-12-63

By WILLIAM D. LAFFLER

NEW YORK (UPI)—Life has a new meaning for Sadie Vimmerstedt because she wrote a letter to singer-composer Johnny Mercer.

She is coauthor of one of the nation's top songs even though she did not write either its music or lyrics. Her almost unbelievable success has earned her the title of "the Cinderella girl of Tin Pan Alley."

Cinderella was a young girl; Sadie is 58 and a grandmother.

The story of Sadie, who lives in Youngstown, Ohio, began five years ago when she wrote a letter to Mercer suggesting that he write a song called "I wanna be around to pick up the pieces when somebody breaks your heart."

"Two years later he answered my letter and apologized for his tardiness," Sadie said in a telephone conversation from her home.

When months and then years went by without another word from Savannah - born Mercer, Sadie apparently forgot about her idea. Then one day she heard again from Mercer.

"He said he didn't want to record the song until he got the best singer," Sadie said. "When he told me that Tony Bennett was going to record it, I really got excited."

Bennett at that time had just become the hottest seller at Columbia Records with the single, "I Left My Heart in San Francisco."

Today Bennett's recording of Sadie's "I Wanna be Around" is moving toward the top of the best-seller charts.

Sadie is grateful to Mercer, because Johnny wrote the music and lyrics but gave her credit as cocomposer and split the royalties with her on 50-50 basis.

"He is a most unselfish man," Sadie said of Mercer. "To me he was a person you could talk to."

Sadie's song sold 15,000 copies the first day it was released. It appears that she will net about $50,000 in royalties by June.

While Sadie is not a professional musician and does not pretend to be anything more than an average Youngstown citizen, she sings in the choir at St. Ann's Roman Catholic Church.

"My husband passed away four years ago, but I don't like being called a widow," Sadie said. "I now sell cosmetics and I love my job."

Her ambition now is to see two men who mean so much to her.

"We are a little trio," she said, "but I've never met Tony Bennett or Johnny Mercer."

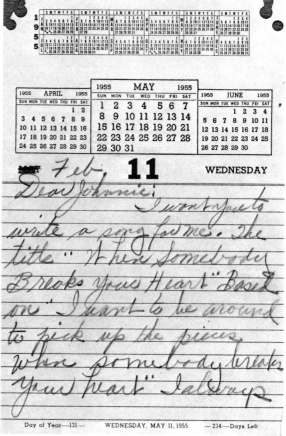

Feb. 11 WEDNESDAY

Dear Johnnie:

I want you to write a song for me. The title "When Somebody Breaks Your Heart" Based on "I want to be around to pick up the pieces when somebody breaks Your Heart" I always

Day of Year—131— WEDNESDAY, MAY 11, 1955 —234—Days Left

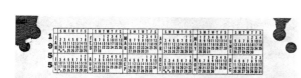

MAY Feb. 12 THURSDAY

left that is the way Nancy Sinatra feels about Frankie boy. I know You could add a little story to the title and Please me. Thank You

Sadie Vimmerstedt
38 W. Auburndale
Youngstown O.

Day of Year—132— THURSDAY, MAY 12, 1955 —233—Days Left

199

Fun on the boulevard: Mercer enjoyed the company of his new friend, Michel Legrand, particularly the visits to the country home of the Legrands where he would play with the kids.

34th Annual
Academy Awards
Presentation

SANTA MONICA CIVIC AUDITORIUM · APRIL 9, 1962

Jack Klugman (pre-"Odd Couple" and "Quincy") helped Jack Lemmon in his Academy Award performance, and the theme song helped a bit too.

Mercer in his favorite
Greek fisherman's cap near Savannah in 1970.

Once Upon a Summertime

1962

Original lyric by EDDIE MARNAY   English lyric by JOHNNY MERCER
Music by EDDIE BARCLAY and MICHEL LEGRAND

Once upon a summertime, if you recall,
We stopped beside a little flower stall.
A bunch of bright forget-me-nots was all
I'd let you buy me.

Once upon a summertime, just like today,
We laughed the happy afternoon away
And stole a kiss in ev'ry street café.

You were sweeter than the blossoms on the
　　tree.
I was as proud as any girl could be,
As if the Mayor had offered me the key
To Paris!

Now, another wintertime has come and
　　gone.
The pigeons feeding in the square have
　　flown,
But I remember when the vespers chime
You loved me once upon a summertime.

The first collaboration with French composer Michel Legrand, who was later to become a good friend with whom Mercer worked on several projects. The song was originally titled "Valse de Lilacs" and was brought to Mercer's attention by Blossom Dearie, an enthusiasm of his from the sixties on. This very pretty song is still generally unappreciated despite records by Sinatra, Barbra Streisand, George Shearing and Anita O'Day.

Charade

1963

Music by HENRY MANCINI

When we played our Charade
We were like children posing,
Playing at games,
Acting out names,
Guessing the parts we played.

Oh, what a hit we made.
We came on next to closing
Best on the bill,
Lovers until
Love left the masquerade.

Fate seemed to pull the strings,
I turned and you were gone.
While from the darkened wings
The music box played on.

Sad little serenade,
Song of my heart's composing,
I hear it still,
I always will
Best on the bill Charade

The Mercer-Mancini magic diminished a little this time out, although the song got an Academy Award nomination. Movie title songs were the name of the game for bigtime songwriters in Hollywood of the sixties. With the Beatles mania still raging, Mercer, like so many others of his craft, was forced to spend most of his time on the sidelines. Even in this less-than-golden period musically "Charade" is a good solid song, nothing to be shrugged off.

Emily

1964

Music by JOHNNY MANDEL

Emily, Emily, Emily
Has the murmuring sound of May.
All silver bells, coral shells, carousels
And the laughter of children at play say.

Emily, Emily, Emily
And we fade to a marvelous view.
Two lovers alone and out of sight
Seeing images in the firelight.

As my eyes visualize a family,
They see dreamily,
Emily too.

The last movie theme song of any importance for Mercer, this one has some tender and poetic pictures in its opening lines. He had a special fondness for children, although this feeling rarely showed up in his lyrics. The movie was *The Americanization of Emily*, starring Julie Andrews and James Garner, and the strong melodic line is by former jazz trumpeter Johnny Mandel, who also wrote "The Shadow of Your Smile," which award-winning song Mercer winningly admits he failed to write acceptable lyrics for. Musicians seem to be drawn to this song a lot (no lyrics necessary generally).

Bon Vivant

1964

Music by ROBERT EMMET DOLAN

Now for the life men dream about,
Days that a king might scheme about.
Once I have got
My palatial yacht,
I shall slowly steam about the brine.
Fie on the word economy,
I'll live a life of bonhomie,
Sail into port
For a night pour le sport
Full of rare gastronomy and wine.

Manchester and Dorchester
And Chichester and Perth
Sailing on the Firth of Forth
Or is it Forth of Firth?

Woppington on Battersea,
The shire of me birth,
In a thatched home of modest worth
   (unpaid for).

Birmingham and Nottingham
And Sandringham and Crewe
Shrewesbury and Tewkesbury
And Shaftsbury and Lewe
Where I starred as Portia
In "The Taming of the Shrew."
As we would say in school,
I've been around the pool
So I'm the bon vivant you want.

A perfect wow of a Mercer fun lyric, during which you can practically hear Bert Lahr foghorning his way through it. It was written for the wonderful Lahr when the show *Foxy* (with Bobby Dolan again) began its pre-Broadway run in—of all places—Dawson City, Alaska. In talking about Lahr much later, Mercer told the audience at New York's 92nd Street "Y": "He endeared me to him." (Haven't you always heard it the other way—"he endeared himself to me"?) The use of British town names was duck soup for Mercer, so much so that he repeated the trick later when writing the London musical *Good Companions*. But even producer David Merrick can guess wrong, and so *Foxy* failed, though one reason, we're told, was Merrick's lack of advertising support.

205

Summer Wind

1965

English words by JOHNNY MERCER
Music by HENRY MAYER

The summer wind came blowing in across
   the sea,
It lingered there to touch your hair and walk
   with me.
All summer long we sang a song and strolled
   the golden sand.

Two sweethearts and the summer wind.
Like painted kites the days and nights went
   flying by.
The world was new beneath a blue umbrella
   sky.
Then, softer than a piper man
One day it called to you.

I lost you to the summer wind.
The autumn wind, the winter winds
Have come and gone
And still the days, the lonely days
Go on and on
And guess who sighs his lullabyes
Through nights that never end.

My fickle friend, the summer wind,
The summer wind, the summer wind.

The last truly "Hit Parade" sort of success for Mercer, this one was helped through the miasma of rock 'n' roll thanks to records by Wayne Newton and Frank Sinatra. Walter Rivers, Johnny's cousin and boyhood pal, wonders from whence came the expression "a piper man"—is there or was there such a thing? This is a perfectly wonderful song to use as a marker of sorts for the passage of Mercer from one period of creativity to another.

Trees
(With sympathy for Joyce Kilmer)

1969

I think that never shall I see
A poem loveless as a tree

A tree whose hungry mouth is pressed
Against some scientific breast

A tree which from no acorn springs
But comes from Mother's barkless rings

A tree that looks to Vitamin A
And lifts her leafless arms to pray

A tree whose beauty life and soul
Starts in some laboratory bowl

A tree who may at birth be found
With nests of nutrients all around

Who must, as one non-sexual cell,
In niacin and thiamine dwell

A tree who may in winter wear
No rain nor snowflakes in her hair

Whose thirst is slaked—if slaked at all
When auxins and cytokinins fall

Who'll feel no sunshine kiss of love
Just an electric light above

A tree, whose very birth may have
Joyce Kilmer whirling in his grave

While GOD, (if he's alive, of course)
Accepts retirement pay by force

A tree improved in every way
For each undappled summer's day

A tree that's neither he nor she
Who'll know no dog, who'll know no bee

Poems are made by fools in love
But only Dr. Linus Winton, biologist of the
    Institute of Paper Chemistry
    —out there in Appleton, Wisconsin—
    can make an entire non-sexual aspen
    grove!

"Four unusual little trees. . . . produced from a tiny plug of unspecialized
non-sexual tree cells, began their existence in a laboratory dish at the
Institute of Paper Chemistry in Appleton, Wisconsin, today."

The New York Times, April 18, 1969

At Christmas time, it's hard to say
The old-time wish a brand-new way
For fashions rise, and fashions fall
But Christmas is the best of all
So prayerfully I lift my pen
To welcome Santa once again
Old Santa of the cherry nose
The apple cheeks, the swirling snows
Who, yearly, with his reindeer comes
To shacks and condiminiums
The only payment for his ride
The knowledge there is love inside
For though love makes the world go round
It's getting harder to be found
And in our riot, war torn land
The Scrooges have the upper hand
We oldsters who were youngsters then
Must set examples once again
And make our fun so unalloyed
That underneath — they're overjoyed!
It's like a man who walks a wire
Above a sea of molten fire
While balancing on cattail stalks
Your Aunt's best china as he walks
For how can anything be solved
If no one smiles — or gets involved?
But I — in my dimwitted way —
Sing out, "A Merry Christmas Day"
The blessing old still ringing true
For you — and you — and you — and you!

While seated 'round your Christmas tree
Think of the trees that used to be
The happy faces of old friends
Whose roles are through — whose playlet ends
Remember how they used to smile
Their glow lit up the world a while
And welcome little ones at birth
Who've just now joined us all on Earth
The old and new — a lovely sight
They made almost as bright a light
As that far tree in Viet Nam
Whose one bright bauble is a bomb
Then go to church and sing — off key!
(. . . as every hymn in church must be!)
Against our good friends wise advice
We'll sing the loudest at the part;
"Still stands thine ancient sacrifice,
"An humble and a contrite heart"
So, friends and neighbors . . . Nashville style
I send you all a great big smile
A great big hug that's full of love
A great big blessing from above
I wish you — in imperfect rhyme
The perfect wish at Christmastime:
Just for a moment — now and then
Be little children once again
Get on the floor with all your toys
And be one of the girls and boys!
Remember — when the tinsel's gone
The Mercers — Ginger, Jeff and John

208

December 17, 1965

Mr. Johnny Mercer
10972 Chalon Road
Los Angeles, California   90024

Dear Johnny:

        What a good warm Christmas card!
But then I would not expect anything less
from a good warm man like yourself. Many
many thanks and the happiest of holidays
to you and Ginger.

                    Sincerely,

                    [signature: Frank]

FL:kp

IRVING BERLIN

December 22nd, 1965

Dear Johnny:

    Only God can make the tree
    Where presents lie for you and me
    But only Mercer makes the rhyme
    That cheers us all at Christmas time

Thanks for the couplet you inscribed and best
Holiday wishes to you and Ginger from us,

      As always,

Mr. Johnny Mercer
10972 Chalon Road
Los Angeles, California

JACK LEMMON

December 28, 1971

Dear John:

    A quick note in the midst of the
Holiday madness just to voice my personal
opinion and that of the rest of my family,
that you should be the first man to receive
an Academy Award for a Christmas card.

    It is absolutely marvelous and far and
away the greatest card that any of us has
ever received. As a matter of fact, I may
frame the damn thing and put it on the piano!
(Surrounded by Mercer songs.)

    Hope to see you soon, and in the mean-
time, pull yourself together--- and may the
coming year bring you all possible happiness,
which, of course, includes another Oscar.

      Best always,

      the Human Hinge.

JL:bg

Mr. Johnny Mercer
1092 Chalon Road
Los Angeles, Calif.

The message is more than the medium.

209

Interview with Johnny Mercer, March 14, 1971:

*Part of the New York 92nd Street "Y" Series of
Lyrics and Lyricists. The interviewer is Maurice
Levine, host of the series.*

Q: I'd just like to ask you a couple of questions, relative to today's songwriters versus those of the past. Were you and your colleagues reworking the single emotion of romantic love? Were you being superficial and impersonal, were you not concerned with the quality of life?

JM: I think we were in more of a rut than the kids are, though I think ours was a more attractive rut.

JM: I think it all springs from the war. They're all scared and they want to tell everybody what they know. They're really children philosophers. They're talking about . . . philosophically, they're trying to say to you, what they want everybody to hear, and so they don't write any tunes. They write to the same tune, they have new words, and I just think it's appalling, but I think that out of it all, there will come a lot of great writers, because there are so many people writing. Almost everybody is a songwriter. There used to be maybe a hundred songwriters or five hundred, now there are maybe fifty thousand or five million. Maybe eight, I don't know. But some of them are good. A few of them have a lot of integrity, like Jimmy Taylor. He's brand new—he sings like he means it. The kid with Blood, Sweat and Tears—he's a marvelous singer. The writers I'm not so nutty about. I'm not so nutty about the Beatles. I think Stephen Sondheim is a wonderful writer. And I think some of these folk writers, the kids, are good, but there's nothing very new. Woody Guthrie wrote before that—before him, Vernon Dalhart used to sing "The Death of Floyd Collins" and those narrative songs, "The Wreck of the Old 97." This whole folk bag is overdone.

This is a kind of a dull answer. When I get serious about things, it's dreary.

Q: Johnny, the unique thing about the *Greatest Songs of the Sixties* is it contains one helluva great tune called "Moon River." Johnny, you may have touched on this and I guess you have, but I'd still like to ask it as a general question, what were your great influences?

JM: Well, I guess, as I say, I started to sing when I was six months old. When I was in dresses, I remember cylindrical records—before the big flat Edison records. And I think in those days, Victor Herbert—the first ones I remember were Victor Herbert and Harry Lauder. Big impression on me. And then as I got a little older, Berlin, although I didn't know who he was, Donaldson, I did know who *he* was—Walter Donaldson—and then later on, Harry Warren.

Then I got up to New York and I became a little more—well, a little more educated, I guess. I found out about Porter and the Gershwins and particularly Rodgers and

Hart. So, when you live in a rural community, you like pop songs and that's what you learn how to write. When you come to New York, it's like starting all over again. So that's my Southern background.

Q: Johnny, surely you must know that now you're the model and the inspiration for a generation of younger lyricists, and here are just a couple of questions I'm going to ask on their behalf and actually at their request, and they're a little more specific, having to do with lyric writing. And here's one I was asked to ask you. What qualities do you look for in a collaborator?

JM: In a collaborator? First of all, great talent and integrity, that's what I like. I like a guy who writes his way and his way is so high that it starts where other guys leave off. I've written with a few like that. I think Kern is everybody's favorite. I think Harold Arlen is an enormous talent. I think Hoagy Carmichael, in his way, starts where most guys stop. And that's the best thing in a music writer, I think.

Other guys may have a little gift this way or that way and they're all different. I prefer to write not with them but away from them. I don't like to get too mixed up with them—very delicate, collaboration.

Q: That leads to that classic question which everyone asks, what comes first, the melody or the lyric, and I gather from what you've said, that you like to have a good melody——

JM: With me, I prefer that.

Q: Yip Harburg said the same thing.

JM: Well, you know why? He feels music like a composer and so do I, so we understand the music. We know where the accents should come, and I don't mean to sound conceited when I say this, but I've often had a lot of good lyrics loused up by writing them first because the guy doesn't understand the meter that I wrote. I'd rather try and catch the mood of his tune than—now, there are some exceptions. Mr. Rodgers is magnificent at writing to words. But I think most guys would rather do it the other way.

Q: You may have answered this next question, which one of the other writers——

JM: I feel like John Jay Anthony. Remember him? Or The Answer Man. What did Durante say? These are the answers, you figure out the questions.

Q: This question is, how did your various composers differ in approach?

JM: They're all different. Every one is different, but you know, there's something funny about songs—it's elusive, it's like you're going out looking for the snark or something that you never heard of, the golden fleece. You don't know where it is, it's just up there somewhere and you can tune in on it, and you get a little glimmer, and you say, ah—you don't even know if it's a word and then it begins to—it's like you're tuning in to a musical instrument that's miles away, and you say, oh, there's something there, if I just dig hard enough, I know it'll come. I think that's the way I write. I think that's the way Yip writes too.

Q: Here's a good question. How do you write for a character and yet emerge with a hit?

JM: Well, it's not easy, but sometimes it helps. For instance, if you're going to write a song for Helen Morgan, you've got to write with a limited range and the qualifications sometimes are an asset, really. Or if you're going to write for Crosby, you know that he's very casual, he sort of talks his songs. If you're going to write for a big singer, then you write a little more operetta. You adapt, you adapt to the artist.

Q: One of the songwriters and lyricists out in the audience wants to know what was the most difficult lyric problem you ever encountered?

JM: Well, I think the thing that scared me the most was when I was about twenty-one, I couldn't even write yet, I was trying to write a show with Vincent Youmans. I would come in petrified every day, and of course I didn't write it. And the next one, I think, was working with Harold on *Saratoga*—outside of meeting that darling Teague DaCosta, that show was a dreary show. Hey, Harold?

Q: Which leads me to another question, which is my own question. Your greatest hits—I'm talking numerically, the greatest number of hits—came from straight pop songs or from the movies, and can you give us some indication of why this did not happen in your Broadway shows? Numerically, I'm talking about.

JM: I don't know. Frank Loesser said "Boy, I wish you could write (he wanted to be my publisher, I think, before he died) I can show you how to get those big songs in shows."—Well, I never had the shows at the time I had my big songs. And you can't let a song hang around too long, somebody else is going to write it. I could never wait. Unless you're a recluse. I just don't think I'm that gifted a show writer, I just don't think I am. I think Lerner is a marvelously gifted show writer. He's literate, he writes scenes well, he writes business songs well. I don't think he knows too much about popular songs, but he gets hits anyway.

Q: Do you think that popular songs and the musical theater are the antithesis of each other?

JM: Sort of. For instance, you talk about the kids writing folk songs. That's the bedrock, that's the grass roots, and if you write something and you say the same thing, you have bad rhymes, but you have a kind of a folk quality. That's the man in the street. But the theatre is as cultivated as you can get. You're going in and you're paying sometimes $50 a ticket nowadays, and you expect to hear music that's comparable to Kern or Arlen and you expect to hear witty, inventive, great lyrics, and I think you're entitled to that for that money.

Q: Well, Johnny, your catalogue in ASCAP is just one of the largest there is, and I took off a day last week just to read your song titles. There seems to be nothing but winners in that catalogue. Tell us about your losers.

JM: Oh, I've had a lot of those. I've got a trunk full of those. Would you like to hear about a real new loser?

It's like how it was with Buddy DeSylva. I used to play him songs and he'd laugh and say "Oh, that's wonderful—can't use it." That's what happened to the lyric I wrote for the song that became "The Shadow of Your Smile." They sent it back and said they couldn't use it. I said, "Well, get Paul Francis Webster" and they did and had a great big hit.

Q: Johnny, what are the three greatest moments in a songwriter's life?

JM: Well, I think the three greatest moments in a songwriter's life are when he first knows he can write a song, when he writes his first song, even when he's fifteen, in my case. The second time is when he gets his first song published, and he's in print, like an author. And then the third time is when he gets his first hit, a real hit song that you hear—you go down the street and people are singing it that don't know who you are, they just love the song—and that's really a thrill. It's still a thrill, right now. Which somehow reminds me of something sort of funny: A few years ago my wife went to Japan with her sister while I was gallivanting around out in California, and she was dancing with a gentleman on the boat and he said, "By the way, what does your husband do?" And she said, "Oh, he's a songwriter?" And he said, "Yeah, but what does he do for a *living?*"

Speaking of which—a few years ago a lady sent me a song title. She worked in a cosmetic counter in Youngstown, Ohio, and I finally wrote the song and I told her we had a record by Tony Bennett. Well, she was thrilled. She's the cutest thing,—she writes me letters all the time:—She says, "You've changed my life, Mr. Mercer, you just don't know." People are coming in the store asking for my autograph, next week I have to go on the radio in Cleveland, and two weeks later, I'm going to Cincinnati. I'm getting to be so famous. Finally, she came to New York and she was on "To Tell the Truth" or something and then she goes to Europe and she says, "Mr. Mercer, I gotta work every day next week—I'm tired, I'm going to get out of show business." [Two stories about a couple of hit songs will wrap it up]

About "Blues In the Night." You know, when I wrote the lyric "My Mama done tol' me" that was way down at the end and Harold said, "Why don't you take that and put it up in the front?"

Another song had a funny beginning: They had a preview of this picture, *Breakfast at Tiffany's,* in San Francisco, and we had one of those conferences afterwards. Didn't go too well. Of course, it was a big hit, but it didn't go too well at this preview, so the producer, Marty Ragin, said, "Well, I don't know what you guys are going to do, but I'll tell you one thing—that damn song can go." That song was, of course, "Moon River."

Happy Ever After

1971

Music by DICK HYMAN

Second mortgage man
Showed me a plan
Easy to swing—with a single little down
   payment,
So I'm savin' up,
Found an old cup,
Makin' it clang—with a gang o' nickels 'n'
   dimes. . . .

Happy ever after,
Are ya gettin' the picture—same as me?
Kids on every rafter,
Runnin' over the nice clean floors,
All mine and yours.
A tiny station wagon,
Automatic disposal in the sink.
When I bring you home a dragon,
You'll fix us both a drink!

Mondays, I'll be off and slavin',
Stashin' stuff in the bank.

You'll be shoppin', blue-chip savin',
Puttin' gas in the tank.
Ajax, Brillo, Instant Bourbon,
TV dinners at night.
Kids all bussin', interurban,
Too darn busy to fight.

Sunshine, flowers, laughter,
What a beautiful lifetime—wait and see.
Happy ever after,
After you say you'll marry me!

Second mortgage man,
Coppin' your plan,
Buyin' a ring with a single little down
   payment.
For it to succeed
Whadda I need?—Little more greed and a
   "Yes indeedy" from you!

What amounts to a posthumous song that composer Dick Hyman only recently began performing. Interestingly, both Hoagy Carmichael and Mercer picked up on this melody when it was released on Enoch Light's record label and easygoing Johnny at first said he would step aside to let his former writing partner do it.

"SATCHMO"

Dear Ginger & Johnny:

I sincerely appreciate your beautiful letter and
your kind expressions of love and sympathy.
Louis and I often talked about you both and the
wonderful memories we shared of your friendship.

Love,

LUCILLE

August 1971

Lucille

Shortly after Louis Armstrong's death, his widow, remembering their mutual admiration, sent this letter to the
Mercers. One of Johnny's favorite stories concerned the
time that Satchmo was emceeing a stage show in a
predominately Black theatre. Satch started to introduce
the next act—a white tap-dancing team—but then, looking into the wings, realized he had forgotten their names.
He grinned, hemmed and hawed for a moment or two,
and then announced, "And now, folks . . . here they are
. . . The Two Ofays!"

Compliments of
SATCHMO

215

Untitled Poem

JOHNNY MERCER

Ain't you proud of me?—I'm a man
I spoil everything that I can
And I'll never be satisfied
Till I've ruined the countryside
I catch all the fish in the seas
Burn up forests and chop down trees
Fill the rivers with sludge and oil
Wash the minerals from the soil
I kill tigers and leopards, too
I put everything in the zoo
(Those I haven't destroyed, I save
To remind me that I'm so brave!)
Soon not one of them will be here
I make everything disappear
Giant turtles and blue sperm whales
Now are rarer than nightingales
I shoot eagles and bears from planes
They're all gone with the whooping cranes
I have mountaintops leveled down
For one ticky-tack hi-rise town
Soon the air will be black as ink
All the water unfit to drink
I raise cattle and pigs for meat
Ducks and chickens are good to eat
As for hummingbirds—they're no loss
They're delicious with bearnaise sauce!
I kill sables and minks for furs
—Some are his'n—and some are hers—
I stuff everything else I can
Ain't you proud of me? . . . . . . I'm a man!
When I've got 'em all on a shelf
I may even destroy myself!

I have children my wife adores
So I send 'em all off to wars

Where they shoot someone else's sons
Ain't that wonderful?—That sells guns
That ain't all—I been on the moon
Like a fly on a macaroon
But them planets are no damn good
Ain't no animals there for food.

Some damn dreamers—and I mean damn
Think they're better than what I am
Say by usin' the sense God gave
There's no species they couldn't save
If we only killed one apiece
We might even make things increase!
Did you ever hear such damn rot?
They don't know of the plans I got
Like the buffalo and the gnu
Like the passenger pigeons too
I plan startin' in on the shrew
Soon, ol' buddy, I'll start on you!
Then, imperious, I will stand
In a waterless, treeless land
On a planet of sand and stone
Picked as clean as a chicken bone!

Well, I'd like to just stay and "jaw"
But in Africa I just saw . . . . . .
Say! . . . . . they tell me in Timbucktoo
There's a panda or two in view
And I know—'cause I seen the map—
Oil lies under the polar cap
So I'm takin' my blastin' rig
That uranium's tough to dig!
Well, ol' buddy, I'll see you roun'
Don't take nothin' that ain't nailed down

216

No music here. . . . Ginger Mercer found this poem among
Johnny's papers. It goes to show the mostly hidden serious side
of his nature.

Some day when you instruct your son
Tell the little chap what I've done
He'll be sort of impressed, I bet
Hell, I haven't got started yet!

There ain't nothin' that man can't do
Ain't you proud of me?
You're one too!

SHINING HOURS

Mercer and Bach in the garden of
La Residence du Bois, Paris, 1973

GINGE & JOHN Glass Pants

Johnny loved this joke: two guys forming a business partnership on New York's lower East Side during the early
1900s decide to have their picture taken together to celebrate the event. The photographer, though very good at his
craft, speaks very little English. He poses the two guys this
way and that, keeps saying "Glass pants." They don't know
what he's driving at. Finally the photographer comes out
from behind the camera, takes one guy's hand and places it
in his partner's hand in a pose of fraternal togetherness.
"Dot's nice," says the photog. "Glass pants."

Frazier

Music by JIMMY ROWLES

1972

Frazier was an aging lion
Living in a cage of iron
In a circus out of Tia Juana.
Frazier was their main attraction
And he gave them satisfaction,
Doing it with talent and with honor.
Growling for his daily dinner,
Frazier kept on getting thinner
On a measly can of Spam and tuna.
Days were lean but he got leaner
So one night in Pasadena
Through the bars he split for South Laguna.
Oh, cruel is fate but it's never too late, said
   Frazier.
I'm ninety-one and I haven't a son, thought
   Frazier,
The blue-eyed truth is I'm ready for
   eusthanasia.
Though matted and tarry, a local safari
   rescued poor old Frazier.

First they combed his tangled tresses,
Housed him with the lionesses,
Thinking him a harmless old grandpapa.
Fed him niocyn and fluoride, B-1, 2, 612
   and chloride,
Clams, cod liver oil and copper.
Younger studs brought in for breeding
Wound up beaten, bruised and bleeding.
Every day the same thing kept occurring.
Stretched out on an old serape
There lay Frazier tired and happy,

All his ladies on the list and purring
Oh, cruel is fate but it's never too late, said
   Frazier,
Announce the feast, I'm king of the beasts,
   grinned Frazier,
But king or not I am certainly hot, yawned
   Frazier
Well, when you're hot and you're hitting the
   spot their action might amaze-ya.

Children by his wives eleven added up to
   sixty-seven.
What nocturnal bliss he must have tasted
For no matter what the night time
Any night time seemed the right time.
Daytime found him fast asleep, just wasted.
When the circus owner found him,
Brought a lawsuit to impound him
Claiming you cats have to go where we go.
Frazier roared hasta la vista
You think all these chicks my sister?
I'm in business for myself, amigo,
Oh, cruel is fate but it's never too late, said
   Frazier,
I thank my stars I'm not behind bars, said
   Frazier.
They pay to see what comes naturally in
   Asia,
No African cat ever had it like that
And that goes for Malaysia.
He's up above, dear Frazier . . . Raising
   cubs, oh Frazier . . . Bless his heart, happy
   Frazier.

A lion isn't a bird but it's still part of the animal kingdom and therefore this story, which got quite a bit of play in the California press and on TV, appealed to Mercer. He had great fun with it and was able to stretch the storyout through several choruses. Jimmy Rowles, the great pianist who sometimes accompanied Mercer, brought it to his attention, wrote the music, and still performs it almost as well as his co-author did.

I'm Shadowing You

1973

Music by BLOSSOM DEARIE

Everywhere you go
I think you ought to know
I'm shadowing you.
Turn around 'n' find
I'm half a step behind,
I'm shadowing you.
You lug, you,
I wouldn't bug you
Except whenever I can.
You see, love,
You are to me, love,
The indispensable man.
After you decide
You want me for a bride
The deed'll be done.
Both of us'll be
So independent we
Will live on the run,
Picketing for every cause,
Fighting all the unjust laws,
Happy as can be,
Just you, J. Edgar Hoover and me.
I'm shadowing you.

Like I said before,
I'm campin' at your door,
I'm shadowing you.
How can you escape,
I'm getting out a tape
And video too.
In Venice
I'll be a menace
In your Italian motel.
In Paris,
I shall embarrass
You on the rue de Chappelle.
After you decide
You wanna be my bride
The deed'll be done.
Both of us'll be
So independent we
Will live on the run,
Picketing for every cause,
Fighting all the unjust laws,
Happy as can be,
Just you, the Secret Service and me.
I'm shadowing you.

Mercer always had an open door for those with special talents, and that certainly worked in favor of someone as unique as Blossom Dearie. She is not only a fine musician but funny and cute to boot. The song may be obscure (only Blossom is known to perform it), but it does represent one of the master's last few examples of the old fashioned boy-girl pop song lifted out of the ordinary with some tricky rhymes and references.

March, 1967: Meeting of the "in crowd", here composed of Blossom Dearie, JM, Jean Bach, and great comedy writer Goodman Ace.

M & M in high good humor. The beard and the glasses remind us of the passing years.

Good Companions

1974

Music by ANDRÉ PREVIN

Good companions stick together,
Sunny skies or stormy weather,
Birdies of uncommon feather,
Come what may.
Even when the rain drops tumble
Good companions never grumble.
Them's the breaks,
As William Shakespeare used to say.
Through the highways
And the byways
Of our native land,
Playing both the big time
And the one-night stand,
Hand in hand,
Good companions that's the ticket,
This old life's a game of cricket,
Sitting duck or sticky wicket,
Work or play,
We're good companions all
And we're on our way.

Frustration clouded a great deal of the period during which Mercer worked with André Previn for the British production *Good Companions*. Previn was often away with the London Symphony Orchestra, making their collaboration difficult, but Mercer was a big admirer of J. B. Priestley, on whose novel the musical was based, and so he hung in there. The result was pleasant and charming if not blockbuster, with Mercer capturing a few nice Britishisms such as "sitting duck and sticky wicket" here. Mercer's old pal Bing recorded the song—which makes for a fitting salute.

HER MAJESTY'S THEATRE

Proprietors:
A.T.P. (London) Ltd.

Chairman:
SIR LEW GRADE

Managing Director:
TOBY ROWLAND

Deputy Chairman:
LOUIS BENJAMIN

General Manager: RAYMOND LANE
Box Office: 01-930 6606

Bernard Delfont, Richard M Mills and Richard Pilbrow on behalf of the Bernard Delfont Organisation Ltd
present

John MILLS · Judi DENCH
The GOOD COMPANIONS

The Musical of the Novel by J.B. Priestley

Christopher GABLE · Marti WEBB

Hope JACKMAN · Malcolm RENNIE
Roy SAMPSON · Jeannie HARRIS · Bernard MARTIN
Ray C. DAVIS

Music by
André PREVIN · Johnny MERCER · Ronald HARWOOD
Lyrics by
Book by

Choreography by
Jonathan TAYLOR · Herbert W. SPENCER & Angela MORLEY
Orchestrations by

Designed by
Malcolm PRIDE · John B. READ · David COLLISON · Marcus DODS
Lighting by
Sound by
Musical Supervision by

Production Associate Peter Rawley

Directed by Braham MURRAY

First performance at Her Majesty's Theatre, Thursday 11th July 1974

222

The GOOD COMPANIONS
SOUVENIR BROCHURE

How 'bout your old Da
Dancing for you?   Dancing for two?
O-ho and a-ha   Terping

You sing oom-pah-pah
I'll dance for two   *Tops* / *Terp* .   a few

Dig my entrechat   Middle ... pipe my entrechat luv
                                     Also my pas-des-deux

And etcetera, luv
[illegible]   Sing tra-la, luv   Oo-la-la-   While
[illegible]   When I entrechat luv
[illegible]   You passe-partout!
[illegible]   Til you go on   turky-trot
                       Put a proper show on
                       On

I'll entertain the queue
And then ..... ta-ta! luv
A great big hurrah, luv!   Tra-la-la, luv .... Here's
Ta, luv .... for you!   Ooo-la-la, luv
                 While you   Watch my entrechat, luv
Go and put the face on   I'll   My ......

Like Paris, lass .
      Paree
   See, lass   oui, lass   Heel & toe &
(Just-) If you follow me, lass   Blackbirds in a row
   I'll bring you in on cue .   And
1,2,3. lass, Keep following me, lass.   On the stage we go
                                         On the spot " "

Ta, luv
Ta, luv
How 'bout your old Da, luv
Dancing for you?

Oom-pah-pah, luv
When I entrechat, luv
You pas des deux!

One, two, three, lass
Just you follow me, lass
I'll bring you in on cue!

And then ...... tada! luv
A great big hurrah, luv
Ta, luv
For you!

When I pas des deux, luv
You pas des too!
First we entrechat, luv
Then pas des deux!

Heel and toe, lass
Down the stairs we go, lass
Wait for the proper cue
(Climb through the window too!)
(Circle the table too!)

Another example of the word puzzling that goes on when putting together a good song. This one became "Ta Luv" in *Good Companions*, but we might wonder whose phone number is at top right.

223

My New Celebrity Is You

1976   Music by BLOSSOM DEARIE

I dig Modigliani,
Jolson doing "Swanee,"
Several Maharanee are my intimates too.
I played with Mantovani,
And that's a lot of strings to get through.
But anyone can see
My new celebrity is you.

I've sung with Ethel Merman,
Swung with Woody Herman,
Played a gig in Germany with Ogerman too.
I nodded at a sermon
Billy Graham barely got through.
But anyone can see
My new celebrity is you.

I'm not a bit
Ashamed of it,
My rapier wit
Kept Serge Koussevitzky in line.
I'd reprimand
The Dorsey band
And right on the stand,
'Cause Annie's cousin Fanny was a sweetie
    of mine.

I've golfed with Lee Trevino,
Won at the casino,
Danced the Piccolino,
When the movie was new.
Spent the night with Dino,
Had to sleep with Jerry Lewis too.
But anyone can see
My new celebrity is you.

I've swooned at Mia Farrow,
Angular and narrow,
Drove her Pierce Arrow
To a Gatsby review.
Though frozen to the marrow,
Who would dream of leaving that queue?
But anyone can see
My new celebrity is you.

Her husband André Previn
Absolutely heaven,
Even Herman Levin
Wants to hire him too.
And as for Lady Bevan
We were both in labor that's true.
But anyone can see
My new celebrity is you.

I played the uke
With Vernon Duke
So well in Dubuque
That Vladimir Dukelsky
Said "Gee!"
My fingering
A certain string
Was such a big thing
That Fanny's cousin Annie's taking lessons
    from me.

I'm quite a fan of Lena,
Close to Katerina,
Very fond of Gina
Lollobrigida too.
And as for Pasadena

Everybody there's an old shoe,
But anyone can see
My new celebrity is you.

I've drunk with Willie Harbach,
Also Roger Staubach,
Wiggled pretty far back,
When you start to pursue.
And talk about your star back,
Tarkenton can scramble some too.
But anyone can see
My new celebrity is you.

I see Muhammad Ali,
Clanking goes my trolley.
Starred in "Hello Dolly"
When it ran out of glue.
And Salvador Dali
Did a little sketch of me too.
But anyone can see
My new celebrity is you.

You need a pair
To give an air
Of fashion and flair,
Have Bob and Danny Zarem fly down.
The older set
Will need a pet
So who do you get?
Well Danny
Has a granny
Who's the talk of the town.

The incidents are many,
Jack and Mary Benny,
Nick and Sister Kenny
Made the scene for me too.
And little Lotte Lenya
Helped to entertain at chez nous
Where everyone could see
My new celebrity is you.

By rights "Good Companions" should be the last song in the book but chronologically this one follows and how can you leave out a tour de force such as this one? Can you believe that the same man who wrote such commercial hits as "Moon River" and "Laura" could take the time to construct a laundry-list song of hip and inside references? But that's our Huckleberry Friend for you—they don't make 'em much anymore.

Having a good time despite the chilly weather in his native Savannah. The window display tells the period.

226

The Last Christmas Card

THIS Christmas card, I think, may be
The last you people hear from me
The reason being, not because
I don't believe in Santa Claus,
But I most strongly disapprove
Of how you gallivanters . . . MOVE!
A half a year is what it took
To change around my address book!
In January cards come back
All saying, "Moved"—"Not here"—"Lost
    track"
In February, one or two
Return across the ocean blue
In March and April, people call
To say "Your card came, after all"
In May and June, I start to think
And get out paper, pen and ink
And stew and wonder how on earth
I'll celebrate our Saviour's birth
And then, as summer wanly smiles,
I busily correct my files!
Old friends deceased, this couple wed
That pair no longer shares a bed
Those children now have different names
Their parents too—have different dames!
With all these different "libs" in sight
The sex is incidental, right?
So I perspire, type, erase
Recalling some forgotten face
And pretty soon the summer's gone
And Autumn puts her colors on
The Bears, the Lions and the Rams

Are at each other's diaphragms
And soon it's time to "have a Merry"
To spike yourselves a Tom and Jerry
So, here is looking at you, pal
Out seated on the old corral
Or in the traffic's roaring boom
The silence of your lonely room
Safe in your boudoir, or your den
There in your tent of oxygen
Before the IRS men catch you
Ol' pal o' mine, here's looking at you!
Like in your bathroom—all enamely
Amid the bosom of your family
Be thankful that's your home address
The world out there is in a mess
So, bank the fire, jump in bed
Await the reindeer overhead
And picture Santa, cheeks aglow
Tiptoeing through the fallen snow
Then, down the chimney noiselessly
To leave his toys beneath the tree
Can you recall when all were young
And Christmas carols first were sung?
How deep the snow! . . . and everywhere!
But now the snow is in our hair
So . . . to the tasks we have to do
While getting kissed—and loaded too
Remembering, thanks to the Lord
There's one gift we can all afford
And here it is . . . from these old versers
The gift of love—from all the Mercers—
                    Merry Christmas!

The Champagne Music of Lawrence Welk

February 16, 1976

Mrs. Johnny Mercer
10972 Chalon Road
Los Angeles, Ca. 90024

Dear Mrs. Mercer:

I just thought you might be interested in the reaction to our recent show, "The Songs of Johnny Mercer".

I, personally, have had more wonderful comments on this show than almost any show we've ever done. Our mail also reflects the same sentiment. Many people have remarked that such a tribute was long over-due. Others were amazed to learn that Johnny had written so many great songs. I tell them what George Thow has often said, "We could do a whole season of Johnny Mercer songs, without repeating ourselves, and every show would be good."

I felt that both you and Johnny would be happy to know how well this show turned out. I hope Johnny was able to see it, and if not, I trust that by now you will have received the Video-tape Cassette Marshall Robbins had asked for.

All of us are hoping that Johnny is making progress, and that his recovery will be quick and complete.

With warmest personal regards to you both.

Sincerely,

Lawrence Welk
LW:ll

July 15, 1976

Dear Mr. Adams:

Johnny Mercer once said he had a "feeling for tunes". No one who ever heard his songs doubts those words. His mellow voice revealed that he was a child of the South; but his phrases were full of affection for people everywhere.

Johnny Mercer's talent was just too big to be applied to any one area of show business. As a performer, he had a special warmth that reached out and made a friend of every audience. We sang his wonderful songs and we listened as his music caught the precise mood of the moment in many motion pictures. Johnny Mercer had a gift all could enjoy.

Today, let me join with countless others in expressing my appreciation for Johnny Mercer's unique and loving contribution to the performing arts. He will long be remembered.

Sincerely,

Gerald R. Ford

Mr. Stanley Adams
ASCAP
One Lincoln Plaza
New York, New York 10023

S I D N E Y Z I O N

Blues in the Night

June opened by giving us Jimmy Carter and ended by taking Johnny Mercer. If there's a better reason for getting out of town I don't want to hear it, and to make sure I don't hear it I'm going so far into the hills that even the meadowlarks won't bother. I never thought I'd pick an apple tree over Sardi's bar, but then who thought we'd have a coronation in New York on the bicentennial? And who could dream that Jimmy Carter's "ideas" on foreign policy would be a headline while Johnny Mercer died on the obit page?

I suppose it's strictly romance, but there must have been a time in this country when people preferred writing popular songs to making unpopular laws. If so, it was in the Twenties, when John Mercer of Savannah, Ga. — see why I put him in the same sentence with a guy like Carter? — came to Tin Pan Alley to go up against the poets in the Brill Building. He was one of the few Southerners ever to make it in that wondrous world, where everything that counted lived in 32 bars; surely he was the only lyricist then or now to write with a true touch of the South. "Lazy Bones," "Pardon My Southern Accent," and "Moon River" were to the South what "Manhattan" was to New York.

Mercer never lost that flavor, the scent of roots that made him the most American of all our song writers, Irving Berlin included. For all his imitators, anyone who knew his stuff could always tell a Mercer lyric; however sophisticated the story line, there was the lovely patented fragment and everybody has his favorite. Mine: "Like the lights home before me ..." Has any kid ever come back from college or the army who didn't feel something the first time he caught the home fire on the way down the block?

It was his knack—his genius—to conjure up novels in a word, a phrase, which however otherwise curious was always perfect in context. Was there ever a better one

than "my huckleberry friend" from "Moon River"?

A few years ago, Johnny went back home to be honored at a municipal celebration. "Savannah's still like it used to be," he said later. "Everybody goes around and sings songs, drinks, and loves one another."

Just like Plains, right baby? But Johnny Mercer had no cross to bear; all he could do was sing and write songs. For my money he was one of the best jazz singers ever; if you can find his sides with Jack Teagarden or Bing Crosby, you'll know. But they are almost impossible to get; more likely, though difficult to pick up, is his LP, "The Best of Johnny Mercer" on Capitol, which label, incidentally, he founded. There is also a great LP he made with Bobby Dari called "Two of a Kind" on Atco, and a recent English disc, "Johnny Mercer Sings Johnny Mercer" by Pye Records.

Still, his lyrics are his immortality, and he wrote for the best composers in the country, including Harold Arlen, Duke Ellington, Richard Whiting, Jerome Kern, Harry Warren, Jimmy Van Heusen, Hoagy Carmichael, Walter Donaldson, Henry Mancini, Gene DePaul, Arthur Schwartz, Bobby Dolan and Michel LeGrand. He also composed a few tunes, like "Something's Gotta Give," "Dream," and "Strip Polka."

Few people under forty know much about Mercer's lyrics, and few over forty know he wrote them, however much they may have fallen in love to them. So herein a brief, hardly all-inclusive list:

Too Marvelous For Words
Satin Doll
That Old Black Magic
Days of Wine and Roses
You Must Have Been a Beautiful Baby
Come Rain or Come Shine
Skylark
I Want To Be Around To Pick Up the Pieces
Jeepers, Creepers
Goody, Goody
Ac-Cent-Tchu-Ate the Positive
Laura
Autumn Leaves
Summer Wind
You Were Never Lovelier
Dearly Beloved
I'm Old Fashioned
The Atchison, Topeka and the Santa Fe'
Hooray for Hollywood
When The World Was Young ("Ah, the Apple Tree")
One For My Baby (And One More For the Road)

Hardly comparable to the Grateful Dead, even if I did leave out "Blues In The Night," which if you want to know why I have 'em, well baby look at you now. ●

230   The Mercer tribute, July 22, 1976, on the stage of the Music Box Theatre, New York. Carl
Rowan reads his column about Mercer while (left to right) Jimmy Rowles, Margaret
Whiting, Harold Arlen, William B. Williams, Alec Wilder, Mel Tormé and Albert Hibler
listen.

Carl Rowan's Tribute

WASHINGTON—Ask me how I'd prefer to judge a society. By its preachers and politicians, its authors or architects? No, I'd first like a look at the output of those who write its popular songs.

In war or peace, hard times or good, it is the popular lyricists who tell us so much about the heart and soul of a nation.

That's why a little bit of me died the other day with the passing of Johnny Mercer. And I'm disappointed that a greater fuss wasn't made over this man who for more than four decades put magical words to tunes and touched, even helped shape, the lives of millions of us.

As a boy of 8 in Tennessee, wading barefoot in a creek looking under rocks for crawfish, I learned about "the work ethic" from Johnny Mercer.

I truly believed that he was telling me something when I sang lines from his "Lazybones":

"You'll never get your day's work done resting in the morning sun. You'll never get your cornmeal made sleeping in the noonday shade."

Now, it seems, Americans learn about the work ethic only from politicians who seek power by berating welfare recipients.

I was 15 and had suffered through at least one high school crush before Mercer wrote a beautiful lyric which taught me that romance is a risky situation where only "Fools Rush In."

"Fools rush in where wise men never go, but wise men never fall in love—so how are they to know?"

But when I was 17, Johnny Mercer let me know that he wasn't really putting down romance. So my heart pounded as I sat in the movie *The Fleet's In.* I've almost forgotten Dorothy Lamour, Bob Eberle, Helen O'Connell, Betty Hutton, Eddie Bracken and William Holden, the stars of that Paramount hit. But I've never forgotten a single word of Mercer's simple but haunting lyric, "I Remember You":

"When my life is through . . . and the angels ask me to recall . . . the thrill of them all. Then I shall tell them I remember you."

That was the same year, 1942, when a college freshman would take two looks at a pretty coed and wonder if he had been struck by what Mercer described so eloquently as "That Old Black Magic" called love.

Someone is forever writing to ask me to list "the six books that most influenced your life." Why don't they *ever* ask me to list the songs that most influenced me?

That summer of '42, while doing household work for a vacationing family up near Monteagle, Tenn., I read a book I recall as *The Quest Eternal* by E. Phillips Oppenheim. It moved me greatly, but today I don't recall how or why.

But I'm sure no book writer influenced me more than did Mercer, whose gloomy hero would in 1943 tell the bartender that he was drinking "to the end of a brief episode . . . Make it one for my baby and one more for the road."

People often wonder whether novelists write biography. I was asking that about Mercer when he wrote: "From Natchez to Mobile, from Memphis to St. Joe, wherever the four winds blow. I been in some big towns. I heard me some big talk. But there is one thing I know: a woman's a two-face. A worrisome thing who'll leave you to sing the blues in the night."

I lot of us learned from Mercer, without paying Dale Carnegie a dime, that you make things happen when you "Ac-Cent-Tchu-Ate the Positive."

And how many millions of Americans must have kissed, loved, broken up, cried to those unpretentiously beautiful lyrics Mercer wrote about "Autumn Leaves":

"Since you went away the days grow long, and soon I'll hear old winter's song. But I miss you most of all, my darling, when autumn leaves start to fall."

It is almost incredible that from boyhood depression days in the early '30s, when I sang "Lazybones," right up till these days when I delight in crooning "Moon River," it has been Johnny Mercer psyching me up, making me a romantic, sending up warning signals about that other sex—yet always telling me that "we're after the same rainbow's end, waiting round the bend."

Johnny Mercer, thank you. I hope you make it to rainbow's end.

232

(Overleaf) The real Moon River: This is Mercer's
home on the outskirts of Savannah; in the rear it
faced onto a winding stream that the city renamed
in honor of the award-winning song.

Song	Publisher
Accentuate the Positive	E. H. Morris
Affable, Balding Me	Chappel
After 12 O'Clock	Southern
Afterbeat, The	Palm Springs Music
Ah Loves Ya	Harwin
Ain't Nature Grand	Robbins
Airminded Executive, The	Commander Publ.
All Through The Night	Witmark
Alphabet of Love Begins and Ends With You, The	Harms
Americano	Commander Publ.
And So to Bed	Famous
And the Angels Sing	BVC
Angels Cried, The	Commander Publ.
Another Case of Blues	Harms
Antonia	Commander Publ.
Any Place I Hang My Hat Is Home	A-M (Chappell)
Ariane	Commander Publ.
Around the Bend	Commander Publ.
Arthur Murray Taught Me Dancing	Famous
As Long As You Live	Remick
At the Jazz Band Ball	Feist
Autum Leaves	Ardmore
Autumn Twilight	Commander Publ.
Baby Doll	Feist
Baby-O	Sands Music
Bachelor Dinner Song	Four Jays
Bad Humor Man, The	BVC
Baiiao	Commander Publ.
Ballad Of Alvarez Kelly, The	Colgems
Barrelhouse Beguine	T. B. Harms
Bathtub Ran Over Again, The	BVC
Be My Guest	Chappell-Mercer
Beautiful Forever	MCA
Bells Of Honolulu, The	Southern
Beneath the Curtain of The Night	Southern
Bernardine	Palm Springs Music
Beyond the Moon	Miller
Big, Beautiful Ball, A	Witmark
Big Daddy	Commander Publ.
Big Movie Show in the Sky, The	Chappell
Bilbao	Harms
Bittersweet	Commander Publ.
Bless Your Beautiful Hide	Robbins
Bless Your Heart	Commander Publ.
Blossom	Commander Publ.
Blue Rain	Burvan
Blues in the Night	Harms
Blues Sneaked in Every Time, The	Paramount
Bob White	Remick-Commander
Bon Vivant	Commander Publ.
Bonne Nuit	Jerome Music
Bouquet	Marpet Music

Boys Will Be Boys	Bourne	Day In, Day Out	BVC
Brasilia	Cromwell	Daybreak Blues	E. H. Morris
Buona Fortuna	Dena Music	Daydreaming	Remick
By the Way	Commander Publ.	Days of Wine and Roses	Witmark
		Dearly Beloved	T. B. Harms
C-A-T Spells Cat	Commander Publ.	Deep South	Bolton
Cakewalk Your Lady	A-M (Chappell)	Deirdre	MCA
California's Melodyland	Commander Publ.	Derry Down Dilly	Miller
Calypso Song	Harwin	(I Ain't Hep to That Step	
Can't Teach My Old Heart		But I'll) Dig It	E. H. Morris
New Tricks	Harms	Dixie Isn't Dixie Anymore	Robbins
Captains of the Clouds	Remick	Dixieland Band, The	Miller-Commander
Caribees, The	E. H. Morris	Do My Eyes Deceive Me?	Bourne
Cast Your Bread Upon the		Dog Eat Dog	Harwin
Water	Commander Publ.	Dog Is a Man's Best Friend,	
Celia's Lament	Commander Publ.	A	Chappell-Mercer
Central Park	Robbins	Don't Ask Too Much of	
C'est La Guerre	Robbins	Love	Harms
Charade	Northern-Southdale	Don't Run Away From the	
Chimney Corner Dream	Cromwell	Rain	Commander Publ.
Chin Up, Stout Fella	Commander Pub.	Don't That Take the Rag	
Cinderella Waltz	Palm Springs Music	Off'n the Bush	Commander Publ.
Cindy	Goldsen	Don't Think It Ain't Been	
Circus Is Coming to Town	BVC-Commander	Charming	BVC
College November	Commander Publ.	Down a Long, Long Road	T. B. Harms
Come Rain or Come Shine	A-M (Chappell)	Down in the Valley	Chappell
Comes The Revolution,		Down to Uncle Bill's	Southern
Baby	Bourne	Down Through the Ages	Harms
Confidentially	Harms	Dream	Goldsen
Conversation While		Dream Awhile	Robbins-Commander
Dancing	Goldsen	Dream Peddler's Serenade	Ardmore
Corn Pickin'	Remick	Drinking Again	Witmark
Could Be	Joy Music	Duration Blues	Goldsen
Countin' Our Chickens	Harwin		
Country's in the Very Best		Early Autumn	Cromwell
of Hands, The	Commander Pub.	Echo of a Dream	Mansion Music
Cowboy From Brooklyn	Witmark	Echoes	Palm Springs Music
Cream Puff	Robbins	Eeny Meeny Miney Mo	Bourne
Cuckoo in the Clock	Bourne	Elevator Song	Chappell-Mercer
Cure, The	Harwin	Emily	Miller
		Every So Often	Four Jays
Daddy Long Legs	Commander Publ.	Everything Happens to Me	Commander Publ.
Dancing Through Life	Commander Publ.	Everything Is Ticketty-Boo	Commander Publ.
Dark Is the Night	Feist	Exercise Your Prerogative	Commander Publ.

Facts of Life, The	Commander Publ.	Hayride	Four Jays
Family Tree	Chappell	He Didn't Have the Know How No How	Goldsen
Fancy Free	Harwin	He Loved Me Till the All Clear Came	Famous
Fare-thee-well to Harlem	Southern		
Fifi	Robbins	He Shouldn't-a, Hadn't-a, Oughtn't-a Swang on Me	East Hill Music
Fine Thing	Paramount		
Fleet's In, The	Famous	He's Dead But He Won't Lie Down	Famous
Fool That I Am	D.B.&H.-Commander		
Fools Rush In	BVC	Headless Horseman	Palm Springs Music
Forever Amber	Robbins	Hello, Out There, Hello	Criterion
Fountain in the Rain	BVC	Her First Evening Dress	Bourne
		Here Come the British	Commander Publ.
G.I. Jive	Commander Publ.	Here Come the Waves	E. H. Morris
Game of Poker, A	Harwin	Here's to My Lady	Mayfair
Garden of the Moon	Harms	Higgledy Piggledy	Commander Publ.
Gee, I Wish I'd Listened to My Mother	Paramount	History of the Beat, The	Commander Publ.
		Hit the Road to Dreamland	Famous
Georgia-Georgia	Commander Publ.	Holy Smoke! Can't You Take a Joke	Joy Music
Get a Horse	East Hill Music		
Gettin' a Man	Harwin	Homecoming	Melrose
Girl Friend of the Whirling Dervish, The	Harms	Hooray for Hollywood	Harms
		Hooray for Spinach	Remick
Glow-Worm	Marks	Hootin' Owl Trail	Chappell
Goin' Courtin'	Robbins	Hoping	Joy Music
Goody Goody	Malneck-Commander	Horseshoes Are Lucky	Chappell
Goose Never Be a Peacock	Harwin	How Do You Say Auf Wiedersehn?	Commander Pub.
Gotta Get Some Shuteye	Bourne		
Great Guns	Feist	How Little We Know	Witmark
Guardian Angel	Commander Publ.	How Long Has This Been Going On?	Bolton
Guitar Country	Northridge-Summit		
		How Nice For Me	E. H. Morris
Half-zies	BVC	Howdy Friends and Neighbors	Colgems
Hang on to Your Lids, Kids	Harms		
Hank	Witmark	I Can Spell Banana	Winston Music
Happy Bachelor, The	E. H. Morris	I Could Kiss You for That	Paramount
Harlem Butterfly	Commander Publ.	I Don't Wanna Be Alone Again	BVC
Harlem to Hollywood	Robbins		
Has Anybody Told You	Bourne	I Fought Every Step of the Way	Chappell-Mercer
Have a Heart	Kacy Music		
Have You Got Any Castles, Baby?	Harms	I Got Out of Bed on the Right Side	Robbins
Have You Written Any Good Books Lately?	Chappell	I Guess It Was You All the Time	Paramount
Having a Ball	Chappell	I Had Myself a True Love	A-M (Chappell)

238

I Knew	*Robbins*	I'm Old Fashioned	*T. B. Harms*
I Like Men	*Robbins*	I'm the Worrying Kind	*TNT Music-Commander*
I Love to Beat the Big Bass Drum	*Four Jays*	I'm Way Ahead of the Game	*Commander Publ.*
I Never Knew	*Commander Publ.*	I'm With You	*Commander Publ.*
I Never Saw a Better Night	*Bourne*	In a Cafe in Montmartre	*Miller*
I Never Wanna Look Into Those Eyes Again	*Palm Springs Music*	In a Moment of Weakness	*Remick*
I Pray	*Commander Publ.*	In My Wildest Dreams	*Robbins*
I Promise You	*E. H. Morris*	In Society	*Commander Publ.*
I Remember You	*Paramount*	In the Cool, Cool, Cool of the Evening	*Famous*
I Saw Her at Eight O'Clock	*Bourne*	In the Valley	*Feist*
I Thought About You	*Burvan*	In Waikiki	*Witmark*
I Walk With Music	*E. H. Morris*	Indian Summer	*Miller*
I Wanna Be a Dancin' Man	*Four Jays*	Indiscretion	*Commander Publ.*
I Wanna Be Around	*Commander Publ.*	It Had Better Be Tonight	*Northridge-United Art.*
I Wanna Be In Love Again	*Cromwell*	It Happened One Night	*Commander Publ.*
I Wind Up Taking a Fall	*Paramount*	It's a Great Big World	*Feist*
I Wish I Had Someone Like You	*Bel Canto*	It's a Nuisance Havin' You Around	*Commander Publ.*
I Wonder What Became of Me	*A-M (Chappell)*	It's a Typical Day	*Commander Publ.*
I'd Know You Anywhere	*BVC*	It's a Woman's Prerogative	*A-M (Chappell)*
If I Could Have My Way	*Miller*	It's About Time	*Miller*
If I Could Only Read Your Mind	*Southern*	It's Easy When You Know How	*Commander Publ.*
If I Didn't Love You	*Commander Publ.*	It's Great to Be Alive	*Chappell*
If I Had a Million Dollars	*Bourne*	I've Got a Heartful of Music	*Witmark*
If I Had My Druthers	*Commander Publ.*	I've Got a Lot in Common With You	*E. H. Morris*
If You Build a Better Mousetrap	*Famous*	I've Got a One Track Mind	*BVC*
If You Come Through	*Commander Pub.*	I've Gotta Be On My Way?	*Witmark*
If You Were Mine	*Bourne*	I've Hitched My Wagon to a Star	*Harms*
I'll Be Respectable	*Harwin*	I've Waited for a Waltz	*Jay Music-Commander*
I'll Cry Tomorrow	*Robbins*		
I'll Dream Tonight	*Witmark*	Jamboree Jones	*Commander Publ.*
I'm an Old Cowhand	*Commander Pub.*	Jeepers Creepers	*Witmark*
I'm Building Up to an Awful Letdown	*Bourne*	Jezebel	*Remick*
I'm Doing It for Defense	*Famous*	Joanna	*Northridge*
I'm Happy About the Whole Thing	*Remick*	Jo-Jo, the Cannibal Kid	*Robbins*
I'm Like a Fish Out of Water	*Harms*	Jubilation T. Cornpone	*Commander Publ.*
		June Bride	*Robbins*
		June Comes Around Every Year	*E. H. Morris*

Just a Fair Weather Friend	*Commander Publ.*
Just a Quiet Evening	*Harms*
Just for Tonight	*Famous*
Just Like a Falling Star	*Bolton*
Just Like Taking Candy From a Baby	*Commander Publ.*
Just Remember	*Southern*
Keep a Twinkle in Your Eye	*Robbins*
Keeper of My Heart, The	*Commander Publ.*
Lady on the Two Cent Stamp, The	*Harms*
Lake Saint Mary	*United Artists*
Larceny and Love	*Commander Publ.*
Laura	*Robbins*
Lawd, I Give You My Children	*Southern*
Lazy Mood	*Goldsen*
Lazy Bones	*Southern*
Leavin' Time	*A-M (Chappell)*
Legalize My Name	*A-M (Chappell)*
Legend of Old California	*Four Jays*
Let That Be a Lesson to You	*Harms*
Let's Go Sailor	*Famous*
Let's Take the Long Way Home	*E. H. Morris*
Life's So Complete	*Olman*
Lights of Home. The	*Ardmore*
Like the Fella Once Said	*BVC*
Li'l Augie Is a Natural Man	*A-M (Chappell)*
Limericks	*Chappell*
Liquapep	*Robbins*
Little Boats of Barcelona	*Crestview*
Little Man With The Hammer, The	*Commander Publ.*
Little Ol' Tune	*Commander Publ.*
Little Old Cross Road Store	*Miller*
Lock the Barn Door	*Criterion*
Lonesome Polecat	*Robbins*
Longing	*Harry Von Tilzer Mus.*
Lorna	*Commander Publ.*
Lost	*Robbins-Commander*
Love Held Lightly	*Harwin*
Love in a Home	*Commander Publ.*
Love in the Afternoon	*Commander Publ.*
Love Is a Merry-go-round	*Shapiro-Bernstein*
Love Is on the Air Tonight	*Harms*
Love Is Where You Find It	*Harms*
Love Me, Love My Dog	*Chappell*
Love Me With Your Heart	*Palm Springs Music*
Love of My Life	*E. H. Morris*
Love Song ("Apache")	*Madrigal Music*
Love With the Proper Stranger	*Paramount*
Love Woke Me Up This Morning	*BVC*
Lovers in the Dark	*Massey-Shenandoah*
Lullaby	*A-M (Chappell)*
Ma Belle Cherie	*Commander Publ.*
Magic Island, The	*Meridian Music*
Make With Kisses	*Burvan*
Man in My Life, The	*Harwin*
Man of the Year This Week, The	*Chappell-Mercer*
Mandy Is Two	*BVC*
Man's Favorite Sport	*Southdale*
Many Ways to Skin A Cat	*Commander Publ.*
March of the Doagies	*Four Jays*
Matador	*Commander Publ.*
Matrimonial Stomp	*Commander Publ.*
Maybe You Know What I Mean	*Southern*
Me and The Ghost Upstairs	*Morris-Commander*
Meant to Tell Yuh	*Christopher*
Meet Miss America	*Bourne*
Meet Miss Blendo	*Chappell-Mercer*
Memory Song	*Goldsen*
Men Who Run the Country, The	*Harwin*
Merry-go-round in the Rain	*Frank Music*
Mexican Moon	*Commander Publ.*
Midnight Sun	*Crystal Music*
Mirror, Mirror, Mirror	*Witmark*
Mr. Meadowlark	*E. H. Morris*
Mr. Pollyanna	*Famous*

Mr. T From Tennessee	Robbins	Ohio	Commander Publ.
Moment to Moment	Southdale-Northern	Old Aunt Kate	Southern
Money Isn't Everything	Commander Publ.	Old Brown Thrush, The	Commander Publ.
Month of Sundays, A	Chappell	Old Glory	Famous
Moon Country	Southern	Old Guitaron	Brasiliance-Commander
Moon in the Mulberry Tree	Herbert Music	Old King Cole	Harms
Moon River	Famous	Old Man Rhythm	Bourne
Moon Shines Down, The	Harms	Old Music Master	Famous
Moon Dreams	Mutual (Chappell)	Old Skipper	Miller
Moonlight on the Campus	Harms	Old Valparaiso Town	Commander Publ.
Moonlight Waltz	Christopher		
Mouthful O' Jam	Bolton	On Behalf of the Visiting Firemen	E. H. Morris
Music From Across the Sea	Miller	On the Atchison, Topeka and the Santa Fe	Feist
Musica Di Roma	Commander Publ.	On the Beam	T. B. Harms
Musical Chairs	Commander Publ.	On the Nodaway Road	Witmark-Commander
Mutiny in the Nursery	Witmark	On the Swing Shift	Famous
My Home Is in My Shoes	Chappell-Mercer	On With the Dance	Harms
My Inamorata	Witmark	Once Upon a Summertime	MCA
My Intuition	Feist	One For My Baby	E. H. Morris
My Love For You	Commander Publ.	One Step, Two Step	Harwin
My Night to Howl	Commander Publ.	One Thing at a Time	Robbins
My Old Man	Commander Publ.	One Two Three	Harms
My Shining Hour	E. H. Morris	Only If You're In Love	Chappell-Mercer
My Valentine Letter	Commander Publ.	Ooh! What You Said	E. H. Morris
		Oops	Feist
Namely You	Commander Publ.	(I Wish It Could Be) Otherwise	Commander Publ.
Naughty But Nice	Four Jays		
Navy Blues	Witmark	Out of Breath and Scared to Death of You	Harms
Night Over Shanghai	Remick	Out of This World	E. H. Morris
Night Song	Commander Publ.		
Nile, The	Robbins		
Nine Thorny Thickets	Commander Publ.	P.S. I Love You	MCA-Commander
Not Mine	Paramount	Pardon My Southern Accent	Bourne-Commander
Not With My Wife You Don't	Witmark	Parting Is Such Sweet Sorrow	Commander Publ.
		Past My Prime	Commander Publ.
O.K. for TV	Chappell-Mercer	Peekaboo to You	BVC
Oh Happy Day	Commander Publ.	Perfect Paris Night, A	Famous
Oh What a Horse Was Charlie	Witmark	Peter Piper	Robbins
Oh What a Memory We Made	BVC	Petticoat High	Harwin
Oh You Kid	Feist	Pineapple Pete	Commander Publ.

Piney Woods, The	*Walt Disney Music*
Pipes of Pan, The	*Commander Publ.*
Politics	*Chappell*
Poor Mr. Chisholm	*E.H. Morris*
Pot and Pan Parade, The	*Commander Publ.*
Progress Is the Root of All Evil	*Commander Publ.*
Put 'Em Back the Way They Wuz	*Commander Publ.*
Que Le Vaya Bien	*Commander Publ.*
Queen of the May	*Commander Publ.*
Quierme y Veras	*Southern*
Rainbows in the Night	*Commander Publ.*
Rainy Night	*Commander Publ.*
Raise a Ruckus	*Robbins*
Ready, Willing and Able	*Harms*
Remember Dad	*Remick*
Respectability	*Commander Publ.*
Ride 'Em Cowboy	*Chappell*
Ride Tenderfoot Ride	*Witmark*
Ridin' on the Moon	*A-M (Chappell)*
Riffin' the Scotch	*Robbins*
Rocky Mountain Lullaby	*BVC*
Rocky Mountain Moon	*Commander Publ.*
Rollin' in Gold	*Commander Publ.*
Rumba Jumps, The	*E.H. Morris*
Run, Run, Run Cinderella	*Commander Publ.*
S.S. Commodore Ebenezer McAfee the Third, The	*Commander Publ.*
Sans Souci	*Chappell-Mercer*
Santa Claus Came in the Spring	*Bourne*
Saratoga	*Harwin*
Satan's Little Lamb	*Harms*
Satin Doll	*Tempo Music*
Say It With a Kiss	*Whitmark*
Says Who, Says You, Says I	*Harms*
Seeing's Believing	*Four Jays*
Sentimental and Melancholy	*Harms*

Seven Little Steps to Heaven	*Harms*
Shameless	*Commander Publ.*
Sharp As a Tack	*Famous*
Shooby-Doin'	*Albert-Commander*
Shorty-George, The	*T.B. Harms*
Show Your Linen, Miss Richardson	*Commander Publ.*
Sighs	*Commander Publ.*
Signora	*Sugarbush Music*
Silhouetted in the Moonlight	*Harms*
Sing You Son of a Gun	*Harms*
Singin' in the Moonlight	*Commander Publ.*
Single-O	*Commander Publ.*
Skylark	*Simon*
Sleep Peaceful	*A-M (Chappell)*
Slogan Song	*Chappell-Mercer*
Sluefoot	*Commander Publ.*
Smarty Pants	*Bourne*
Sobbin' Women	*Robbins*
Some Place of My Own	*Commander Publ.*
Something Tells Me	*Witmark*
Something's Gotta Give	*Commander Publ.*
Song of India	*Criterion*
Sorry	*Arwin*
Sounds of the Night, The	*Arch Music*
South Wind	*Robbins*
Spring Is in My Heart Again	*Miller*
Spring Reunion	*Four Jays*
Spring Spring Spring	*Robbins*
Square Dance	*Chappell*
Square of the Hypotenuse, The	*Commander Publ.*
Star Sounds	*Cromwell-Commander*
Storm, The	*Palm Springs Music*
Strawberry Lane	*Paramount*
Strip Polka	*E.H. Morris*
Sudsy Suds Theme Song	*Famous*
Summer Wind	*Witmark*
Sweater, a Sarong and a Peekaboo Bang, A	*Famous*
Sweet Angel	*Robbins*

Sweet Little Lady Next Door	Miller	Tomorrow You Belong to Uncle Sammy	Paramount
Sweetheart Tree, The	Southdale-Witmark	Tonight Is Mine	Walt Disney Music
Swing Into Spring	Commander Publ.	Tonight May Have to Last Me All My Life	Kacy Music
Swing Is the Thing, The	Robbins	Too Marvelous For Words	Harms
Swing Your Partner	Feist	Top Banana	Chappell-Mercer
		Trav'lin' Light	BVC
Tailgate Ramble	Goldsen	Two Hearts Are Better Than One	T.B. Harms
Take a Crank Letter	Chappell	Two of a Kind	Commander Publ.
Talk to Me, Baby	Commander Publ.		
Talkin' in My Sleep	Miller	Until We Kiss	Harms
Tangerine	Famous	Unnecessary Town	Commander Publ.
Technique	Palm Springs Music		
Temporarily	Colgems	Yodel Blues	Chappell
Tender and True Love	Commander Publ.	Yogi Who Lost His Will Power, The	Paramount
Tender Loving Care	Kacy Music	You	T.B. Harms
Texas Li'l Darling	Chappell	You and Your Love	Robbins
Texas Romp and Square Dance	Commander Pub.	You Can Say That Again	Robbins
Thank You, Mssrs. Currier and Ives	Four Jays	You Can't Always Have What You Want	Commander Publ.
Thanksgivin'	Southern	You Can't Run Away From It	Colgems
That Old Black Magic	Famous	You Grow Sweeter As the Years Go By	Commander Publ.
That's for Sure	Chappell-Mercer	You Have Taken My Heart	Joy Music
There's a Fella Waiting in Poughkeepsie	E.H. Morris	You Know You Don't Want Me	Zeller Music
There's a Ring Around the Moon	T.B. Harms	You Must Have Been a Beautiful Baby	Remick
There's a Sunny Side to Every Situation	Remick	You or No One	Harwin
There's Nothing Like a College Education	Bourne	You Were Never Lovlier	T.B. Harms
There's Room Enought For Us	Commander Publ.	Your Heart and Mine	Robbins
These Orchids	T.B. Harms	Your Heart Will Tell You So	Famous
They Talk a Different Language	Chappell	Your Make Believe Ballroom	Leon Rene
13th Street Rag	Robbins	You're a Natural	Witmark
This Time the Dream's on Me	Harms	You're So Beautiful That	Chappell-Mercer
Three Guesses	Harms	You're the One for Me	Paramount
Thumbin' a Ride	Colgems	Yours For Keeps	Commander Publ.
Time Marches On	Bourne	You've Got Me This Way	BVC
Time to Smile	Denric Music	You've Got Me Where You Want Me	E.H. Morris

You've Got Something There	Harms
Wait and See	Feist
Wait for the Wagon	Robbins
Wait Till It Happens to You	Harms
Waiter and the Porter and the Upstaris Maid, The	Famous
Walkin' With My Shadow	Mills
Way Back in 1939 AD	E.H. Morris
Way to a Man's Heart, The	Commander Publ.
Wedding in the Spring	T.B. Harms
Weekend of a Private Secretary, The	Remick-Commander
Welcome Egghead	Commander Publ.
Welcome Stranger	Robbins
We're Working Our Way Through College	Harms
What Was Your Name in the States?	Robbins
What Will I Do Without You	Harms
Whatcha-ma-call-it	Commander Publ.
What'll They Think of Next	E.H. Morris
When a Woman Loves a Man	Joy Music
When Are We Going to Land Abroad	Whitmark
When I'm Out With the Belle of New York	Four Jays
When Love Walks By	Feist
When Sally Walks Along Peacock Alley	BVC

When the World Was Young	Criterion
When We Ride on the Merry-go-round	Bolton
When You Are in My Arms	Bourne
When You Hear the Time Signal	Paramount
When You're in Love	Robbins
Whichaway'd They Go	Chappell
While We Danced at the Mardi Gras	Miller
Whistling for a Kiss	Harms
Whoopin' and A-Hollerin'	Chappell
Who's Excited	World
Why Can't It Be Me	Robbins
Why Don't Men Leave Women Alone?	Commander Publ.
Why Fight This	Harwin
Wild Wild West	Feist
Windmill Under the Stars	T.B. Harms
Windows of Paris	MCA
Wings Over the Navy	Witmark
With You, With Me	Bedford Music
Wonderful Wonderful Day	Robbins
Word a Day, A	Chappell-Mercer
Word to the Wise Will Do, A	Archie Bleyer
World Is My Apple, The	Harms
World of the Heart, The	Frank Music
Would Ja For a Big Red Apple?	Harms
Wrap Yourself In Cellophane	Southern

Johnny Mercer's Movie Contributions

COLLEGE COACH (1933) Warner Bros.

Music: Sammy Fain, Arthur Johnston Lyrics: Sam
  Coslow, Johnny Mercer
No individual songs found

Dick Powell, Ann Dvorak, Pat O'Brien

TRANSATLANTIC MERRY-GO-ROUND (1934)
Small/UA

Nancy Carroll, Mitzi Green, The Boswell Sisters

"If I Had a Million Dollars" (M: Matt
  Malneck) (P: Bourne, Inc.)

FOOLS RUSH IN (1934)

"I'm Building Up to an Awful Let-Down"
  (M: Fred Astaire) (P: Bourne, Inc.)

OLD MAN RHYTHM (1935) RKO (Mercer
appeared in film)

Betty Grable, Buddy Rogers

"I Never Saw a Better Night" (M: Lewis E.
  Gensler) (P: Bourne, Inc.)
"Old Man Rhythm"
"Boys Will Be Boys - Girls Will Be Girls"
"When You Are in My Arms"
"There's Nothing Like a College Education"
"Comes the Revolution Baby"

TO BEAT THE BAND (1935) RKO (Mercer
appeared in film)

"If You Were Mine" (M. Matt Malneck)
  (P: Bourne, Inc.)
"Eeny Meeny Miney Mo"
"I Saw Her at Eight O'Clock"
"Meet Miss America"
"Santa Claus Came in the Spring"
  (M: Mercer)

LET'S MAKE MUSIC

"Central Park" (M: Matt Malneck) (P: Robbins
  Music Corp.)

RHYTHM ON THE RANGE (1936) Paramount

Bing Crosby, Roy Rogers, Martha Raye

"I'm an Old Cowhand" (M: Mercer)
  (P: Leo Feist, Inc.)

THE SINGING MARINE (1937) Warner Bros.

Dick Powell, Jane Wyman, Jane Darwell (Chor.
  Busby Berkeley)

"Night Over Shanghai" (M: Harry Warren)
  (P: Remick Music Corp.)

READY, WILLING AND ABLE (1937) Warner
Bros.

Ruby Keeler, Lee Dixon, Winnie Shaw, Jane Wyman,
  Allen Jenkins

"Just a Quiet Evening" (M: Richard A.
  Whiting) (P: Harms, Inc.)
"Sentimental and Melancholy"
"Too Marvelous for Words"
"When a Blues Singer Falls in Love"
"Handy With Your Feet"
"Little Old House"
"The World Is My Apple"

HOLLYWOOD HOTEL (1937) Warner Bros.

(Dir/Choreo: Busby Berkeley)

Dick Powell, Rosemary Lane, Frances Langford,
  Benny Goodman Orch.

"Let That Be a Lesson to You" (M: Richard A.
  Whiting) (P: Harms, Inc.)
"Can't Teach My Old Heart New Tricks"
"I've Hitched My wagon to a Star"

"Silhouetted in the Moonlight"
"Hooray for Hollywood"
"Sing You Son of a Gun"
"I've Got a Heartful of Music"
"Have You Got Any Castles, Baby?"
    (Background) (see VARSITY SHOW)
"Bob White" (Background) (P: Remick Music
    Corp.)

VARSITY SHOW (1937) Warner Bros.

Dick Powell, Priscilla Lane, Rosemary Lane, Carole
    Landis, Fred Waring Orch.

"Old King Cole" (M: Richard A. Whiting)
    (P: Harms, Inc.)
"Love Is in the Air Tonight"
"Moonlight on the Campus"
"On With the Dance"
"You've Got Something There"
"Have You Got Any Castles, Baby?"
"We're Working Our Way through College"
"When Your College Days Are Gone"
"Little Fraternity Pin"
"Let That be a Lesson to You"

GOLD DIGGERS IN PARIS (1938) Warner Bros.

Rudy Vallee, Rosemary Lane, Hugh Herbert

"Daydreaming (All Night Long)" (M: Harry
    Warren) (P: Music Publ. Holding Corp.)

"My Adventure"

COWBOY FROM BROOKLYN (1938) Warner
Bros.

Dick Powell, Ann Sheridan, Pat O'Brien, Priscilla
    Lane

"I'll Dream Tonight" (M: Richard A. Whiting)
    (P: M. Witmark & Sons)

"Ride, Tenderfoot Ride"

"I've Got a Heartful of Music" (Used in
    HOLLYWOOD HOTEL) (P: Harms, Inc.)

"Cowboy from Brooklyn" (M: Harry Warren)
    (P: Music Publ. Holding Corp.)

GARDEN OF THE MOON (1938) Warner Bros.

(Dir/Choreo: Busby Berkeley)

John Payne, Margaret Lindsay, Pat O'Brien

(Lyrics: Mercer & Al Dubin)

"Garden of the Moon" (M: Harry Warren)
    (P: Music Publ; Holding Corp.)
"Love Is Where You Find It"

"The Lady on the Two Cent Stamp"
"Confidentially"
"The Girl Friend of the Whirling Dervish"

GOING PLACES (1938) Warner Bros.

Dick Powell, Anita Louise, Allen Jenkins, Ronald
    Reagan

"Jeepers Creepers" (Oscar Nom.) (M: Harry
    Warren) (P: Music Publ. Holding corp.)
"Say It With a Kiss"
"Mutiny in the Nursery" (M: Mercer)
    (P: M. Witmark & Sons)

HARD TO GET (1938) Warner Bros.

Dick Powell, Olivia deHavilland, Charles Winninger

"You Must Have Been a Beautiful Baby"
    (M: Harry Warren) (P: Music Publ. Holding
    Corp.)
"There's a Sunny Side to Every Situation"

JEZEBEL (1938) Warner Bros.

Bette Davis, Henry Fonda, George Brent, Margaret
    Lindsey

"Jezebel" (M: Harry Warren) (P: Music Publ.
    Holding Corp.)

THE DUDE RANCHER

"Howdy Stranger" (M: Richard A. Whiting)
    (P: Music Publ. Holding Corp.)

WINGS OF THE NAVY (1938) Warner Bros.

John Payne, Olivia deHavilland

"Wings Over the Navy" (M: Harry Warren)
    (P: Music Publ. Holding Corp.)

MR. CHUMP (1938) Warner Bros.

Johnny Davis, Lola Lane, Penny Singleton

NAUGHTY BUT NICE (1939) Warner Bros.

Dick Powell, Ann Sheridan, Gale Page, Ronald
    Reagan, Helen Broderick

"Hooray for Spinach" (M: Harry Warren)
    (P: Music Publ. Holding Corp.)
"I'm Happy About the Whole Thing"
"In a Moment of Weakness"
"Corn Pickin'"

YOU'LL FIND OUT (1940) RKO

Kay Kyser Orch.

"I'd Know You Anywhere" (Oscar Nom.)
  (M: Jimmy McHugh) (P: Bregman, Vocco &
  Conn, Inc.)
"(Ting-a-ling) The Bad Humor Man"
"I've Got a One-Track Mind"
"You've Got Me This Way"
"Like the Fellow Once Said"
"Don't Think It Ain't been Charming"

ALL THROUGH THE NIGHT (1940) Warner
Bros.

"All Through the Night" (M: Arthur
  Schwartz) (P: M. Witmark & Sons)

SECOND CHORUS (1940) Paramount

Fred Astaire, Paulette Goddard, Artie Shaw & Orch.

"Love of My Life" (Oscar Nom.) (M: Artie
  Shaw) (P: Edwin H. Morris & Co., Inc.)
"Poor Mr. Chisholm" (M: Bernie Hanighen)
"Me and the Ghost Upstairs" (M: Bernie
  Hanighen)
"I'll Dig It" (M: Hal Borne)

THREE AFTER THREE (1940)

"What'll They Think of Next" (M: Hoagy
  Carmichael) (P: Edwin H. Morris & Co., Inc.)
  (also in Broadway show "I WALK WITH MUSIC")

LET'S MAKE MUSIC (1940) RKO

YOU'RE THE ONE (1941) Paramount (Songs
Reg. w/ASCAP—1940)

"Strawberry Lane" (M: Jimmy McHugh)
  (P: Paramount Music Corp.)
"The Yogi (Who Lost His Willpower)"
"You're the One (for Me)"
"I Could Kiss You for That"
"Gee, I Wish I'd Listened to My Mother"*

BLUES IN THE NIGHT (1941) Warner Bros.

Priscilla Lane, Betty Field, Jack Carson, Elia Kazan,
  Lloyd Nolan, Richard Whorf

"Blues in the Night" (Oscar Nom.)
  (M: Harold Arlen) (P: Remick Music Corp.)
"This Time the Dream's on Me"
"Hang on to Your Lids, Kids"
"Says Who? Says You, Says I"

BIRTH OF THE BLUES (1941) Paramount

Bing Crosby, Mary Martin, Brian Donlevy, Eddie
  'Rochester' Anderson

"The Waiter and the Porter and the Upstairs
  Maid" (M: Mercer) (P: Famous Music
  Corp.)

NAVY BLUES (1941) Warner Bros.

Jack Carson, Jack Oakie, Ann Sheridan, Jack Haley,
  Martha Raye

"You're a Natural" (M: Arthur Schwartz)
  (P: M. Witmark & Sons)
"Navy Blues"
"In Waikiki"
"When Are We Going to Land Abroad?"

THE FLEET'S IN (1942) Paramount

William Holden, Dorothy Lamour, Eddie Bracken,
  Betty Hutton, Jimmy Dorsey Orch.

"Tangerine" (M: Victor Schertzinger)
  (P: Famous Music Corp.)
"The Fleet's In"
"Arthur Murray Taught Me Dancing in a Hurry"
"If You Build a Better Mousetrap"
"I Remember You"
"Not Mine"
"When You Hear the Time Signal"
"Tomorrow You Belong to Uncle Sam"

YOU WERE NEVER LOVELIER (1942) Columbia

Fred Astaire, Rita Hayworth, Larry Parks, Adolph
  Menjou, Xavier Cugat Orch.

"Dearly Beloved" (Oscar Nom.) (M: Jerome
  Kern) (P: T.B. Harms, Inc.)
"You Were Never Lovelier"
"I'm Old Fashioned"
"On the Beam"
"The Shorty George"
"Wedding in the Spring"

STAR SPANGLED RHYTHM (1942) Paramount

Bing Crosby, Bob Hope, Dorothy Lamour, Mary
  Martin, Dick Powell, Fred MacMurray, Eddie
  'Rochester' Anderson, Vera Zorina, Diana Lynn,
  Cass Daley, Dona Drake, Susan Hayward, Betty
  Hutton, Johnny Johnston, Eddie Bracken, (and
  others)

"That Old Black Magic" (Oscar Nom.)
  (M: Harold Arlen) (P: Famous Music Corp.)
"Old Glory"
"On the Swing Shift"
"Sharp as a Tack"
"Hit the Road to Dreamland"

"A Sweater, a Sarong and a Peek-A-Boo
    Bang"
"I'm Doin' It for Defense"
"He Loved Me Til the All Clear Came"

CAPTAINS OF THE CLOUDS (1942) Warner
Bros.

James Cagney, Brenda Marshall, Dennis Morgan

"Captains of the Clouds" (M: Harold Arlen)
    (P: Famous Music Corp.) (Official Song of the
    Royal Canadian Air Force)

RIDING HIGH (1943) Paramount

Dick Powell, Dorothy Lamour

"He Loved Me Till the All Clear Came" (M: Harold
    Arlen) (P: Famous Music Corp.) (also in "Star
    Spangled Rhythm")

THE SKY'S THE LIMIT (1943) RKO

Fred Astaire, Joan Leslie, Robert Benchley, Robert
    Ryan

"My Shining Hour" (Oscar Nom.)
    (M: Harold Arlen) (P: Edwin H. Morris &
    Co., Inc.)
"One for My Baby (and One More for the
    Road)"
"(I've Got) A Lot in Common with You"
"(Hector) Harvey, the Victory Garden Man"
"Cuban Sugar Mill"
"Hangin' On to You"

THEY GOT ME COVERED (1943) Goldwyn/RKO

Bob Hope, Dorothy Lamour, Otto Preminger

"Palsy Walsy" (M: Harold Arlen) (P: Mills Music,
    Inc.)

TRUE TO LIFE (1943) Paramount

Dick Powell, Mary Martin, Franchot Tone, Yvonne
    De Carlo

"Mr. Pollyanna" (M: Hoagy Carmichael)
    (P: Famous Music Corp.)
"Old Music Master"
"There She Was"

HERE COME THE WAVES (1944) Paramount

Bing Crosby, Betty Hutton, Sonny (Bowen) Tufts,
    Ann Doran

"Ac-Cent-Tchu-Ate the Positive" (Oscar
    Nom.) (M: Harold Arlen) (P: Edwin H.
    Morris & Co., Inc.)

"Let's Take the Long Way Home"
"Here Come the Waves"
"There's a Fella Waitin' in Poughkeepsie"
"My Mama Thinks I'm a Star"
"The Navy Song"
"I Promise You"

TO HAVE AND HAVE NOT (1945) Warner Bros.
(Songs Reg. w/ASCAP—1944)

Humphrey Bogart, Lauren Bacall, Hoagy
    Carmichael, Walter Brennan

"How Little We Know" (M: Hoagy Carmichael)
    (P: M. Witmark & Sons)

LAURA (1945) 20th Century-Fox

Gene Tierney, Dana Andrews, Clifton Webb

"Laura" (M: David Raksin) (P: Robbins Music
    Corp.) (NOTE: Lyric written after release of film)

HER HIGHNESS AND THE BELLBOY (1945)
M-G-M (Song Reg. w/ASCAP—1944)

Hedy Lamarr, Robert Walker, June Allyson, Agnes
    Moorehead

"Dream" (M: Mercer) (P: Michael H.
    Goldsen, Inc.)

OUT OF THIS WORLD (1945) Paramount

Eddie Bracken, Diana Lynn, Cass Daley, Olga San
    Juan (Bing Crosby—voice only)

"Out of This World" (M: Harold Arlen)
    (P: Edwin H. Morris & Co., Inc.)
"June Comes Around Every Year"
"I'd Rather be Me"

THE HARVEY GIRLS (1946) M-G-M

Judy Garland, John Hodiak, Angela Lansbury, Ray
    Bolger, Kenny Baker, Marjorie Main, Cyd Charisse,
    Virginia O'Brien

"On the Atchison, Topeka and the Santa Fe"
    (OSCAR) (M: Harry Warren) (P: Four Jays
    Music Co.)
"Swing Your Partner Round and Round"
"Oh, You Kid"
"In the Valley (Where the Evening Sun Goes
    Down)"
"Wait and See"
"It's a Great Big World"
"My Intuition"
"The March of the Dogies"
"The Wild, Wild West"

"The Train Must be Fed" (P: Robbins, Feist &
  Miller)
"Hayride"   (P: Robbins Feist & Miller)

CENTENNIAL SUMMER (1946) 20th
Century-Fox

Jeanne Crain, Cornel Wilde, Constance Bennett,
  Lillian Gish, Walter Brennan

"Two Hearts Are Better than One" (M: Jerome
  Kern) (P: T. B. Harms, Inc.)
"Two Hearts Together"

FOREVER AMBER (1947) 20th Century-Fox

Linda Darnell, Cornel Wilde, George Sanders

*"Forever Amber" (M: David Raksin) (P: Robbins
  Music Corp.)*

DEAR RUTH (1947) Par.

William Holden, Joan Caulfield, Edward Arnold, Billy
  DeWolfe, Mona Freeman

"Fine Thing" (M: Robert Emmett Dolan)
  (P: Paramount Music Corp.)

MR. PEABODY AND THE MERMAID (1948)
Universal

William Powell, Ann Blyth

"The Caribees" (M: Robert Emmett Dolan)
  (P: Edwin H. Morris & Co., Inc.)

ALWAYS LEAVE THEM LAUGHING (1949)
Warner Bros.

Bert Lahr, Virginia Mayo, Milton Berle, Ruth Roman

THE PRETTY GIRL (1950) Columbia

Robert Cummings, Joan Caulfield, Elsa Lanchester,
  Melville Cooper

"Fancy Free" (M: Harold Arlen) (P: Harwin
  Music Corp.)
"Calypso Song"
"Ah Loves Ya"
"The Petty Girl"

MY FAVORITE SPY (1951) Paramount

Bob Hope, Hedy Lamarr

"I Wind Up Taking a Fall" (M: Robert Emmett
  Dolan) (P: Paramount Music Corp.)

HERE COMES THE GROOM (1951) Paramount

Bing Crosby, Jane Wyman, Louis Armstrong,
  Dorothy Lamour, Cass Daley

"In the Cool, Cool of the Evening" (OSCAR)
  (M: Hoagy Carmichael) (P: Famous Music
  Corp.)

EVERYTHING I HAVE IS YOURS (1952) M-G-M

Marge and Gower Champion, Monica Lewis

"Derry Down Dilly" (M: Johnny Green) (P: Miller
  Music Corp.)

THE BELLE OF NEW YORK (1952) M-G-M
(***Reg; w/ASCAP—1945)

Fred Astaire, Vera Ellen, Marjorie Main, Keenan
  Wynn, Alice Pearce, Gale Robbins

"Bachelor Dinner Song"   (M: Harry
  Warren) (P: Four Jays Music Corp.)
"A Bride's Wedding Day Song"
"I Love to Beat the Big Bass Drum"
"I Wanna Be a Dancin' Man"
"Naughty But Nice" (P: Robbins, Feist &
  Miller)
"Baby Doll"
"Oops!"
"When I'm Out with the Belle of New York"

THOSE REDHEADS FROM SEATTLE (1953)
Paramount

Rhonda Fleming, Gene Barry, Agnes Moorehead,
  Teresa Brewer

"I Guess It Was You all the Time" (M: Hoagy
  Carmichael) (P: Famous Music Corp.)

(other songs in score written by Livingston &
  Evans)

DANGEROUS WHEN WET (1953) M-G-M

Esther Williams, Fernendo Lamas, Charlotte
  Greenwood, Jack Carson

"I Like Men" (M: Arthur Schwartz) (P: Robbins
  Music Corp.)
"C'est La Guerre"
"I Got Out of Bed on the Right Side"
"Fifi"
"Ain't Nature Grand"
"Liquapep"
"In My Wildest Dreams"

TOP BANANA (1954)

Phil Silvers, Rose Marie, Jack Albertson

SEVEN BRIDES FOR SEVEN BROTHERS (1954)
M-G-M

Howard Keel, Jane Powell, Jeff Richards, Russ
    Tamblyn, Marc Platt, Julie Newmar

"Wonderful, Wonderful Day" (M: Gene de
    Paul) (P: Robbins Music Corp.)
"Lonesome Polecat"
"Goin' Co'tin' "
"Bless Your Beautiful Hide"
"June Bride"
"When You're in Love"
"Spring, Spring, Spring"
"Sobbin' Women"
"Lament"

APACHE (1954) U-A

Burt Lancaster, Jean Peters

"Love Song" (M: David Raksin) (P: Madrigal
    Music Co.)

TIMBERJACK (1955) Republic

Sterling Hayden, Vera Ralston, David Brian, Hoagy
    Carmichael, Adolphe Menjou

"He's Dead But He Won't Lie Down"
    (M: Hoagy Carmichael) (P: Famous Music
    Corp.)

THAT'S LIFE (Song Reg. w/ASCAP—1955)

"The Art of Conversation Has Declined" (M: Alan
    Bergman) (P: None listed)

I'LL CRY TOMORROW (1955) M-G-M

Susan Hayward, Eddie Albert

"I'll Cry Tomorrow" (M: Alex North) (P: Robbins
    Music Corp.)

SPRING REUNION (1957) U-A

Betty Hutton, Dana Andrews

"Spring Reunion" (M: Harry Warren) (P: Four
    Jays Music Co.)

DADDY LONG LEGS (1955) M-G-M

Fred Astaire, Leslie Caron, Fred Clark, Thelma Ritter,
    Terry Moore

"Something's Gotta Give" (Oscar Nom.)
    (M: Mercer) (P: Robbins Music Corp.)
"Daddy Long Legs"
"Sluefoot"
"C-A-T Spells Cat"
"Welcome Egghead"
"Guardian Angel"
"Texas Romp and Square Dance"
"Dancing Through Life"
"The History of the Beat" (That'll Get It)
"Blues Theme"
"Dream"
"Thunderbird"
"How I Made the Team"
"Ballets: Guardian Angel, Carnival In Rio,
    Daddy Long Legs, Hong Kong Cafe"

YOU CAN'T RUN AWAY FROM IT (1956)

Columbia

June Allyson, Jack Lemmon, Paul Gilbert, Charles
    Bickford

"Whatcha-ma-call-it" (M: Gene de Paul)
    (P: Columbia Pict. Music Corp.)
"Temporarily"
"Howdy Friends and Neighbors"
"Thumbin' a Ride"
"Old Reporters Never Die"
"You Can't Run Away From It"
"It Happened One Night" (P: Commander
    Publications)

BERNARDINE (20th Century-Fox)

Pat Boone, Janet Gaynor

"Bernardine" (M: Mercer) (P: Palm Springs Music
    Co.)
"Technique"

MERRY ANDREW (1958) M-G-M (Songs Re.
w/ASCAP—1957)

Danny Kaye, Pier Angeli, Salvatore Baccaloni,
    Robert Coote, Rex Evans

"The Pipes of Pan" (M: Saul Chaplin)
    (P: Commander Publications)
"The Square of the Hypotenuse"
"Everything Is Tickety-Boo"
"You Can't Always Have What You Want"
"Chin Up, Stout Fellow"
"Salud (Here's Cheers)"
"Buona Fortuna"

250

LOVE IN THE AFTERNOON (1957) Allied Artists

Gary Cooper, Audrey Hepburn, Charles Boyer

"Love in the Afternoon" (M: Matty Malneck)
    (P: Commander Publications)
"Ariane"

THE MISSOURI TRAVELER (1957) Disney

"The Piney Woods" (Biarn's Song) (M: Jack
    Marshall) (P: Walt Disney Music Co.)

PETER GUNN (1959)

"Joanna" (M: Henry Mancini) (P: Northridge
    Music Co.)

LI'L ABNER (1959) Paramount (See BROADWAY
SHOWS)

Peter Palmer, Leslie Parrish, Julie Newmar, Stubby
    Kaye

THE FACTS OF LIFE (1960) U-A

Bob Hope, Lucille Ball

"The Facts of Life" (Oscar Nom.) (M:
    Mercer) (P: Commander Publications)

BREAKFAST AT TIFFANY'S (1961) Paramount
(Song Reg. w/ASCAP—1960)

Audrey Hepburn, George Pappard, Patricia Neal,
    Buddy Ebsen, Mickey Rooney, Martin Balsam

"Moon River" (OSCAR) (M: Henry Mancini)
    (P: Famous Music Corp.)

TWO OF A KIND   (Song Reg. w/ASCAP—1960)
Columbia

"Two of a Kind" (M: Johnny Mercer)
    (P: Commander Publications)

MR. HOBBS TAKES A VACATION (1962) 20th
Century-Fox

James Stewart, Maureen O'Hara

"Cream Puff" (M: Henry Mancini) (P: Robbins
    Music Corp.)

HATARI (1962) Paramount

John Wayne, Elsa Martinelli

"Just for Tonight" (M: Hoagy Carmichael)
    (P: Famous Music Corp.)

DAYS OF WINE AND ROSES (1962) Warner
Bros.

Jack Lemmon, Lee Remick, Charles Bickford

"Days of Wine and Roses" (OSCAR) (M:
    Henry Mancini) (P: M. Witmark & Sons)

HOW THE WEST WAS WON (1962) M-G-M

Henry Fonda, Debbie Reynolds, Lee J. Cobb, Carl
    Malden, Thelma Ritter

"Raise a Ruckus" (M: Trad.—Arr: Robert Emmett
    Dolan) (P: Robbins Music Corp.)
"What Was Your Name in the States?"
"Wait for the Wagon" (Wait for the Hoedown?)

CHARADE (1963) Universal

Audrey Hepburn, Cary Grant, Walter Matthau,
    James Coburn

"Charade" (Oscar Nom.) (M: Henry
    Mancini) (P: Northern Music Corp. &
    Southern Music Corp.)

LOVE WITH THE PROPER STRANGER (1963)
Paramount

Natalie Wood, Steven McQueen, Edie Adams

"Love With the Proper Stranger" (M: Elmer
    Bernstein) (P: Paramount Music Corp.)

THE PINK PANTHER (1964) U-A

Peter Sellers, David Niven, Capucine, Claudia
    Cardinale

"The Pink Panther (incid. music)"
    (M: Mercer-Henry Mancini-Franco Migliacci)
    (P: United Artists Music Co., Inc. & Northridge
    Music Co.)

THE AMERICANIZATION OF EMILY (1964)
M-G-M

Julie Andrews, James Garner, James Coburn

"Emily" (Oscar Nom.) (M: Johnny Mandel)
    (P: Miller Music Corp.)

THE GREAT RACE (1965) Warner Bros.

Natalie Wood, Tony Curtis, Jack Lemmon, Keenan
    Wynn

"The Sweetheart Tree" (Oscar Nom.)
    (M: Henry Mancini) (P: East Hill Music Co.,
    Inc.)

"He Shouldn't-a, Hadn't-a, Oughtn't-a Swang on Me"

NOTE: "The Sweetheart Tree" Not on ASCAP list.

MOMENT TO MOMENT (1965) Universal

Jean Seberg

"Moment to Moment" (M: Henry Mancini) (P: Southdale Music & Northern Music)

JOHNNY TIGER (1965) Universal

Robert Taylor

"The World of the Heart" (M: Johnny Green & Mercer) (P: Frank Music Corp.)

NOT WITH MY WIFE, YOU DON'T (1966)
Warner Bros.

Tony Curtis, George C. Scott, Virna Lisi

"A Big Beautiful Ball" (M: Johnny Williams) (P: Harms, Inc.)

"My Innamorata"

BAREFOOT IN THE PARK (1967) Paramount

Robert Redford, Jane Fonda, Mildred Natwick, Charles Boyer

"Barefoot in the Park" (M: Neal Hefti) (P: Famous Music Corp.)

CIMARRON STRIP (1967)

"Tomorrow Never Comes" (M: Morton Stevens) (P: April Music, Inc.)

DARLING LILI (1969) Paramount (Songs Reg. w/ASCAP—1970)

Julie Andrews, Rock Hudson

"Whistling Away the Dark" (Oscar Nom.) (M: Henry Mancini) (P: Holmby Music Corp. & Famous Music Corp.)
"The Little Birds (Les P'Tits Ciseaux)" (P: Holmby Music Corp.)
"Darling Lili"
"The Girl in No Man's Land"
"I'll Give You Three Guesses"
"Skal"
"Smile Away Each Rainy Day"
"Good Will Ambassador"

KOTCH (1971)

Walter Matthau

"Life Is What You Make It (Theme from Kotch)" (M: Marvin Hamlisch) (P: Ampco Music, Inc.)